Bon Courage!

by

Rodney Freeman

with illustrations by Bob Dewar

Published in 2009 by YouWriteOn.com

Copyright © Text Rodney Freeman

First Edition 2009

The author asserts the moral right under the Copyright, Designs and Patents Act 1988 to be identified as the author of this work.

All Rights reserved. No part of this publication may be reproduced, stored in a retrieval system, or transmitted, in any form or by any means without the prior written consent of the author, nor be otherwise circulated in any form of binding or cover other than that in which it is published and without a similar condition being imposed on the subsequent purchaser.

Published by YouWriteOn.com

To Helen Sudell, the Chief Editor of Pavilion Books in 1991, who although unable to publish this book at that time wrote me the nicest letter imaginable. And to Gordon Maunder, my chum of many years, who chivvied me relentlessly.

ABOUT THE AUTHOR

Rodney Freeman is a retired Chartered Accountant who has suffered from itchy feet ever since he can remember. His long distance walks have taken him through Uganda, France, Germany, Czechoslovakia, Italy, Poland and New Zealand.

He has learned the basics of six foreign languages to help him survive 'on the hoof', and gets a real kick out of wandering into some rural backwater and discovering whether the locals can understand him.

ACKNOWLEDGEMENTS

How many men have a wife who would let them wander off on holiday on their own for a month?

How many men have a daughter who would turn a pile of loose sheets into a bound book (the one and only copy of the real first edition)?

How many men have a daughter-in-law who would be willing to prepare their book for publication while bringing up three small children and holding down a part-time job?

And how many nations have such lovely people scattered through their countryside, willing to chat to a strange man, feed him delicious food, listen to his version of their native tongue and give him cheerful encouragement? *Vive la France!*

'Vous n'avez pas composté, Monsieur!'

CHAPTER 1

ATLANTIC

'Vous n'avez pas composté, Monsieur,' growled the ticket inspector, leaning over me accusingly as the train swayed gently from side to side.

Well, I'm a gardener by inclination, and composting is one of those eco-friendly things you do amongst the cabbages. It has nothing to do with travelling by train from Bordeaux to Arcachon at the start of an epic journey. So I looked at him in bewilderment.

'Vous n'avez pas composté!' he repeated more loudly, tapping my ticket with his finger and gazing at me as though I were some miserable miscreant dragged from the bowels of the Bastille and destined for the guillotine.

It was most unfair. I had clearly asked at the booking office for a single ticket to Arcachon, and that was what the ticket said. Admittedly I had attempted first to buy a ticket at the confectionery stall when I arrived breathless off the airport coach after waiting for my rucksack to appear as the last item of luggage off the flight, but there was no doubt that I had a valid ticket. So what was all this nonsense about compost?

Madame opposite, who had given me a smiling welcome when I hauled myself panting aboard the train, came to my rescue, although her little grand daughter seated next to her clearly suspected that I had criminal tendencies. She explained to the conductor that I was a foreigner who was probably enjoying his first trip on FNCL. She pointed to the hieroglyphics stamped across one end of her own ticket and imitated for me the motion of inserting it in a machine.

And then it dawned on me. In the mad rush to catch the 2.20 train I had bolted from the ticket office out through the doorway where a ticket inspector would normally have been standing, past a funny little machine where other travellers were pausing and had pelted down the platform shouting desperately to the guard who was about to close the last door on the train. Obviously the little machine was a composting point.

The conductor listened to my friend, shrugged his shoulders and moved on down the carriage, satisfied that I was an imbecile rather than a criminal. I was relieved to see the little girl now eying me with curiosity in place of horror.

That's the thing about travelling. You are never quite sure when you can relax and let someone else do the worrying. Normally it's the moment when I sink into my seat on the aircraft having sweated round the M 25, fought my way across the airport to the check in point and tracked down the departure gate. I guess that when Agricola brought his Roman legions over from Gaul he must have heaved the same sigh of relief when the last legionary was loaded and he could hand over responsibility to the ship's captain. And you can bet that some officious bursar asked to see his ticket even then.

We were rattling along happily through sandy pine forests with occasional sleepy level crossings as the map indicated we should be. It was not that I distrusted French railways; FNCL had a very good reputation. But it was reassuring to note that we were passing through Marcheprime because this confirmed that we were actually travelling west towards Arcachon and not south towards Langon or east towards St. Foy la Grande. A large sea lagoon ought to appear soon. Yes, there it was; the Bassin d'Arcachon.

The tide must be out because the little creeks were almost empty of water although this did nothing to detract from their beauty. Rows of brightly coloured sailing boats and fishing boats were moored to the banks beside tiny hamlets against a green backdrop with sparkling blue beyond. We stopped once or twice for local shoppers to get off and then rolled gently through the outskirts of a holiday town and stopped at a white-washed station with beds of bright flowers. Well, this was it. On your feet. No more wheels until you reach the Mediterranean. I swung the pack onto my back, buckled the waistband firmly around me, stuck *Série Verte* map number 46 into my belt and carefully lowered myself to the platform.

According to the map Arcachon faced north, overlooking a large salt water lagoon, protected from the Atlantic by a long spit of land running southwards to end at Cap Ferret and containing a nature reserve with a name which could be freely translated as "Bird Island". The place had been developed in the nineteenth century from a sleepy fishing village minding its own business to a seaside resort fed by the railway with a diet of Parisians eager to escape the summer heat of their city.

I headed north through neat white-painted streets getting accustomed once more to the terminology: *Boulangerie*, a source of delicious newly-baked bread which needs to be consumed immediately because it becomes inedible after a few hours; *Charcuterie*, the home of a variety of ghastly sausage-like creations of mixed and mysterious origin; *Boucherie*, a reasonable equivalent of a butcher's shop, with a heavy emphasis on veal; *Epicerie*, a small grocer, usually stocking a good choice of cheeses; and, of course, the inevitable *Supermarché*, carrying everything from toilet rolls to Tubourg lager.

Neatly side-stepping a car which tried to fool me by approaching on the righthand side of the road and ignoring my right of way at a pedestrian crossing, I arrived at a tree-lined promenade with the sparkling waters of the " Bassin " spread out before me. This seemed as good a place as any to start the photographic record of an epic journey and a short pier reaching out into the water ahead of me appeared to provide a good vantage point. I walked out along the concrete causeway and turned to see whether the wind-rippled waters, baking beach and plane tree lined promenade would frame an interesting picture. Pentax Zoom 70 was halfway to my eye when he was brought abruptly to a stop in mid-air. Along the beach, scattered amongst tiny children building sandcastles, medium-sized children throwing zimmers and large children punishing beach balls was the most comprehensive and breath-taking display of bare bosoms I had ever seen. I lowered Pentax Zoom 70 and groping my way to a low wall eased off the pack and sat down. Were you permitted to take pictures or would the heavy hand of the Gendarmerie fall upon your arm if you attempted to capture this Eden for posterity? I glanced around nonchalantly but no-one seemed to be paying me the slightest attention or even to be aware of my quandary. The warm breeze continued to raise little wavelets on the surface of the water, a cloudless metallic sky poured early September heat onto curving kilometres of sand, and the bronzed bosoms reclined in elegant contentment.

I reached once more for Pentax Zoom 70 and then remembered that he was attached to the pack by a cunning arrangement which allowed him to rest on my chest ready for instant use on the move. I detached him and searched through the viewfinder for a good composition. As every photographer knows, the camera never captures what the eye sees, although it can select a composition which the eye has missed. On this occasion Pentax Zoom 70 refused to co-operate. I zoomed in and out but the lagoon, beach and promenade remained obstinately flat and uninteresting. All that featured was a line of snaking seaweed deposited by the tide and a sprinkling of electric-powered boats looking like armchairs reclining between twin buoyancy tanks. Bosoms vanished into obscurity. I took one unexciting picture in each direction and walked to the end of the pier to watch a catch of fish being packed into crates.

Enough of loitering. The plan for the day was to skirt round Arcachon on the seaward side and head south down the coast to le Pilat-Plage as the jumping off point for the first full day of walking. I set off along the promenade in the direction of Cap Ferret and the open sea trying to settle into a rhythm which would carry me safely along for the next month. The French were renowned for taking their holidays in August and returning to work promptly as the month came to an end but here on Saturday 2nd September they still swarmed lazily between the beach and the cafes as though the summer would never end. And certainly the summer showed no inclination to bring itself to an end. In the town the temperature had been sufficient to make the tar melt in patches on the road and out here by the water opinion was evenly divided between those who were putting a final touch to their tan and those who preferred to let the warm Atlantic breeze fan them in the shade. I examined them all with intense approval. They were coming to the end of their holidays and I was just beginning mine. That in itself was enough to make me love them all. My head, arms and legs already tanned by an exceptional English summer soaked up the sun with a feeling of deep anticipation as I strode along.

A voice suddenly broke in upon my thoughts and I realised with a start that for the first time a Frenchman was engaging me in conversation. He was a man of homely and grizzled appearance whom I had just overtaken. For some reason I judged him to be not a holiday-maker but a local.

" Monsieur ?" I enquired politely, slowing down and turning with a smile. He gestured at the pack and from his questioning tone I gathered that he was enquiring how far I intended to walk with it. I had prepared for this moment. "From the Atlantic to the Mediterranean", I responded proudly.

" Ah, non !" he replied, stopping in his tracks and earning a censorious glance from the owner of two long and slender legs who bumped into him. I assured him that I had a whole month in which to achieve this but he was anxious about the size of my load and gestured again at the pack enquiring its weight. For this question I was not so well prepared and my mental arithmetic stalled at the task of converting approximately 20lbs into kilograms. I multiplied instead of dividing and came up with an answer of 40 kilograms.

" Formidable !" he exclaimed, again stopping and causing confusion to the pedestrian traffic. We walked together for a little way and then he wished me a warm *" Bon Voyage "* as I moved on ahead again. Re-checking my calculations I realised that I had claimed to be carrying well in excess of what the marines took when they yomped across West Faulkland without the benefit of footpaths and carrying all their clothing, equipment, bedding and food. No wonder he had been impressed.

The promenade petered out, as is the habit of all promenades at some point, and offered a choice of soft, dry sand ridged with occasional concrete outcrops or a diversion back into residential streets. I chose the latter forgetting that the French do not understand the purpose of pavements in residential areas. They seldom make them more than two feet wide and have a nasty habit of scattering lamp posts carelessly in the middle of them. A walk along them is therefore punctuated by frequent diversions onto the road in deference to elderly ladies airing their dogs or young ladies hiding behind dark glasses and insisting upon right of way.

'Formidable!' he exclaimed.

Avoiding the temptation to investigate every little alley which led back to the beach and gave access only to private stretches of sand I stuck to the road which eventually swung round and joined the beach again. It climbed a little rise through pine trees and looked down on a miniature view of sunshades casting circular pools of shade on the sand where couples lounged sipping their drinks. I paused to capture the scene and Pentax Zoom 70 clicked, and wound on rather slowly. A group of youngsters playing volleyball were framed between pine trunks. I stopped again to catch a picture of them in action. A blonde young lady wearing nothing but a blue towel wrapped around her middle squealed as she reached for a high ball and laughed up at me. Pentax Zoom 70 clicked and his automatic winding mechanism wound on again even more slowly; I tried to blame it on the rich diet which I was feeding to him but a feeling of unease began to stir.

The promenade swung fully south at last and gave an impressive view of dazzling sea, sandbars, paddling families and athletic windsurfers. I stopped for a further snap. Pentax Zoom 70 clicked once again and the film began to grind forward. Then it stopped, paused, and finally began to rewind itself. I stood there in horror. Only seven exposures out of thirty-six and now he was rewinding himself! The journey of a lifetime was going to be ruined by a defective camera. My thoughts flicked back over the years to a similar moment of frustration standing in a distant corner of Uganda between Lake George and Lake Edward gazing at an enormous green snake lying coiled in the middle of the dirt road. I had just used the last exposure of my first reel of film in a brand new 35mm Voightlander Vito B camera and I had not the slightest idea how to rewind the film into its cassette and load another one. On that occasion I had waited until nightfall, missing countless pictures of elephant and hippopotamus, and fumbled in the darkness of a hotel bedroom until I had mastered the mysteries of modern camera design.

On this occasion I retired to the shade of a pine tree and considered the alternatives. Walk back into Arcachon, whose suburbs were coming to an end and seek advice at a photographic shop? That would delay arrival at a hotel this evening. Change the film now and hope for the best? That might just sacrifice another film and prove nothing. Wait until reaching the hotel and then insert a new battery and a new film? I might miss the picture of a lifetime this very afternoon. I groaned with indecision, hoisted the pack once more and set off back into Arcachon, then changed my mind after a few yards and turned south again.

And as I walked a memory was triggered, a memory of sitting in a dusty sunlit classroom where this journey might be said to have been born. We were listening to 'Gad' Gillard whose idea of teaching English to thirteen year olds was refreshingly unconventional. He held that reading aloud the books of good English authors was the only sure way of inculcating into reluctant heads the rules of grammar and proper use of language. He did not ask members of the class to read aloud in turn as they would be unlikely to do full justice to the piece. He himself read the book to the class, and did it very well. We sat enraptured week after week by John Buchan and Sir Arthur Quiller Cooch. 'Gad' was also a good raconteur and was willingly diverted into reminiscence. One morning we had seized on a passing reference to France and drawn out of him a fascinating tale of a walking holiday round Brittany shortly after the first World War. He and another young bachelor master had set off on foot round the coast moving in leisurely fashion from one fishing village to another, exulting in sea, rocks and birds, living at peace with the world and talking through the long evenings. It had fired my imagination and started a craving to walk through foreign lands which had been impossible in a childhood overhung by the Second World War.

Cycling, hitch-hiking, national service and long student vacations had taken me to many fascinating places in the next few years until marriage and a young family had limited holidays to caravanning near the sea. But the itch had returned more persistently than ever, not to be ignored, not to be bought off with compromises, and certainly not willing to wait for retirement. The years were passing with horrifying speed; fortieth birthday, fiftieth birthday. Lord, I would soon be knocking on sixty at this rate. The itch was to walk, to see it all at first hand, to smell the country, to feel its texture, to meet it face to face in unarmed combat without wheels or engines, relying only on legs, lungs and heart. I remembered the final moment of decision very clearly. I had committed myself by telling Jenny what I was going to do. It had been a June morning two years ago in a little village in the Haute Savoie. That morning was still crystal clear in my mind.

I had stared at the little flower in disbelief. Sweat ran down my face and salt stung the corners of my eyes before I could wipe it away. My chest heaved as I gulped greedy draughts of alpine air to cool an over-heated body driven step by stumbling step up the last hundred feet. The little thing winked up at me from a sheath of ice. It could not be that cold up here. I straightened up and plucked the damp shirt away from my skin. Immediately a cold shiver ran up my back in spite of the sunshine. I stared again at the tiny yellow anemone nestling in the grass, stiff in its frosty jacket. It must be a tough existence blooming in the warmth of the day and being plunged into an icy straightjacket each night without even the chance to snuggle back into a tight bud again.

I walked on a few yards in the sunshine of the open slope, still not at the top but high enough. That last bit must be a local joke. No-one could possibly call it a track, or even a footpath or sentier or whatever the term was. It had been an ambitious scramble on hands and knees up a torrent of loose boulders, and yet there were tyre marks. There must be a more civilised approach to that building at the bottom or there would be no sense in renovating it.

I had slipped out of my side of the bed at seven o'clock, dressed as quietly as possible, tip-toed (well, alright, clumped slowly) in my boots down the stairs so as not to wake Eleanor and Geoff, and fought my silent daily battle with the front door key. No-one else shared my conviction that the first three hours of daylight were the best; pastel shaded peace undisturbed by man's machinations, lit by a low sun which made every blade of grass a crystal glory and revealed a world never seen before in just this way, on just this day.

Vilagerel nestled halfway between the valley floor and the high wooded ridges which I had reached. In early June the snow was in full retreat up the side of the valley but still held its grip on the mountain tops across the other side. I stood and drank it in yet again, savouring the added pleasure of seeing it from a point an hour and a half higher up. On those high ridges the snow seemed heedless of the sun's warmth. It cloaked every rock face and filled the long gullies with smooth drifts. It picked up and absorbed gentle colours from the young morning sky. Its purity pulsed across the divide which lay between us. I wanted to capture it irretrievably so that I could relive this ecstasy again and again.

Then an even more ecstatic thought occurred to me: coffee, and hot bread with butter and honey. I set off down a decent looking path which had the virtue of at least pointing in the right direction. Then I stopped again, and in that moment all the vague intentions and yearnings of the years crystallised into a firm purpose. If this is what I really enjoyed doing, getting out into the open countryside and walking for hours from one glory to another, then I must organise myself to do it properly. There was the whole of France just waiting for me. I would stick a pack on my back and actually do it.

This momentous decision being reached I looked at my watch and found with horror that it was already past breakfast time. No time now for following careful gradients and signed footpaths; just a precipitous plunge down the hillside through dew-soaked pastures of gentian and campanula. Across the traverses linking hairpin bends, past slowly chewing cows whose bells clanged tunefully as they looked up, and into the woods above Vilagerel. It was a plunge from the first days of spring at the edge of the receding snowline down to the warmth of an early June summer in the valley below.

"Good walking, darling?" she enquired as I clomped into the dining area of the gite.

"Gorgeous! I've decided I'm going to walk right across France from one side to the other one day."

"Yes, darling. Have your breakfast quickly because you've been an awful long time and Eleanor and Geoff are twitching gently. They want to go off shopping."

So much for my momentous announcement. It had been relegated to the level of a domestic inconvenience, so I had poured a large cup, a really large French cup, of coffee and attacked a chunk of baguette voraciously, adding generous dollops of butter and honey.

And now I was starting that journey on foot right across France. Unfortunately the expectation of walking beside the Atlantic with elegant bodies reclining at my feet once again petered out with the promenade at a collection of cafes and gift shops. Peering down the coast I could see no joy in following the beach. At regular intervals the sand vanished and left Atlantic waves crashing against concrete walls. There was nothing for it but to turn inland and follow a typical coastal road unsure of its true identity with drifting sands encroaching here and there on the tarmac surface and sudden forks trying to divert it towards the sea but leading only to the driveways of seaside mansions. It wound its way into the mini resort of Pylat-sur-Mer and deposited me right outside a photographic shop in a small shopping centre.

I entered and explained my problem. The proprietor showed no surprise. "Some films do have a minor fault which causes the mechanism to rewind," he assured me. "Your camera is o.k." he added, disclosing a surprising ability to diagnose the problem without even looking at the camera. I left the shop feeling re-assured, but determined to insert the spare battery that evening after reading the instruction book carefully.

The feeling of frustration lifted as I continued on my way at a slower pace now that the heat of the day had begun to take its toll. Every few hundred metres (yes, I must think in metres now and not yards) a little side avenue reached down to the sea between large houses in extensive gardens but the result was always the same; a little isolated beach or quayside with small waves crashing enthusiastically against walls of concrete. It was easier to stick to the road. A glance at my watch indicated that it was time to take a break. It was well past forty-five minutes since the last rest and there was nothing to be gained by making my legs weary. At the next right turn I walked down the usual quiet avenue to the point where it dived steeply towards the blue waves. A family was spread out comfortably on a little platform a few feet above the water. I walked halfway down the flight of steps towards them, swung the pack off my back and extracted a Mars Bar and one of the water bottles. It was good to lie back in the sun with legs stretched out comfortably and my shoulders relaxed. The waves washed up and down hypnotically. I closed my eyes. It had been a long day since five o'clock that morning.

The voice which drew me back to wakefulness was incomprehensible. Ah, it was French. I could tell by the accent. But it was still incomprehensible. I blinked and sat up. A tanned youth with an incipient moustache was sitting beside me chatting in a friendly manner. He was part of the family group. I listened intently and caught the odd word here and there. He was fixing me with a friendly but peculiar stare; his eyes seemed to swim in and out of focus continually. I understood an occasional phrase and volleyed the conversation back with some difficulty. This was dreadful. How would I ever converse meaningfully if my comprehension of spoken French was so abysmal?

The mother glanced across with a welcoming smile and I felt reassured and strove to continue the exchange with my friendly conversationalist. Then it began to dawn on me. He was not mentally normal; perhaps he had a drugs problem; he certainly found it difficult to concentrate his thoughts. I took the initiative and asked him if he was a student or did a job of work. He paused and frowned. A younger brother climbed up the steps and joined us, saying quietly, "He is ill". I nodded and felt relieved that I could understand the younger brother with relative ease. We joined in a three-way exchange. The younger brother had been to London with a school party and had inspected the Tower, the Houses of Parliament and Trafalgar Square. I explained that I worked next door to Madame Tussaud's and after a while he went off proudly to report the fruits of his discussion to Mama.

I looked at my watch. It was time to move on and to make sure of a hotel room for the night. I stowed the water bottle, swung on the pack, positioned Pentax Zoom 70, adjusted all straps and turned to my friend who was watching me with fascination. I extended a hand and we grasped firmly, man to man, to his obvious delight. Then I turned to Mama with a wave. She waved back and mouthed her thanks for my patient attention to her family. I remounted the steps thinking sadly that the mentally sub-normal retain the habit of trust and openness much better than the rest of us who consider ourselves so well equipped to wrestle with the world's problems. That little interlude had been worthwhile.

A glance southwards from the steps at the end of the avenue had revealed a mountain of sand rising up from the sea a few kilometres further on; the famous Dune du Pilat, highest sand dune in Europe, frustrated in its march inland only by the planting of extensive forests. The resort of le Pilat-Plage lay at the foot of this extraordinary formation and marked the resumption of sandy beaches. It revealed a good selection of seaside hotels as I walked into it along a well shaded road. None of them appeared to be particularly busy. I could take my time in selecting one.

However, the first stop must be the local epicerie in order to ensure that tomorrow's lunch was safely on board before the day's journey began. Madame obligingly provided a thin slice of cheese as a sample to taste. I purchased 200 grams of that, a pack of butter and a couple of tomatoes. To this was added the local evening paper with the two-fold objective of re-awakening my long dormant vocabulary and discovering topics of current interest to debate with the locals.

The Hotel Ttiki Etchea (yes, I was puzzled by the name too) was next to the sea and reasonably priced. Madame escorted me to a single room with a shower. There was no view of the sea, but the sound of the surf came clearly through the window once the shutters had been thrown open. After unpacking I slipped on swimming trunks under my shorts, stuffed the white hotel towel out of sight in a plastic bag, and headed for the sea. At some point this journey had to start in the Atlantic Ocean so I had better make sure I waded into its waters now in case I forgot in the excitement of the morning.

The sun was dipping rapidly towards the horizon, the breeze had suddenly become distinctly cool, and the sea had unaccountably turned grey during the last half hour. A full-blooded plunge into the depths had somehow lost its attraction. I sat a few feet from the water's edge and weighed the matter carefully. The breeze became even cooler and the waves seemed to wash up and down the steep little beach with unnecessary enthusiasm. There might be nasty currents here. There might be underwater rocks. It would be foolish, I reasoned with myself, to court a calamity such as severely grazed toes. All I had to do was actually touch the water in order to justify the claim of starting from the Atlantic coast. I unlaced my boots slowly, peeled off the two pairs of socks with studied deliberation, began to unbutton my shirt, and stopped. A few strides and the swirling water was washing up to my calves and down again. I stood there for a moment or two feeling slightly pathetic and unadventurous and then decided that it was time to phone home and report that I was still alive at the end of the first day.

    The telephone kiosk had an unhelpful air about it as though it was determined to challenge the audacity of anyone who thought that he could, in a matter of seconds, use its facilities to chat to someone on the far side of the Channel. I wrestled with the door, which was hinged in a peculiarly French way and seemed to want to sweep me away instead of letting me in. I read the instructions carefully and pondered on whether to insert a five franc, a two franc or a one franc coin. One franc looked rather mean, but five francs might be excessive. I settled on two francs but took the precaution of lining up a row of other coins for instant access. OK, here we go. The code for England is 1944, followed by the Ipswich code 0473, followed by the six digits for Lavender Cottage. There was a series of unpromising clicks followed by a continuous single tone. That hadn't got me very far. Try again with a helpful pause between the sections of dialling. No better. The only good news was that each time the receiver was replaced my two francs reappeared. I tried fast dialling, slow dialling, syncopated dialling, persuasive dialling, robust dialling, but nothing was going to rattle this telephone kiosk. It had never heard of the European Community or, if it had, it recognised only a continental version. Well, *tant pis*, as they say in these parts. Lavender Cottage would have to hold its breath for another day. I had tried.

CHAPTER 2

SAND

It was a restless night. The occupant of the next room snored with shuddering vigour and my mind was too full of uncertainties to relax into complete oblivion. Would I make it all the way across on foot or would I finish up in some remote valley with crippled legs and an empty wallet? Would I get lonely and depressed? Did the footpaths really exist, or had they fallen into disuse years ago? And, above all, did the Mastercard sign at the hotel door really include Access, or was the credit card in my money belt going to be a useless piece of plastic leaving me short of currency before I had got half way?

After several hours I switched on the torch in desperation. It was six o'clock and still pitch black. I turned over and promptly fell into a deep sleep from which I emerged with a start to discover that it was seven-twenty. Damn! I had intended to be in the dining room on the dot of seven o'clock when they started serving breakfast. I leapt out of bed, hauled on clothes, stitched myself into boots and hurried to the dining room. The cheerful waiter who had served dinner the previous evening was not in evidence but a waitress brought me a generous pot of coffee, hot milk, and a basket of assorted bread and croissants with butter and jam. I polished off a croissant, which was more substantial than it looked, and sat eyeing the bread with interest. I couldn't eat it now but it was just what was needed for lunch and would save a journey to the Boulangerie before setting off. I picked it up furtively, thought of tucking it inside my shirt, but decided to be brazen. The waitress raised no objection when I waved the bread at her as I went out to re-pack the haversack and settle the bill.

I held my breath as Madame examined the Access card and exhaled thankfully when she took an imprint and handed it back to me without even checking the signature. Few things irritate me more than attempting to imitate a signature scribbled on a narrow strip on the back of a piece of hard plastic. I had once been summoned to the recesses of Selfridges to be cross-examined on the 'phone by someone in Southend because of my miserable failure to reproduce the nasty squiggle on the card. Madame did not embarrass her guests by such a vulgar precaution as checking their signatures. She asked where I was going and blinked in astonishment when I said that the Mediterranean was my destination. The snorer of the night before joined us and enquired my route. I explained that the first day would take me south down the coast to Biscarrosse after an initial look at the Dune. Both of them agreed without hesitation that the Dune was not to be missed. Madame beamed with pleasure when I thanked her for an excellent start to my journey and we shook hands all round before I departed and turned south down the road.

    I was dragged from a brief reverie by a shout from the cheerful waiter of the night before who was coming towards me on his way to work. He was pointing back towards the hotel where the snorer was hurrying after me trying to attract my attention.

    "The route to the Dune, Monsieur. It is down that road," he shouted, pointing down a road which went due east from the hotel. I stared at him in puzzlement for the Dune stood out plain for all to see to the south of where we were.

    "It is the best route, Monsieur. You approach the Dune from behind. If you go that way it is very hard." He did a remarkable imitation of Beau Geste lost in the Sahara and crawling up a sand dune on hands and knees. I got the message and retraced my steps to the turning he had indicated. It was the first of many occasions on which a brief chat was to save me setting off in the wrong direction.

    My boots fell on a carpet of pine needles on the road which led away from the sea. After two minutes I became conscious of a feeling of strain in my left thigh. Oh no, not now! I had trained steadily for twelve months to become fit enough to carry this pack for twenty five miles a day without falling apart. Well don't panic, you ass! Just do what you've learnt to do. Stop for a moment, flex the muscles and walk on carefully with everything relaxed.

    The road dutifully carried me round in a semicircle and a mile further on it swung me back west through a scattering of bars and other tourist traps nestling in the shade of some woodland. It wound through shuttered gift shops and empty car parks and suddenly emerged at the foot of a monstrous heap of drifting sand hundreds of metres high sweeping contemptuously into the woods, submerging trees in its path and diminishing everything around it. I stopped and gawped at it in disbelief. Two bicycles linked with a padlock and chain stood at the foot of a flight of wooden steps which crawled its way up the massive heap into the sky above. There must be literally hundreds of steps, each one six inches above the other. What was that going to do to the muscles in my left thigh? Oh, shut up and relax. You haven't come this far just to turn round and walk away.

  I started up the steps with care, using the hand rails on either side to pull myself up gently. Twelve steps up and then a short horizontal platform, another twelve steps and another platform, another twelve steps and... It was not yet nine o'clock and the air was deliciously fresh but the sweat began to trickle into my eyes. The stairway rose above the tops of the trees and the countryside began to stretch out below me. Twelve steps and another platform, twelve steps and another platform... A helicopter started its engine somewhere below me and I turned round to search for it. Twelve steps and another platform, twelve steps and another platform... Calves, knees and thighs combined to carry me thankfully up the last flight of steps and I stood and stared at the surface of the moon.

  Well, check with Neil Armstrong if you like, but it looked just like the moon to me. Each footfall of a perspiring tourist had left a mini crater in the last slope up to the final crest. There was no sign of vegetation or animal life. In some miraculous way even the non-biodegradable litter scattered generously by the human race in every beauty spot had vanished from view. I felt alone as I dug my boots into the shifting, slipping surface and plodded my way up to the ridge. The snorer had been right; this was not a phenomenon to be challenged head on in its raw state; if I had tackled the north face in macho style clawing my way up naked sand slopes there could only have been one outcome; a sweaty bundle caked in sand rolling back and coming to rest ignominiously against the trunk of a half submerged pine tree.

  From the top of the final ridge golden flanks of sand curved away smoothly north and south into the morning haze. Straight ahead a shoulder dipped down into the water and submerged itself reluctantly in a series of sand bars and lagoons. A handful of yachts were anchored in the calm water. Behind me the avalanche rolled without a pause into the woods below.

Delicious peace. A tingling sensation of freedom and escape, to be here alone without even a breeze stirring, just an occasional bar of muted bird song from below. I walked slowly along the ridge dragging reluctant boots with me and watching the sparkling grains of sand cascade gently back into the inverted cone of each footprint. Surely the whole place was being gently trodden down by visitors and would be nothing more than an inconspicuous hump in a few decades. No, that was wrong. According to the Michelin Guide Book it was actually piling up even higher each year driven by a combination of wind and currents. Well, no wonder we were getting short of sand on our favourite Cornish beaches; it was being shipped f.o.b. to Aquitaine where they already had a vast surplus. Undoubtedly a matter for an E.E.C. regulation.

I turned round and started back aware of the minutes ticking by relentlessly and the day's march still ahead of me. Yuck! Someone had left a nasty bundle of rubbish over there. I struggled over indignantly to see whether it could be dragged back down the steps. Well, fancy being daft enough to ditch a whole sleeping bag and a cooking stove. Some idiots must have had a party and departed carelessly in the dark. The sleeping bag wriggled gently and separated itself into two sleeping bags. I paused in embarrassment, unsure whether to call out a greeting or steal away unobserved and leave them with an unspoiled illusion of isolation. The decision was made for me; a young man's tousled head appeared, put on spectacles and mumbled a sleepy " B'jour ". My fingers itched to bring Pentax Zoom 70 into action but gentlemanly instincts prevailed.

An equally tousled female head popped out of the second sleeping bag and grinned at me. The man sat up and enquired whether I had just arrived by way of the steps and, being assured that I had, fired another question which went past me at speed. I asked for it to be repeated slowly.

"Oh, you are English", he said, and began to form the question in English. "Did you see..." I waved my hands emphatically and with supreme but unfounded confidence demanded , " En Francaise, s'il vous plaît" .

He passed a hand over his face and groaned at the effort of making an Englishman understand French at nine o'clock in the morning and began patiently to put his question again in French with an English accent and just a hint of sarcasm. This earned him a rebuke from the girl. I grasped that the question had something to do with the bottom of the steps and involved a mysterious " *vélo* ". The dictionary was in a side pocket of the haversack and I was about to disassemble everything and get to the bottom of the matter when inspiration came to the rescue. " *Les bicyclettes* !" I cried, and hastened to reassure them that their bicycles were waiting in good order down below.

They were on a two week tour covering the enormous distances on which French cyclists seem to thrive; from Paris to the sea, a plunge south to the Pyrenees, and a quick run back north. The idea of moving from coast to coast on foot astounded them and they were interested to know whether I would arrive by Christmas. They had wanted to watch dawn break from the top of the Dune and had come up in the darkness to see the sun rise at six o'clock and then, warming themselves with a brew of coffee, had curled up to sleep.

I bade them farewell and returned to the steps to begin a jolting descent. My left hip regarded this as an act of deliberate provocation and issued a curt warning. I paused at each horizontal platform and flexed the whole leg like a mother soothing a petulant child. We arrived at the bottom without serious disagreement.

There now occurred one of the many "firsts" of the journey. The map (*Série Verte No. 55, 1 cm pour 1 km*) showed the little red line of footpath number 8, or to give it its proper name " *Sentier de Grand Randonné Numéro 8* ", calling in at the back of the Dune on its journey south to Biscarrosse. According to the map it actually ran out of steam on a minor road just north of that town, obviously not considering the remaining two kilometres worth the effort. It suited my purpose well. The day's plan was to move down through low wooded hills touching a long inland lake at intervals and to reach a convenient jumping off place from which to head eastwards without getting entangled in Bordeaux. The lake, Lac de Cazaux, was supposed to be a bird reserve and would probably be a mess of reeds ringed with the camouflaged lairs of ornithologists.

I looked around me. There was only one way to go, so I went, full of trust in French cartographers and keeping a wary eye open for white and red marks which would indicate the official footpath.

To my delight, and almost my unbelief, two rectangular daubs of paint, white above red, appeared within seconds inviting me to turn off down a little path through the trees. A shiver of excitement ran through me. Off the metalled road where tourists drove in the security of their cars and cyclists raced along on wheels; into the real France on foot. Lord, into your hands.

The path ran between scrubby oak trees under the shade of tall pines. It threaded its narrow way through clumps of heather and round bushes of broom. Its sandy surface was covered in a fine carpet of brown needles which deadened any sound of footfalls. The only sound was the occasional scratch of a branch against the haversack as it brushed through one of the denser patches of foliage. A brown and black squirrel raced round a tree and peeped down at me. The route curved gently and undulated over small rises. Several of the pine trees had V-shaped cuts from which resin ran into little cups, and I remembered reading about this local industry in a tourist leaflet. The Dune was lost to view. There were no landmarks, only an encircling ring of woodland which opened itself to the sky.

The path forked. I faltered, chose the right, scanned the tree trunks nervously for confirmation, and breathed again after nearly missing the red and white daub on a rock at ground level. So, the rules were that they splashed paint on anything solid? Without warning the path arrived at the side of a little road, crossed it, and continued up a slope on the far side. I checked my watch. It was ten o'clock and time for a rest even if I didn't feel the need for it. I had spent a year learning the hard way and this was not the moment to jettison all that accumulated experience. Unload, take a few swigs of water to maintain body moisture and then stretch out flat for a few minutes. It worked wonders. I sat up refreshed and filled in a page of the diary which a thoughtful niece had provided.

A peculiar scraping sound drifted faintly through the trees and urged investigation. I loaded up again and set off in pursuit. An ancient grey Deux Chevaux Renault was parked on the track which had now widened considerably. I paused, scanning the woods for an explanation of the noise, and spotted a movement amongst a group of taller pines. A deeply tanned man in old clothes and a battered Trilby hat was wheeling a small tub from one tree to another. It must be collection time for the pine resin.

"Are you collecting the resin, Monsieur?" I enquired politely.

He eyed me in a guarded manner as one might a suspected undercover VAT man checking on unregistered activities. As he appeared reluctant to admit to commercial activity I added hurriedly, "I am English."

Suspicion vanished. "And I am Spanish," he responded with a grin. We were both foreigners in France but brothers in the E.E.C. I inspected his mobile tank. It reminded me of the pots of delicious dripping which my mother used to save from beef joints. White formations encrusted the sides of the tank and white globules floated in a light brown liquid. I was permitted to photograph him in action unhooking cups from the bark and scraping the contents noisily into the tub. How on earth was this contraption loaded into the car and transported to the processing place and, come to think of it, why wasn't he standing on tall wooden stilts like the ones shown in the coloured brochures? I chickened out of this linguistic challenge and continued on my way.

Walking across a *Série Verte* map with a scale of 1 cm to 1 km comes as a nasty shock after cruising comfortably across an Ordnance Survey map with a scale of 2 cms to 1 km since it naturally takes twice as long to progress across the map. As I strode on I began to heap curses on the Spaniard's head. At every rise in the track his wretched little car had churned the surface into a trough of loose sand through which each step demanded herculean efforts. One boot slid backwards before the other boot could gain any purchase and every little hillock on the path became an absurd obstacle. I heaved a sigh of relief when the path emerged onto another minor road since it was better to suffer contact with civilisation than dissolve into the sand.

The GR swung along cheerfully down the road with unmistakeable markings appearing on rocks, electricity poles, concrete posts, the backs of road signs, and any other object which the artist had thought would enjoy relative permanence. When it took to the woods again I consulted the map eagerly to establish progress. No, this couldn't be the spot; it wasn't far enough along the route; I must have come further than that; there must be another junction between footpath and road further south on the map. There was, but it made no sense. The road had definitely not passed the various features which would precede that junction. The unpalatable conclusion was that progress to date was unimpressive, one might even use the term 'disastrous'.

I followed the markings obediently into the woods again and found a good track with welcome shade after the exposure of the roadway. After a while the next road duly presented itself and the footpath followed it once more. This procedure repeated itself several times until the markings turned off decisively into a stretch of woodland which would take me to the shores of the lake. I took another breather in a cool glade and re-examined the map. Not half way yet and the hours were ticking past. Don't panic, you've covered the worst bit back where Pedro's car had churned up the path, I consoled myself.

I had stopped confidently beside a splash of white and red on a piece of fencing and although the way ahead was not immediately apparent there was the comfortable assurance of being on the planned route.

Starting off in the direction which naturally followed from the point of arrival revealed no markings; neither did a broad sweep in two semi-circles; nothing, and no obvious alternative route. With slight misgivings I started off again in the direction of my first choice. It soon left the cover of the trees and emerged into scrub taking on at the same time an entirely different character and becoming a chaos of sand ten metres wide which could only have been created by heavy machinery moving in and out to harvest the timber. I examined it with disgust; the achievements of Pedro's car were ineffectual scratchings compared to this orgy of ridges and furrows. The original path, even if this was indeed the route, had been obliterated without trace and a few tentative steps revealed that even the bottoms of the furrows were a shifting morass. Sand from the ridges had slid back into the valleys and nowhere was there a solid base. I climbed the little bank at one side of the track in the hope of finding firm ground along the edge but discovered that the surroundings were covered in inpenetrable low-lying vegetation, thorns and briars creating an entanglement which required one high step after another in order to make any progress at all. I gave up and returned to lumberjack's highway. It was worse than that horrible dream in which some dreadful but indefinite "thing" is pursuing you and your feet are caught in deep sucking mud which requires a super-human effort to make each step to safety. In the dream you are spared the added inconvenience of a blistering overhead sun whose heat is thrown back from glittering sand underfoot.

I forced my way forward one step at a time with moisture streaming from every pore. After five hundred metres I stripped off the pack and sank gasping into the pathetic shade of a baby pine tree which had escaped the slaughter. I dug into a side pocket of the haversack, extracted my sun hat and sat there panting. This was a nightmare; virtually no progress at all and the conditions were getting worse, but there was no point in going back. So, take a swig of water and press on again.

Rounding a slight bend I saw that the present horror appeared to peter out halfway up a low hillside. The promise of change spurred me on. Slipping and staggering up the final incline I detected a pathway leading into the gloom of a mature grove of evergreen oaks and stumbled the final distance, driving myself across a short stretch of blessedly firm soil to sink down onto the grass in a cool cavern of peace, flat on my back with arms and legs outstretched.

Only an empty stomach kept me awake. The slices of hotel baguette felt leathery but with a dollop of butter and a chunk of cheese they became a delicacy. A tomato and several swigs of warm water provided the liquid and my remaining London Airport Mars bar constituted dessert. Life flowed back into limbs which had begun to lose hope. Biscarrosse before nightfall became once more a possibility and with a bit of luck I might just reach the Mediterranean by the end of the month.

The path had returned to single person proportions and headed on up the slope with a firm surface which was a joy to tread. After a few minutes it became even firmer and I looked down to discover a thin line of concrete just wide enough to walk on comfortably. What unknown benefactor had provided this, and why? Whatever the reason the concrete ceased as inexplicably as it had begun but it was swept from my thoughts by the first view of the lake.

This was no reedy ornithologist's backwater. Conical sails were dotted on clear sparkling water as far as the horizon and family groups clustered in little sandy bays. I sped down the incline eagerly and crept into the cover of some overhanging bushes to strip off boots and socks and wade into the blissfully cool water. Twenty metres from the shore the water changed from a sandy hue to deep blue indicating a sharp change in depth. Along this line a sprinkling of yachts and power boats were moored and people swam lazily around them. I fished out my swimming trunks and followed their example doing a lazy backstroke out across the shallows. Bliss, absolute bliss; I could feel my whole body drawing in the moisture gratefully.

A passing day hiker from the direction of Biscarrosse confirmed that I could follow the shore to the bottom of the lake along the narrow band of firm wet sand which edged the water and provided a perfect walking surface. If the GR8 wished to twist and turn through the woods inland it could do so without me. The lake threw up a cool radiance which was irresistible and I set off along the waterline dodging vegetation and making brief detours inland only when forced to do so by stretches of wind blown reeds.

It was at the end of one of these little detours that I met them. A girl of exquisite proportions, in nothing but the briefest of bikini singlets and leaning slightly backwards, was being gently and willingly propelled by a young man away from a boat at the water's edge and into the shade of the woods. She leaned back on him and they moved slowly in step together as one body, his hands clasped lightly across her stomach. She smiled at me through half closed eyelids displaying her beauty without the slightest embarrassment. Their intentions were obvious. I went hot and cold simultaneously and uttered a strangled greeting, to which they nodded an absent-minded reply. My mind reeled with disturbing images and I reminded myself severely that I was, and looked, fifty-four even if for the moment I felt only twenty-four. I walked on cursing my bodily feelings and wondering what I would stumble upon next. Fortunately it was nothing more erotic than a little quayside in a tiny bay with blackberry bushes growing in profusion. I paused, and attempted with some success to satisfy my bodily longings by feeding them a generous ration of ripe fruit. Splashing my hands and face in cold water and feeling somewhat calmer I continued along the wet sand and rounded a little headland to discover the attractions of Maguide spread out before me. They included caravan sites, yacht moorings, an enclosure for learner sailboard enthusiasts, and a bar with an extensive patio. I made a beeline for the last of these since warm water will sustain life adequately but gets a bit boring after a few hours. A swift survey of the rows of bottles behind the counter revealed only one thing with a familiar name, Heineken, the stuff with that exaggerated advertisement on television about reaching those parts of the body which other drinks cannot. At least I recognised its name so I ordered a bottle. A young lady aged about twelve served me and in my best accent I enquired the price. Her younger sister, all of eight years old, interrupted this commercial discussion and said in a very precise tone eyeing me deliberately, "Twelf franc, please."

    I surrendered without a struggle, emptying my Lloyd's Bank plastic bag on the counter and declaring solemnly after selecting two coins, "ten and two makes twelve".

    The cool breeze coming down the lake fanned me under the shade of a large table parasol. I watched the antics of a learner sailboarder with pleasant feelings of superiority and began to think that Heineken had a certain justification for their claim, even if the price was exorbitant. I had a profound thought: civilisation is the ability to walk through beautiful natural surroundings isolated from man and the motor car and slip back into their company whenever you feel like a cool drink. Feeling rather smug after this profound thought I loaded up and continued the trek southwards. Inhabitants of Maguide who had purchased plots of land with private access to the lake shore looked up in astonishment and indignation as a stranger tramped along the water's edge on the margin of their estates. A certain determination in his bearing must have dissuaded them from confrontation, or possibly the thought that this must be the last ignorant foreigner who would disturb their peace this summer.

The lake tried to fool me by unfolding one little inlet after another but I wasn't falling for that old trick. Years of sailing and walking along East Anglian rivers and estuaries had taught me that your destination is always twice as far away as it looks and there is no such thing as a straight shoreline. I was therefore still feeling well disposed towards the world when I crossed the bridge at the foot of the lake, selected a short cut into the town and finally tramped down the main street. The Hotel Poseidon faced me squarely but I decided not to be blackmailed in this blatant manner and walked past it to weigh up the competition. After another fifty metres my legs issued a joint ultimatum pointing out that they had been on the go without anything worth calling a rest from eight o'clock until six-thirty. I conceded defeat and retraced my steps to the Hotel Poseidon.

The town of Biscarrosse itself had been around for quite a few years. Don't ask me when it was founded, and stop reading now if you are one of those earnest people who soaks up dates and historical minutiae like an avid sponge. These pages are intended to give you a two-legged vision of La France as she slipped into the last Autumn of the 1980's. Correction, this book is intended to give its author the satisfaction of obtaining double value for one holiday, experiencing it and then re-living it once more and discovering some interesting bits which he has already forgotten.

Anyway, I was about to explain that Biscarrosse is quite a mature little town situated about five kilometres inland as the seagull flies and not to be confused with Biscarrosse-Plage its younger cousin sitting right on the coast. My confident guess is that Biscarrosse itself was once a little fishing village on the edge of the Atlantic but gradually shifted inland as the dunes piled up inexorably to the west and left it with two lakes and a canal in meagre substitution. Judging from appearances the inhabitants are no longer bothered about this, perhaps because the tourists now take their litter away to the coast. The Plage was an optional diversion on my itinerary but had been booted out at about two o'clock when time was running short and Lac de Cazaux began revealing its delights.

The Poseidon Hotel was one of the newer pieces of Biscarrosse. I arrived in the wake of a young couple clad from head to foot in black leather and hot off the saddles of their monster Harley-Davidson. They swaggered in like swarming cavalry who had swept across the plains of France and dismounted to receive the fealty of a conquered town. Standing behind them bare-kneed, bare-armed, and bare-headed, self-powered and toting a month's baggage, I had the satisfaction of sneering at them inwardly whilst outwardly maintaining the civility of a fellow guest.

"Une chambre a un lit, s'il vous plaît, " I trotted out confidently.

"Oui, Monsieur ". I was conducted across a new courtyard at the rear of the hotel which was clearly used for large functions at the height of the season, and shown up a flight of steps to a well appointed little room tucked into the very roof. The ceiling followed the slope of the roof and was clad in light wood panelling. The walls were freshly painted in cheerful colours, a modern painting hung on the wall, and all the fittings were brand new. On the other hand the only natural light came through two roof lights which defied all attempts to open them, and for hours the room had been absorbing the heat of the day. Nevertheless I liked it; it had a welcoming feeling. I took a long cool shower, washed a shirt and two pairs of socks and hung them out to dry in the faint breeze which blew across the balcony at the head of the steps. No-one complained or even appeared to notice.

I unpacked my Marks & Spencer yellow slacks from their plastic bag at the bottom of the rucksack, put on my Marks & Spencer lightweight black casual shoes and Marks & Spencer black socks, slipped into a clean cotton shirt and, feeling perfectly dressed, descended to see what was on offer in the dining room.

You are probably tired of being told this, but the French really do know about food. Their chefs are artists as well as cooks. The first course was presented on a delicate bed of seaweed covered in ice; on this there was arranged a mouthwatering selection of baby lobsters and large shrimps. I just sat and admired it for a few minutes, sipping a cool glass from my half bottle of Muscadet. I can't recall all the details of that meal but it included sole, a selection of cheeses, water ice and black coffee. None of the courses was very large. Each one was a work of art. I lingered, jotting down the day's events in the diary and finally rose when I found myself alone in the dining room.

After all this self-indulgence I suddenly remembered the telephone. Help! Was it an hour earlier or an hour later at home? Oh yes, thank goodness, it was an hour earlier than here. I inserted myself into the dimly lit cubicle, lined up a selection of coins on the shelf and dialled. The result was the same as on the previous evening. Several more attempts were no more encouraging. In despair I went to Madame and requested her aid. She checked the international code I had used, asked for my home number and busied herself in the cubicle with the aid of a directory. After one or two false starts she turned and signalled to me to take the receiver.

"OK, Monsieur?"

I took the receiver and listened. A homely bleep-bleep greeted me. I gave her the thumbs up sign and waited. "Hello," said a young lady's voice.

"Bonjour, Mademoiselle ."

"Daddy! Where are you?"

I gave a dramatic account of the battle so far, claiming that only a year's intensive training had enabled me to survive, and finished with a glowing description of the recent meal. Envious noises came back in reply with an assurance that all was well at home.

I asked Madame for the secret of her success and was told to omit the 'O' from the beginning of the regional code. So simple when you know. I looked at the piece of paper with the row of numbers and decided that I could scrap it. Start with the year of the 'D' Day landings (1944), chop out the 'O' and dial the home number. It was memorised.

I climbed the steps back up to my room feeling confident of a solid night's sleep. It had been a twenty-five mile day and tougher conditions than I had dreamed of. Add to that a good dinner and a half bottle of white wine and the result must surely be oblivion.

The room was still very warm even with the door open. I stripped off and lay under the sheet on a comfortable bed but sleep eluded me. Every muscle in my legs tingled gently after the struggle although nothing was sore or strained, which was great news and a vindication of all the weekend efforts over the past year. Twelve months ago I would have folded up in a heap before reaching the lake. I lay on my back contentedly without any worries and waited for sleep which would not come. Thoughts drifted gently a few feet above a relaxed body but for the first time in years I felt no concern at not sinking into unconsciousness. Two or three times I got up to take a long drink as dried out tissues reabsorbed moisture and the body restored its natural water table.

By seven o'clock the sky was brightening. I had been offered breakfast at eight-thirty but had negotiated eight o'clock and by that time I was packed and ready to move off immediately after coffee and croissants . By eight-thirty I was off down the road having settled up by Access once more. I topped up my supplies with half a baguette and two tomatoes and headed down to the main crossroads to find the D652 which would take me out of town in the right direction. There was no GR across the Landes but the map showed several tracks or minor roads running east-west across the flat country to the valley of the Garonne. The junction was an unmistakeable cluster of five roads. I checked carefully which of them was the D652, cross-checked with the names on the other signposts, double checked once more, and faced east into the rising sun which was just topping the trees beyond the town. Looking down the road I felt a sudden and unexpected thrill of excitement. This was the real beginning. The whole of France now lay in front of me and I had a whole month in which to walk across it. It was really happening at last; in fact, anything might happen. I began walking eastwards into the dazzling rays of the sun.

The D652 was only the means of getting out of town. The plan that day was to reach a place called le Muret via woodland tracks. The map supported by tourist brochures indicated that the Landes was flat wooded country intersected by occasional roads and practically uninhabited. It was fairly obvious that le Muret with its sister hamlet of Saugnacq existed only as a staging post on the trunk road from Bordeaux to Bayonne. In fact the whole area looked so uninhabited that I had taken the precaution of booking the next two nights accommodation in hotels.

The outskirts of Biscarrosse had the air of a booming frontier town expanding into the virgin land around it. Everything enjoyed masses of space. A new furniture store stood in acres of parking space; a garage had vehicles strewn around it in various degrees of abandon; new houses were staked out with ample land which was doubtless destined to become colourful gardens but was currently no more than scorched earch and struggling brown grass. With so many new developments it was impossible to guess which of the rough tracks to the left was supposed to link with the long black line running across the map towards le Muret. Suddenly I was passing the entrance to a small aerodrome on my right. I stopped and checked the map carefully. My actual and intended courses were diverging slowly but inexorably at an angle of 30°. I had missed the turning but there was no point in going back as another track to the left would appear soon and link up with the intended route. A few minutes later the substitute track appeared. It had an informal look about it and bore the wheel marks of heavy vehicles. A cluster of signs at the entrance conveyed information to anyone who had the right code but none of them positively forbade entry in plain language. All right, in we go.

To describe it as woodland might not be a falsehood but certainly fails to give a true impression. It was forestry, tall straight conifers standing in ranks. Frequent clearings showed that logging was in continuous progress and a few hundred metres ahead of me there were signs of activity. I glanced at my watch and found to my amazement that an hour had passed already. Undo top buckle, pass Pentax Zoom 70 carefully over top of head, undo waist buckle, swing pack to the ground, extract water bottle and take a swig. Relax. Lying on my back I was struck by a horrible thought. I had no recollection of returning the Access card to its separate recess in the money belt after settling the bill that morning. My doubt grew rapidly into deep concern. The card was absolutely critical; cash and travellers cheques could not keep me going for a month of nightly accommodation in hotels. I sprang up, unbuttoned my shirt and checked the money belt. Cash, yes; travellers cheques, yes; Access card, no. Blast! It would take an hour to retrace my steps to the hotel and another hour to get back here again. And what if the card wasn't at the hotel? Stop and think, you idiot; just go back over everything you did after breakfast.

I had taken the card out of its securely zipped compartment before going down to the reception desk in order to avoid the embarrassment of unbuttoning my shirt in front of Madame. I had been wearing my new bright red cotton wind jammer purchased from the Yacht Chandlery in Pin Mill because it was quite cool. Wait, I must have put the card back into one of those unbuttoned pockets in the front of the wind jammer.

I dived into the rucksack showering its contents on the grass. Anorak, lunchbox and baguette were strewn in all directions. I pulled the jacket out of its plastic bag and fumbled in the lefthand pocket. Empty. Into the righthand pocket. Oh, thank goodness, thank goodness. It would have been agony to go all the way back there. I looked at the card and swore never, never, to put it anywhere other than straight back into its proper place and zip it in immediately after use even if it meant unbuttoning myself in front of the most severe Madame in the smartest of hotels. The lesson had been learned. I shivered at the mental picture of the little card falling noiselessly out onto a bedroom carpet as I folded the red jacket and slid it back into its plastic bag.

With that feeling almost of light headedness which accompanies narrow escapes from disaster I set off again down the track, snapping an occasional picture to capture the atmosphere of the morning. Pentax Zoom 70 had behaved perfectly after being given a new battery and a new film. The logging team returned my greeting cheerfully without any attempt to charge me with trespass or search me for hidden matches with which I might have set light to half of Aquitaine. By the way, Aquitaine means "land of waters" if you will excuse the insertion of a little useless historical detail. The Romans apparently found a slushy mixture of sand and water when they arrived on the scene and some public spirited person must have done a thorough job of separating the two elements. If you start a fire these days there is precious little water with which to put it out anywhere between the Atlantic Ocean and the Garonne valley.

I reached a 'T' junction which was in agreement with the map and turned confidently due east once more, but a feeling of unease grew as I realised that the woodland track of my imagination, and as depicted in tourist literature, was rapidly developing into a route nationale for heavy logging machinery. The stuff wasn't actually moving at the moment but I had seen it lurking and grumbling amongst the trees, great multi-wheeled monsters with gangling claws that could pick up a tree as though it was nothing more than a pencil and drop it with precision on a trailer with twenty other trees, the whole assembly then to be towed along by another diesel powered monster which would make a British Rail 125 look like a flashy Hornby toy. Picture the effect of these brutes lumbering up and down an unpaved track. Yes, you're there in one; ridges and valleys of deep shifting sand.

To be fair, it was not quite as bad as the day before. There was usually a sort of verge at each side covered with a thin layer of pine needles, wood chippings and other assorted dead vegetation which provided a delicate carpet with some semblance of solidity if boots were placed carefully. This relief came only in patches. Wherever two vehicles had passed the entire track had been pounded into a good imitation of granulated sugar, the sand having now taken on a bleached white appearance. And it was useless to contemplate getting off the track as an inpenetrable mass of seedlings and briars swarmed below the mature trees. I became an expert in assessing the degree of stability of the surface ahead of me. Telltale wisps of grass and a small struggling broom bush indicated that monster wheels had missed that stretch; a crust-like surface suggested no disturbance since it had last rained; and a really wide furrow might actually have quite a firm bottom. I debated with Pentax Zoom 70 the merits of this self-inflicted punishment.

'It's devastatingly boring.'

'But it's an experience; you won't forget today.'

'If I don't watch the level in the second water bottle very carefully I may not even survive to remember it.'

'Yes, but it's an exceptional experience, better than plodding along noisy tarmac roads somewhere up near Bordeaux.'

'It's plain boring.'

'You'll enjoy looking back on it. Make sure you take some photographs to catch the atmosphere.'

'You can't photograph heat and the damn flies are too small to be photographed even with a zoom lens and even if they did sit still for more than two seconds together!'

'If you can't somehow capture the atmosphere of this lot on celluloid you're not the artist I thought you were.'

'OK, OK, you win, but that blasted railway had better turn up before too long.'

The simplest and most effective solution of course took quite a time to dawn. I was mesmerised by the track itself but many stretches had a drainage ditch eight feet deep and five feet wide running alongside the track. I peered into it. It might be unconventional to walk in a ditch but one must not accept the limitations of convention so I clambered down and was soon speeding along on firm ground hindered only by occasional rocks and junctions with side tracks. It didn't last long but it provided welcome relief from the monotony above.

The timing of rest breaks had to be flexible. Relaxation demanded a flat shady piece of ground with some slight covering of grass and I was beginning to sense that such places occured at the junctions with minor tracks and on the edge of fire breaks where a belt of maize might have a clear cultivatived edge. At one of these a pair of deer took dainty steps out of the trees and into the maize before catching the slight movement of a camera and leaping back into cover.

The line on the map was straight and the track across the ground was straight, interminably straight, as straight as the sun's rays which struck relentlessly into the blistering white of the sand. This wasn't a Roman road but if the Romans built roads as straight as this they must have been poor psychologists. It was enough to drive you round the bend. All sense of distance vanished; there was no feeling of achievement in reaching landmarks; there were no landmarks. There was just the sun, the sand, and the straight trees. Progress could only be estimated by the passing of time. I consulted the map; during the day I would cross four minor roads and a railway, enjoy two changes of direction, and pass one group of houses before reaching the N10 and le Muret.

The hint of a distant rumble vibrated across the heatwaves. I wiped the sweat out of my eyes and looked at an unnatural hump on the horizon. Maybe it wasn't a mirage after all.

A quarter of an hour later I stood on the bridge and looked down at twin lines of shining FNCL rails vanishing into infinity north and south under a lacy netting of wires, behind me the forest and in front of me a cultivated plain of maize. Nothing moved in the heat. Even the flies appeared to have stayed back in the forest. I took a few swigs of warm water and calculated that I was three-fifths of the way to le Muret but ahead of me was a tarmac road which might be hard to walk on but would be heaven after a day and a half of sand. I photographed the railway line for the record and carried on.

Highway engineers must be a peculiar breed of people, schizophrenic and changeable in their moods, frequently leaping out of bed on the wrong side before launching into the day's construction. How else can you account for the incredible variations in camber and surface which you meet in the space of two kilometres on the D348 (beware of driving along it; it takes you as far as the railway line, does a neat circulation round a heap of stones and takes you back where you started from). Having in the morning become an expert in spotting firm sand I became in the afternoon an expert in avoiding hip-displacing cambers. To begin with I stuck to the highway code and faced the on-coming traffic, not that there was any but one likes to observe the niceties, but my left hip sent a message advising me to thumb a lift if I wanted to make le Muret before dark as the left-hand side of the road had developed a forty-five degree slope. I crossed to the right-hand side keeping both ears tuned for traffic creeping up behind. This side was reasonably level if one discounted the potholes but it too began to develop a slant until my right ankle radioed a distress signal. I returned to the left-hand side which was now back on an even keel but was oozing hot tar so I transferred to the crown of the road until a yellow van claiming to be La Poste forced me to give way.

A broad green verge appeared magically on the left-hand side and beckoned me. I moved over gratefully and was enjoying the soothing rustle of grass under my boots when one foot disappeared with spine-jarring suddenness into a well camouflaged six-inch drainage channel. Actually it wasn't well camouflaged as it was marked by a strip of lush green grass but I learned this too late. It became too nerve racking to watch for these green strips and alter the length of my stride so I returned to the road and followed a zig-zag course from one horizontal patch to another taking a rest on my back now and again in patches of shade gazing up at a deep blue sky through a lattice of leaves and pine needles.

My shadow which had trailed behind in the early morning and crept up unnoticed beside me at midday was now moving jauntily ahead as the temperature began to drop, and it outlined a strange hump-backed creature whose legs became disproportionately long. The distant rumble of heavy trucks announced the approach of the N10. I urged on my flagging legs towards it and guided them straight into a wayside bar. A Heineken from the refrigerator slid down my hroat and reached the remotest corners of my being. I promised never to sneer at that television advertisement again even if they went on showing it until the year 2000. A second Heineken followed the first. The barman had visited London on his way to Dublin and produced a touring map of the United Kingdom. In the top right-hand corner of the page for South East England an estuary ran into the North Sea. I placed my finger triumphantly under the name of a little village and showed him where I had travelled from.

Thankfully the N10 had bypassed le Muret and left the hotel Grand Gousier in peace. Yes, they had a reservation. They hoped Monsieur would enjoy his stay. Dinner was at seven-thirty.

Sitting at the dinner table I discovered that "salade landais" included tasty slivers of ham and goose. It was followed by smoked salmon. I sat in an almost deserted dining room jotting down the day's events and adding Tursan to the list of enjoyable dry white wines.

* * * * * *

The great brute was taller than me. True I was sitting down at the breakfast table and he was standing on all four paws but he actually managed to look down on me in a patronising manner. He must have been the occasional barker of the night before. There was nothing malevolent in his manner; he was not one of your nasty all-aggression Alsatian types; more of a black retriever parentage, fed on large helpings of "Growmore" since he was weaned. He inspected each guest in turn and concluded that we were all respectable citizens who could be relied upon to pay before departing. Nevertheless, there was no harm in a peaceful display of strength. These days one never knew; an awful lot of outsiders had been let into the E.E.C. after De Gaulle had lost his grip.

I paid the bill with Access. The Maître was on duty and did not even flicker the corner of an eyebrow when I unbuttoned my shirt. I enquired the location of the Post Office and the boulangerie. He kindly offered to post the five cards for me but regretted that the boulangerie would not be open for at least another half hour. Half-an-hour of early morning coolness was not to be wasted and as it was already eight-fifteen I set off at once.

A reconnoitre the previous evening had confirmed the accuracy of the map. There was the remains of an overgrown track running between plots of land soon to be developed between the old road and the new bypass. It was going to become a matter of routine to scout round each evening before dark and check the next morning's route. A speedy start in the right direction each morning was a psychological boost and avoided that frustrating process of plunging first in one direction and then in another, and even then being not quite sure.

I reached the N10 bypass in a matter of minutes and, dodging through the stream of heavy trucks, threw myself in two perilous stages across the dual carriageway. The Highways Department had forgotten to create a pedestrian crossing when constructing the new road. Slithering into the safety of the trees on the far side I smiled with satisfaction. This was genuine natural woodland. A mixture of pine and indigenous oak threw a canopy over the track which was covered in a soft compost of leaves. Shafts of sunlight filtered through the haphazard pattern of trees. It was icy cool, unbelievably invigorating. Nothing moved except the birds. The insects opened one eye and snuggled back into their beds waiting for the temperature to reach a respectable 28 o C before risking pneumonia. Pentax Zoom 70 slowed me down by frequent demands to edge behind the trunk of a tree and

... actually managed to look down on me in a patronising manner.

capture low flying beams of sunlight which gave a clean fresh early morning shimmer to everything they touched. Now and again we compromised by turning round to get the sun behind us.

An hour of pure magic ended at Pont de Saugnacq where the track joined a minor road to negotiate the cleft of a sharp valley carved out of the flat Landes by the Eyre river. I had forded one of its tributaries a little earlier in a green ravine draped with ferns and tiny flowers in a moist mini-climate of its own.

The road crossed the Eyre on a new bridge high above the water, curved its way out of the valley and twisted eastwards through a more commercial stretch of woodland. Stacks of cut timber stood beside the road. A development of new houses appeared standing in generous wooded plots and shuttered against the world. The shuttered windows of the houses made them seem deserted, but closed wooden shutters kept out the glare of the sun and maintained a cool interior within the stone walls. Whether the owners were in residence or away at work it wasn't possible to tell, but they were taking no chances with casual visitors. At each green plastic-covered wire mesh boundary a ferocious dog would materialise to justify the notice on the gate announcing "*Chien sauvage*". Dog breeding, and feeding, must be a major industry in France. Every detached house seems to require at least one.

Alsatians are the most popular choice, closely followed by bulldogs, with ethnic minorities of Doberman and other species struggling to gain a foothold in the league table. They would rush up in a frenzy of barking and pound up and down the boundary dashing behind hedges to reappear at another vantage point and verbally savage me. At first I crossed the road in an effort to reduce the fury of their barking but this had no effect at all and since they made no attempt to leap over their fences and pursue me I adopted a policy of totally ignoring them. This also failed to reduce the crescendo of barking but it gave me the moral advantage; until, that is, I began to feel sorry for the poor brutes whose only entertainment in life was trying to scare the pants off passing pedestrians. They enjoyed such a limited lifestyle compared with that of Wooster, the companion of my training walks at home. Named after one of P.G. Woodhouse's most famous characters,

Wooster became expert at spotting the preparations for a walk and would prance around with delighted barks whilst I got myself ready. First he recognised the significance of the rucksack; then he realised that the boots were an equally good sign; soon my appearance in thick woolly socks and shorts would alert him; next he learned to spot when the plastic water bottles were being filled; and eventually he developed an early warning system which was capable of picking up a quiet question at the lunch table, 'are you going for a walk, darling?' One eye would open fractionally and one ear would flicker imperceptibly, but to the seasoned observer this denoted a wide awake walk addict faking sleep and just waiting for confirmation before erupting into an impatient frenzy. As soon as we emerged from the back door he would scour the garden for a stick and rush off to drop it ten yards ahead of me. Turning and crouching beyond it he would then challenge me in eye to eye combat to walk past the stick without picking it up. If I ignored it he would assume a look of utter amazement and dart back to regain it, repeating the same procedure fifty yards further on. There was a range of excuses for not bending down to pick up these offerings: 'that's just a twig; it's not worth playing with' or 'that's too heavy, I can't throw that very far' or 'you haven't carried it far enough yet.' Finally one of us would break. Either he would go off to sniff the hedgerows or I would bend my knees with a grunt and fling the article ahead of us, at which he would race off and perform extraordinary feats of catching in mid-air or on the first bounce. His most impressive feat was fast braking with four paws grinding into the ground, rump high in the air and jaws snapping. After a spectacular recovery he would trot ahead with his golden retriever tail waving triumphantly and give me a longer than usual respite. When we reached the river the stick would be dropped at the water's edge and he would wade into the water to make it quite clear where the stick was to be thrown.

  As the expeditions became longer and included stretches of road, walks through grazing cattle, visits to pubs and tearooms and excursions into farmyards I chose the soft option and left him behind at home. His howls of indignation pursued me for several minutes after the door closed behind me.

I paused for the first rest of the day and inspected my feet carefully. There had been blood on my Marks & Spencer ski socks for the first time in a year the previous evening from a slight rub, not a blister, on my right heel. It looked a little raw so I applied a plaster.

The next track left the road before it reached the hamlet of Biganon. I looked at Biganon on the map, decided that it was unlikely to support a Boulangerie , and vetoed a detour into the village. This new track did not have a natural woodland atmosphere and was changeable in nature. At one point it came close to the shifting sands class but was rescued by persistent clumps of little yellow flowers which held the sandy surface together and suffered the full weight of my footfalls. In the run up to ten o'clock (the official moment of transfer to excessive heat) it went through another exquisite stretch of woodland; tall mature pines meeting overhead and giving plentiful shade, green and brown bracken covering the ground densely and glinting in the sunlight, a fine track of silver sand twisting slightly on its course, and the straight stems of the pines making a stippled pattern of light and dark with their sunny and shaded sides. The air was perfumed with gently warming resin and slowly decaying autumnal bracken.

I was just congratulating myself on the excellence of my route planning and giving a pat on the back to " *Série Verte* " when the track ended abruptly in a ploughed field. Well, they do this sort of thing to you in Suffolk too. You have a choice of plunging headlong across the furrows if you think the farmer is trying it on or skirting neatly round the outside of a mega-field. Wishing to follow a course due east in accordance with the map I chose the first alternative, and soon began to regret it. The ploughed field turned out to be several hectares prepared for the planting of baby trees and consisted of a series of north/south ridges and valleys requiring a four foot leap to progress from one ridge to the next. Nothing to a fit man, you will say. Quite a test, I will respond, when you are carrying a sizeable pack, taking off from a crumbling platform and performing all this under a rapidly heating sun.

Halfway across this scene of havoc I gave up the struggle to maintain course and took an escape route south down one of the ridges. At the edge of the field a half-hearted path wandered off through the trees to the edge of a maize patch. A couple of deer who had been taking a free lunch cleared off in disgust and I spotted a promising looking green patch running down the far side of the maize and plodded over to it only to discover that it was a drainage ditch. But drainage ditches are usually crossed by tracks at some point. Peering in one direction I could see where it vanished into a large concrete tunnel. This was all becoming distinctly hit and miss and I had an uneasy feeling that the clear eastward-leading track on the map was vanishing over the horizon while I became entangled in remote recesses of agricultural France. As I pursued the ditch towards its expected junction I realised that I was about to pass under one of those mammoth electric power grids which run for miles across the country and in a flash of inspiration I consulted the map. Sure enough a peculiar double line lay across the map with such unerring straightness that the eye almost dismissed it as an unnatural imposition like the square marks of the grid. If it was followed north-east it would inevitably cross my planned route and enable me to pinpoint my position once more.

  Long distance walking exposes you to all sorts of new sensations. Ten minutes later I could have told you just how that chap Speke (or was it Burton?) felt when he came across the source of the Nile and stood looking at the water pouring out of a big hole at one end of Lake Victoria. I stood looking at a beautiful V-shaped junction of tracks with megawatts of electricity pouring through the sky overhead. I dare say Edmund Hilary got a taste of the same thrill when he arrived at the top of Everest.

  Patting myself on the back I set off crooning a cheerful song. After a few yards, realising that something was amiss, I stopped and tried to put my finger on it. My left cheek felt unusually warm. Good heavens, the sun had moved round to the north!

  'If you stopped thinking yourself so clever and paid more attention to elementary matters you might stand a faint chance of making Villandraut tonight,' muttered Pentax Zoom 70.

  'The cartographer must have got his angles wrong at the junction. It was very confusing,' I replied.

  'You were so full of yourself you forgot which direction you were approaching from.'

'Well, what does it matter? I corrected myself before I had gone twenty yards.'

'What would have happened if the sun had been invisible? You'd have walked south for miles.'

'Alright,' I conceded, 'I'll be more careful in future.'

The track had settled itself comfortably beside a narrow irrigation canal running across a prairie of maize. The next trees were far in the distance. The sun had turned up the temperature to number six on the gas oven. A large bush overhanging the path ahead suggested a rendezvous with lunch. Then I remembered that the Boulangerie at le Muret had been closed and that Biganon had been rated a non- Boulangerie hamlet. I examined the contents of my plastic lunchbox. It's amazing how far you can walk on a hot day on two Twix, sixty grams of cheese, and two small containers of water. I lay on the path in the shade allowing my system to digest all three courses. A lone cyclist took a thoughtful detour around me as I pondered once more the problem of the previous day. Straight lines are boring but you cover the ground fast. My priority in the first three days must be to cover the ground fast and get to the great river systems of southern France.

The horizon of trees arrived and with it a minor road with patches of shade on one side. The tarmac felt hard to walk on and diversions became welcome. A gravelled clearing in the trees drew me in to inspect a small monument. I read the wording and removed my sunhat.

"St Symphorien remembers its heroes of the FFI, Burtchard and Laffon, martyrs of The Resistance", and immediately underneath on a separate plaque "The FTPF of St Symphorien to their comrades of the Maquis, Burtchard and Laffon, murdered on this very spot on 24th August 1944 by the Bosches".

I stood there quietly. It must have been a messy, confused and brutal war in this part of France. You were not in uniform and therefore were not entitled to the status of Prisoner of War if caught by the Germans. Different Frenchmen had differing ideas of what should happen when the Germans finally left. There must have been many scarcely distinguishable shades of activity moving from collaboration through non-involvement to passive resistance and positive action. I was to find many similar wayside remembrances on my route, all perpetuating the bitterness of a war fought quietly and ruthlessly without rules and I began to examine them with increasing interest. Each little village and hamlet had one thing in common with every village and hamlet in England, a 1914/18 War Memorial standing in the churchyard or at its central point. The wording was brief, solemn, and respectful. "To our glorious dead, they died for France", the list of names being unbelievably long by comparison with the size of the community at whose heart it stood, with family names repeated many times. As in England, a smaller addition usually commemorated the dead of the next conflict but here there was a distinction between the two countries. In England one finds wording such as "And to those who gave their lives 1939/45" but in France the few names on the second memorial would each have a date in 1940 against them. In one narrow sense the war had ended for many Frenchmen in 1940 as the French army no longer existed on formal battle fields. The heroes of 1943 and 1944 were to be commemorated at the places where they fell individually, crossroads and hillsides near their own birthplaces.

I replaced my sunhat and walked on deep in thought wondering what rifts still existed between families in these quiet villages and wondering whether German tourists were still regarded as Bosches deep down below the surface life of a new European Community. Some wounds are long in healing.

A road sign announced St Symphorien. It was early afternoon. The side streets were battened down, every window shuttered and every door closed against the glare of the sun. I brushed the sweat sideways off my eyebrows for the hundredth time and struggled on towards the square. A group of six pollarded plane trees provided some shade in the centre, their lower trunks gleaming even whiter than the stonework of the Mairie and other buildings, but the only movement was in the solid shade of the south side. Here a bar was open. A group of youngsters lolled listlessly at tables on the pavement and a car radio blared pop music in defiance of the life-sapping heat. I downed a Heineken and complimented the manufacturers once again on the truthfulness of their advertising; every limb and extremity benefited within moments of the injection. I ordered another one and on the back of this business persuaded the barman to fill up a water bottle with ice-cold water.

I leaned back with my head resting against the wall and half closed my eyes. The shade was soothing and the world was at peace apart from the vibrant car radio. There was a rumble across the cobblestones and a blue van drove into the square and stopped outside the impressive gate of the gendarmerie. I viewed the scene distantly. It was like sitting in the darkness at the back of an old fashioned cinema watching one of those marvellous Laurel and Hardy films. From one side of the van there emerged carefully a tall thin gendarme of solemn face who mournfully opened the gates and latched them back securely against the walls. From the other side erupted a short cheerful gendarme of enormous girth whose pistol holster bounced merrily on his hip with every movement and who proceeded to shake hands warmly with a score of people who materialised from nowhere, firing off a salvo of merry quips which rang round the square. The gates clanged shut behind the van; the gang of hand shakers vanished as mysteriously as they had materialised. The square settled back into afternoon torpor. I eyed the empty Heineken bottles suspiciously. If that scene had really happened Pentax Zoom 70 would have been twittering like mad but he was still hanging docilely from the rucksack on the pavement beside me. Perhaps I had dozed for a moment.

I looked at the map again; only a third of the day's journey left to cover and I had a choice of the D3 all the way or the D3 for a couple of miles and then tracks and minor roads in a gentle arch which looked scarcely any longer. At St Leger-de-Balson I decided that the D3 was noisy and lacked shade and opted for the woodland tracks. Perhaps it was a bad choice. There were too many tracks and none of them seemed to point in the right direction. After a frustrating hour in pleasant surroundings I gave up the hunt for Privaillet (a delightful woodland hamlet astride a little stream, although I never reached it to confirm this) and relying on the sun made my way back to the D3 and waded into the oncoming evening traffic. The village of La Burthe toiled lengthily past me, the Ballion river eventually flowed beneath me, and a final long straight stretch of road showed the outskirts of

Villandraut. This was the second and last hotel booking I had considered it prudent to make and Madame was expecting me.

The dining area was outside under an awning lit by lights which played on the fountain beside which I was sitting, splashed by occasional drops of water. The evening life of Villandrant enacted itself in front of us. A game of boule was being played over on the left. Couples sauntered quietly out of the shadows and gazed at the diners who gazed contentedly back. A giant timber lorry ground past with its heaped burden, narrowly missing a row of lamp posts. The saumon fumé was excellent, the quail even better. I savoured the half bottle of Entre Deux Mers and eyed the couple at the next table curiously. Their familiar exchanges with the waiter indicated that they were locals. Their dinner consisted of two stuffed baguettes, each a full two feet long. I marvelled as they chomped their way through inch after inch. The stuffing appeared to be a mixture of salad and charcuterie . It was just about a dead heat between my five courses and their two feet of baguette, but they finished with a glazed look on their faces and had to move their chairs steadily back from the table to accommodate their stomachs. I guess it was good value if you had eaten nothing all day.

There was no hint of a breeze that night. I looked at my slowly dripping socks and shirt, wrapped them unobtrusively in a Marks and Spencer plastic bag and took them down to the kitchen. The waiter understood my request. I then retired to bed for a third mysterious night of total physical relaxation without sleep. The odd thing was that I didn't feel tired in the mornings and I hadn't yawned once since landing at Bordeaux Airport.

CHAPTER 3

VINEYARDS

After breakfast I paid the bill before going upstairs to complete my packing. The reception desk stood in a corner of the dining room. It was apparently the convention to serve breakfast indoors. Madame was an attractive lady in her thirties and she watched with a smile as my shirt buttons came undone for the Access card and then, producing a bulging plastic bag and glancing at the other guests, she whispered, "Your socks are not yet dry, Monsieur". I replied in an equally conspiratorial whisper, "They will dry in the sun on top of my pack, Madame."

Today was to be a relatively short journey to make up for the long march across the Landes. A brief walk down into the valley of the Garonne and across the river would lead to the beginning of the long GR6 which was to take me up the Dordogne valley and well into the mountains. A brochure had suggested that the Gorge du Ciron was an unspoiled and little known gem worth a detour and the map indicated that a mile or two of walking south down this little river valley could be followed by a turn east to the village of Uzeste before striking northeast for the substantial town of Langon.

I left the hotel in a leisurely frame of mind and headed for the bridge over the river. An idyllic scene awaited me. The path dropped down into a dewy meadow and crossed to the side of a scarcely moving river. In the still waters the overhanging trees were perfectly reflected, an image of utter peacefulness in the early morning sun. Greens of every hue blended together and swam in the water. The air was deliciously fresh and still. It was so exquistely beautiful that I hardly dared tread the ground for fear of breaking the spell. The path joined a track which drew me along sometimes beside the river and sometimes away from it. The track was of pure silver sand, firm underfoot, its two lanes divided by a grassy hummock. I walked along softly, totally entranced.

The harmony was disturbed by the rattle and clatter of a car which caught me up and passed by. Round the next corner I saw that the driver had stopped and was busy hacking off the long arms of briar which had sprouted during the summer and threatened to stop all movement. He was large in all directions with a complexion the colour of well matured claret and he was weilding a wicked looking scythe, slashing through thick stems and kicking them into the undergrowth. I caught him up and he greeted me with a blast of alcoholic breath. His little dog poked its head out of the car window and wagged its tail vigorously. Four minutes later he passed me again and once more I caught up with him, this time stopping for a brief chat. With another alcoholic blast he enquired my destination. I explained that I intended to take a turning to the left and head for Uzeste. He confirmed that this was possible but cautioned me in a friendly manner and with expansive gestures to keep to the track and avoid disturbing the game. I assured him that I would. His accent intrigued me. The little dog had leapt out of the car and was sniffing me with interest. I enquired its name. " Jarrrn ". The word was long drawn out, a provincial equivalent of the neat Parisian " Jean ". The third time I caught him up I realised that I was talking to the local gamekeeper and enquired about the game. He stuck his thumbs in the lengthy belt which looped below an ample stomach and leaned back on the bonnet of his car. Fish, duck, duck eggs; a broad sweep of the hand hinted at other unnamed delicacies. He pushed a greasy beret to the back of his head and muttered something about Les Allemagnes and La Chasse which conveyed a general impression that some visitors to the area were not to be trusted and had a nasty habit of removing eggs.

We parted for the last time at the junction with the track to Uzeste but by this time I had so fallen in love with the Gorge du Ciron that I decided to follow it on to Pont le Trave and double back later on. An extra two hours? So what! How often in a lifetime did one walk into the Garden of Eden? I passed a lake with a shed for ducks to nest in. I walked along a silver track through glades of woodland trees with the sunlight filtering through the leaves and throwing patterns on the bracken. I smelled damp autumn and the delicate decay of leaves. I sang inside myself and thanked the Lord for sharing Creation with me.

… and he was wielding a wicked looking scythe, …

Uzeste has thick plane trees which cast luxurious shadows in the middle of the square. It has little shops with baguette , cheese and tomatoes. It has a Mediaeval church which stands open all day. I sat on a seat under the plane trees and drank water still cold from a night on the window sill. Life was quite perfect.

The sun climbed high again and the road began to throw up the heat in earnest. I crept into a wood of oak and chestnut for lunch and eased off my boots and socks. Acorns plopped gently into the grass around me. A woodpecker laughed and flew off through the trees. I lay on my back and gazed up at the canopy of leaves shielding me from a deep blue sky. The lower branches of the trees were dead; they had served their purpose and perished; the upper branches climbed on up to the light. A faint wind disturbed them and a changing pattern of sunlight struck through the leaves. A family of long-tailed tits hopped and flew past within a few feet chattering quietly to each other.

That afternoon a fairytale chateau stood on a hillside across the valley and beckoned. It flew a long tapering pennant of the kind used by damsels in distress in the story books of early childhood. Crenellated battlements, towers and embrazures slowly became distinct and separate as each curve of the road brought a closer view. It vanished for a while as the road dipped into the thick woods at the bottom of the valley and reappeared as it climbed out again. A smart signboard announced "Chateau de Roquetaillarde". The chateau stood at the end of an avenue of mature trees in open parkland. There was only one snag; the coachloads of assorted Americans, Germans, and Swiss who had paid, or were about to pay, the entrance fee. I took a last look at the pennant snaking lazily in the breeze high above and departed before the memory was scarred with ice-cream and picture postcards.

The hamlet of Mazeres was sunk in afternoon sleep. Not a dog moved. A bright red sign advertised Kronenbourg. I tried the door. It opened and in the dim interior an elderly barmaid was deeply engrossed in a game of cards with three elderly men. She got up promptly to serve me and returned just as promptly to the cloth-covered table.

Vineyards began to appear in the late afternoon but it was a long trek into Langon through messy suburbs of light industry and out-of-town shopping. I reached the old town and after finding the bridge across to St Macaire on the north bank retraced my steps to discover a bar. There was one nestling in a side street beside a garage. I slipped off the pack, hoisted myself onto a bar stool and sat down, Heineken in hand. It was five thirty, time for the older inhabitants to reappear as the heat began to subside and consider a bit of evening shopping and socialising. A gentleman long since retired and doubtless spinning out his years on a meagre pension shuffled into the bar in carpet slippers; a beret of indeterminate colour was pulled forward over his forehead to form a peak; his thick long sleeved woollen shirt was buttoned tightly to the neck; heavy corduroy trousers kept cold draughts away from his legs. I mopped the sweat from my brow and settled back in fascination to watch. He eyed the assembled company, made a careful selection and shuffled across to grasp someone at the bar in a solemn handshake; his target, a mere septuagenarian, returned the greeting somewhat wearily and turned to continue his conversation. The ancient one drooped forlornly and was on his slow journey back to the door when his acquaintance relented and summoned him back. Another acquaintance also had a flash of generosity and within seconds two wine glasses filled to the brim with a dark ruby liquid were standing on the counter. Not a drop was spilled from either of them.

    I crossed the Garonne by the new high road bridge with a sense of achievement and a feeling that the first chapter was closing behind me. The hillsides ahead on the south facing slopes were covered with vines and had a rocky exposed look about them. St Macaire a couple of kilometres upstream is an old fortified settlement built immediately above the flood plain. Massive stone walls rise thirty feet from the fertile fields below. A large church dominates a town of three storey buildings packed together round narrow twisting streets. I checked into the Hotel Des Arts and was given a high-ceilinged room facing a quiet back street. The dining room looked dim and unused so I declined the offer of a meal and went out to explore. The newer northern half of the town lay across the main road although the entire town had now been bypassed by an improvement of the N133. A modern hotel with an outside dining area looked irresistible. I wandered back to the Hotel Des Arts two hours later in tranquil mood. The diary was up-to-date and I was on schedule. Tomorrow was the start of the GR6. I had reviewed the contents of the haversack after the almost crippling heat of the past three days and in anticipation of the steeper hills ahead. One thick shirt, two guide books and a few other oddments had been weeded out and must be sent home. Every ounce saved would reduce the strain on shoulders, thighs and calves.

I slipped naked between the sheets with the window wide open onto the quiet narrow street and fell, for the first time in three days, into deep unconscious slumber.

A noise of terrifying velocity jerked me physically off the mattress. The sound waves crashed down the narrow street reverberating off the walls of the houses. My feet hit the floor in terror. The siren wound down for a few seconds and stopped as abruptly as it had started. I sat on the edge of the bed with my heart pounding. A child was crying in terror in another room as its mother tried to comfort it. A dog raised its voice and joined the list of complainants but there was no noise of rushing fire appliances and the town did not appear to be evacuating itself. I slipped between the sheets again and tried unsuccessfully to sink back into deep slumber and pick up the threads of the dream from which I had been so rudely shaken and in which I had just entered a dormitory occupied by my mother-in-law and other shadowy figures; it was cluttered with beds and arm chairs but there was no bed available for me and I was offered an arm chair; I had just announced indignantly "I have walked all the way across France, and I'm not sleeping in an arm chair tonight!"

* * * * *

Post Offices are the same all the world over. They don't open until nine o'clock in the morning. The hotel Des Arts had offered cold stale baguette for breakfast, justifying the decision to dine out the previous evening, and now there was an enforced hour's delay in which to examine the town before posting home the parcel of excess baggage. I stocked up with lunch supplies, took pictures of sunlit walls and shadowed streets, and discovered the offending siren. It was perched on the rooftops at a cunning vantage point from which it could blast its summons into every little alleyway of the town. It looked an innocuous piece of machinery in the light of day silhouetted against a blue sky.

Madame at La Poste was a motherly sort who produced an official box in which to put my plastic bag of oddments and wrapped it securely in yards of sticky brown tape. La Poste and the Post Office between them later insisted on opening it up in spite of my clear list of contents and delivered it in a sorry melange at the other end. Fortunately it had not included any of my precious films.

I crossed the N113 by the railway line at the precise spot where the GR6 began on the map but there were no red and white daubs to be seen. A track up the hillside pointed in the right direction so I followed it. It divided amoeba-like at the slightest provocation as it climbed up through tiers of vineyards. I gave up looking for daubs and guided myself by the sun and the contours of the hillside until I struck a little paved road which ought to lead into Le Plan. The sight on the slopes below was truly amazing. Neat rows of vines criss-crossed every curve of the hillside, their rectangles switching this way and that to catch the sun and ripen a heavy harvest. The depth of green varied according to the angle at which the sun struck each little plantation. Those immediately below me exposed the stoney soil between the rows and looked thin and grey. Those to each side of me presented a solid wall of green and appeared rich and fruitful. Most had already been picked but here and there a little family group worked, bending low with large baskets beside them.

From the top of the hill there was a view of the tiled roofs of Le Plan through which the elusive GR6 was supposed to run its course. The lady at the Mairie was charming and recalled that there was supposed to be a footpath in the area but was unable to tell me where it started or where it went to. I studied the map carefully again and began to understand the nature of the GR6. It was not so much a footpath as a suggested route for pleasant walking. Between St Macaire and Sauveterre de Guyenne, the objective for the day, ran the D672 coloured yellow on the map denoting that it was a fairly well-used road, which was confirmed by the vehicles buzzing past every few moments. The GR6 recognised the walker's preference for peace and quiet and took him in a series of loops along minor roads to left and right of the direct route, occasionally selecting an unmetalled track. I studied the signposts in the centre of Le Plan, made a choice which corresponded with the red dashes of the GR6 on the map, and set off down a slope into a valley of mixed woodland, vineyards and crops. The traffic vanished, to be replaced by rural solitude. There were small farms with wandering ducks which did not feel the need for guard dogs. There were old stone-built houses, creeper-clad with streams of clear water running by. The little road wound up and down and round about. I was not getting much closer to Sauveterre but I was feeling the countryside, touching its texture, discovering the dwelling places of centuries, feeling their smooth walls, walking round old corners where wooden carts had wound their way during the unchanging millenia before the motor car. This had been my purpose. I was content for the moment.

    I came to a 'T' junction, consulted my watch and sat down in the shade. The postman passed me for the second time and we waved. I took a swig of water, admitted reluctantly that progress was dangerously slow and glanced at the gnarled tree trunk above me. A peculiar patch of colouring caught my gaze and held it. I started to my feet and examined it in amazement. There was no doubt. Years ago someone had carefully applied a splash of white paint and a splash of red. The growth of lichen and the twisting of the bark would soon obscure it forever, but its existence was beyond doubt. No wonder it was only a vague memory to the young lady in the Mairie. It might well have stood untouched since before she was born. Its position even confirmed the route to be taken.

    I moved on thoughtfully. This western extremity of the GR6 must have been little used for years otherwise surely the French equivalent of the Ramblers Association would have demanded a new coat of paint. A track forked off to the left towards a Chateau. I was nearly past it when a splash of white and red caught my eye and, sure enough, the red line on the map parted company with the road for a short distance to take in a funny shaped black splodge on the map. I tried to consult the index at the edge of the map and then realised it was one of the maps which I had cut in half to save weight. It may sound a paltry saving in weight but when you realise that the entire route required twelve " Série Verte " maps and as I only needed one half of most of them you will appreciate the saving that had been made. The sign on the map was a sort of squashed rectangle with insect legs indicating a Chateau or castle (or a Schloss, if you happened to have strayed into Germany by mistake) and this one turned out to be the home of Toulouse Lautrecht. Apart from guided tours it supplied the public with postcards and refreshments so I wrote a postcard to my mother and drank some mineral water.

Have you sometimes wondered how they manage to pick grapes mechanically? The citizens of St Andre du Bois were hard at it and I can describe the process to you in detail if you are interested. If not, skip a paragraph. First make sure your vines are planted in dead straight rows with room for a tractor to pass between them and to turn round at the end. Next, grow your vines precisely to a height of two metres and a width of thirty centimetres so that they fit conveniently within a piece of machinery on wheels which has a similar sized passage running through the middle of it (a sort of inverted 'U' shape). Allow your grapes to ripen in the sun and eliminate weed growth which may gum up the machinery. Attach the machinery to one side of your tractor (don't attempt on any account to tow it directly behind) and switch on the power. Tow the machinery over the row of vines so that a battery of stainless steel rods vibrates with a loud clatter and knocks hell out of the vines causing the grapes to fall into channels on either side and to be collected somewhere within the equipment. When the equipment is full to the brim with mashed looking grapes stop next to a large mobile metal container and discharge them. Finally, employ an attractive young lady clad in a straw hat, mauve 'T' shirt, blue zip-up jeans and fashionable sandals to walk down the row after you with a pair of secateurs snipping off the bunches which you have missed. If she is prepared to wiggle her hips enchantingly as she bends over and to wear her blonde hair in a pony-tail which pokes out saucily beneath the sunhat it all adds to the bouquet.

All this time the hands of my watch had been revolving relentlessly. I climbed back out of the fascinating side valley and did a stretch on the D672 which ran economically along the spine of the hills and had just undergone an improvement. I had to admit that it presented pleasant long distance views. The postman passed me for the eighth time. A cheerful gentleman in an early post-war Renault offered me a lift, the only lift offered on the entire journey. I declined it with equal cheerfulness.

Signals from down below told me that lunchtime was approaching. There was a stretch of road half a mile ahead shaded on one side by tall trees and offering a grassy bank. A car pulled up there and a couple disembarked, set up folding chairs and tables and brought out a large picnic box. I drew abreast of them, paused, and slipped off the pack commenting that it was indeed time for lunch. The man eyed with some disfavour the sweat-stained tramp who sat down with his feet dangling in the ditch and gulped from a plastic water bottle. His wife, however, responded to my comments courteously and with growing interest. They were retired; returning from a holiday in Spain. He had been a taxi driver. I explained the saying "busman's holiday" in English and he thawed and joined in the conversation. It was a pleasantly sociable lunchtime. They departed with good wishes and I stretched myself flat on the verge for a few moments of total relaxation.

A mini van braked sharply, ran off the road a hundred yards further on, turned with difficulty and came slowly back to stop beside me. Four young heads poked out of various windows and enquired if I was injured. Their concern was most touching and I sat up to assure them that all was well and that I was only resting before walking on. They shouted approval, drove a short distance down the road, executed another difficult turn which nearly caused a collision, and came past once more on their original course tooting encouragement on the horn.

The heat built up relentlessly throughout the afternoon. In a countryside given up wholly to vineyards the sun beat down on the soil and the landscape took on a parched look; straight rows of vines intersected by occasional straight rows of poplars, hard rectangular lines with brown grass gasping in between. Most of the vineyards had been harvested. Here and there a heavy crop of dusted blue grapes still hung voluptuously in the shadows of the leaves straining at their skins. The occasional bunch of red roses bloomed at the end of a row of vines, presumably an invitation to the bees to pollinate the vines in spring.

Along the road was displayed a string of tempting advertisements inviting the traveller to pause and taste this year's new wine with a view to purchase. " Dégustation " was the rich suggestive word for tasting; it conjured up pictures of an orgy in a cool dark " cave " as the large buildings were called which housed the wine presses and the storage tanks. Remembering the agony of walking eight miles along the Stour foreshore after two of Tony Reading's large gin and tonics one Sunday lunchtime I gritted my teeth and strode past.

The evening found me plodding up a long hill into Sauveterre. I swung the pack off my back and sank down onto a low stone wall. Was this really a holiday? Was I really enjoying thirst, aching legs, weary ankles and tired shoulders? Oh, shut up! This is just the late afternoon blues. You'll be all right after a shower and a pint of lager. I turned round to look back at the distant hills and groaned in disbelief. Only twenty yards away on the other side of a high wire fence was a school swimming pool. Blue waters tantalised, beckoning me to strip off and plunge into cool depths, sweeping away grime, strain and weariness. But there was no way in; it was deserted. On with the pack again and up the hill.

But now things began to look more promising. The busy road leading into Sauveterre swung away round the outside of the old walled town and, passing through a solid stone gateway wide enough for only one vehicle, I came into a narrow shaded street with shops and old houses opening staight onto the pavement. This was the sort of town which harboured ancient inns with thick stone walls and cool interiors. A couple of hundred yards further on the town square appeared. On three sides of it the pavements were set back under stone arches giving shelter from the sun and providing a shady ground level arcade beneath the buildings. And there was a hotel sign, and another! I headed for the nearer one which looked ancient and enticing. It was closed, as deserted as the swimming pool.

With slight feelings of unease I pressed on among the dawdling evening shoppers to the other hotel. Ah, there was plenty of life here with a reception area and bar combined as usual. I heaved my pack to the ground and asked for a single room.

"Tout plein , Monsieur." Full; it was not so much the news itself as the offhand manner of his response which hurt me. I hoisted the pack and trudged out to continue the search in side streets. A cheerful garage mechanic confirmed that there were only two hotels in the town. Was this going to be my first night under the stars? I had never felt more desperately in need of a long, cold shower and a comfortable bed. A lady behind the counter of a bank smiled pleasantly and I sought her advice. She thought for a moment and then said, "Just outside the town, by the crossroads, there is a hotel by the filling station."

I thanked her, although it sounded rather unpromising, and walked on as directed. My worst fears were confirmed. Outside another stone gateway the bypass reappeared at a busy intersection with traffic lights. Right on the intersection was a filling station with integral bar/hotel for long distance drivers. A four-square, unprepossessing, noisy, modern, characterless eyesore. So much for my dream of cool cloisters and the taste of real France.

Yes, they had a room. It was cool. It was the corner room right over the petrol pump but a delicious breeze blew straight through it. The windows were wide open and wooden shutters kept out the glare of the sun. I unpacked, stood under a stream of cool water in the shower and then lay down on the bed with outstretched arms letting the breeze caress my whole body. I could walk into town and find a place for a decent meal; a filling station was unlikely to rank highly for cuisine. After a while I stirred myself into action, washed the day's socks and sweat-soaked shirt, threw in the lightweight Marks & Spencer shorts as an after-thought, opened the bathroom shutters and treated the users of the bypass to a private viewing of my laundry. Downstairs the bar offered a Heineken as a preliminary move to checking out the restaurants of Sauveterre.

It was clearly a social centre as well as a bar for passing motorists. The locals arrived in their overalls straight from the day's work and greeted each other. I settled down to listen and learn. Those ordering a drink usually had their glasses filled with a pull from each of two levers. I caught the word " panaché " and, finding my glass empty, decided to investigate. I stood at the bar, pointed at the two levers, and said " panaché " with a slight question in my voice. Without hesitation Madame reached for a glass and drew one long stream of beer and another of lemonade. Shandy, not a bad idea! I returned to my seat against the wall and sipped. Extremely refreshing and very smooth, it slid down the throat without the slightest interruption. I was converted on the spot. Now don't get me wrong; Heineken had seen me across the Landes, right through the grim desert tracts of Aquitaine, had taken me into the valley of the Garonne and pulled me out of it by my boot straps. I shall never, never forget it. Emotional tears still spring to my eyes as I watch that noble advertisement on television telling the world the truth; Heineken does reach those parts of the body which other lagers fail to penetrate. But the world moves on. One must be open minded and adventurous, willing to adapt and to encourage fair competition. Au revoir Heineken; bonjour, panaché.

An enormous unkempt gentleman entered in a dirty cotton shirt which was utterly inadequate for the task of covering his beer gut, ragged shorts and open sandals. Clearly a local character he was welcomed into a group at the far end of the bar and became its centre of conversation. I strained my ears to catch the gist of the exchange but the accent defeated me. None of the words were recognisable. After a few minutes the large gentleman looked up and called across to Madame in unmistakeable cockney.

"Come orn luv; let's 'ave some service. Ah bin workin' 'ard all day. Ah need a drink". I froze in my seat, the glass of shandy locked in mid air on its journey to my lips, appalled at this invasion of the French airwaves. The other occupants of the bar appeared quite unmoved. Madame wrinkled her nose but moved across to take an order. The hum of conversation continued. Now that my ear was atuned to the right accent I leaned closer and discovered that he was not attempting to speak French. His entire conversation was in uncompromising cockney flavoured with rhyming slang and amazingly there appeared to be a genuine conversation in progress on such matters as house building and car repairs.

As he obviously knew his way around I decided to consult him on the best place to eat in town. During a convenient lull in conversation I edged up to him.

"You seem to know your way around these parts pretty well. What's the best place to eat?" He eyed me for a moment adjusting his ears with visible difficulty to BBC English.

"You can eat 'ere, mate. It's the best grub for miles around and they're lovely people too. The menu's on the wall over there."

It turned out that he was converting a derelict house into a holiday home with the use of local labour. The last I saw of him he was packing several of his friends into his car for a run round the local "pubs".

Such a clear recommendation for dinner could not be ignored and, abandoning any plan to examine the restaurants in town, I went out map in hand to check the start of the route for the next day. By a stroke of good fortune it left Sauveterre at the road junction under my window. Within less than a kilometre it left the D670 and switched onto a narrow side road; and, what was more, the white and red daubs were there to prove it!

I returned to the hotel in good spirits, removed bone dry shirt and shorts from their vantage point above the traffic lights and descended the stairs in high anticipation. The dining room, neatly set with cutlery and table lamps, was shuttered and deserted. Had he been kidding me? I consulted my watch. It was seven thirty, the universal time for commencement of dinner in France. I stood there nonplussed. A couple descended the stairs, nodded a greeting and disappeared down a dim passage towards the kitchen regions. I hesitated and then followed them.

It was a school dining hall in miniature. Rough wooden tables stood in rows, end to end, with a single gangway running down the room. Two groups of diners were already busy. No staff were in evidence so I seated myself across the gangway from the couple who had greeted me and looked for a menu. There was nothing in sight except a paper tablecloth. It was hot in here; the only window was a large plate glass shopfront window looking onto a pavement and it had no moving parts. I began to have doubts again but the other diners seemed cheerful enough. Yes, it was decidedly hot. I reached down and surreptitiously eased off the black lightweight shoes. Madame across the gangway spotted my maneouvre.

"Oh, yes, it is so hot!" she exclaimed kicking off her own shoes and giving me a grateful smile.

A waitress in an apron appeared from nowhere, placed an open bottle of red wine and a jug of water at each of our tables and disappeared as quickly. That's funny; neither of us had placed an order. My bottle bore no label of any sort. I glanced sideways; neither did theirs. Monsieur half filled his glass with wine and topped it up with water; Madame followed suit. I poured some wine into my glass, sniffed tentatively and took a sip. Not bad at all; I took another sip. The waitress reappeared placing at each table soup bowls, a large tureen of soup and a basket of bread. The soup was delicious with tasty bits and pieces floating in it; the bread was fresh and crisp. I resisted the temptation to empty the tureen and the basket as there were clearly more important things to follow.

"You are on holiday?" I ventured in response to a further encouraging smile from Madame. They were on their way home to Brittany after a lovely holiday in the Pyrennees. I said that my son had cycled through the Pyrennees to Andorra the previous year. They rolled their eyes and laughed. The tourists in Andorra!

"I see that you mix water with the wine," I said to Monsieur. "It is more thirst-quenching," he explained, "but each to his own taste." I experimented. He was right. The cold water and warm wine blended well and produced a long and refreshing drink.

"And you are on holiday too?" enquired Madame. I went into the now well practised explanation and her mouth fell open in incredulity.

"On foot!"

"That must be getting on for a thousand kilometres!" exclaimed her husband in amazement.

"Well, it depends which route I take," I added modestly, but he was already turning to the other diners who had by now gathered at neighbouring tables.

"You hear that?" he called out, "this chap is walking from the Atlantic to the Mediterranean!"

The hum of conversation rose. Most of the newer arrivals were locals who called out to the waitress and greeted one another with warm hand shakes. It was a social gathering which welcomed travellers to its bosom and used them as a topic for conversation.

"Walking to the Mediterranean? He must be mad!"

"Does he want to know a good hotel in St Foy?"

"I can give him a lift tomorrow" (loud laughter).

It was fun. This was the real France tucked away in a back room with plates wiped clean with bread after each course and kept for the next one. We got up and helped ourselves to hors d'oeuvre from a mammoth display outside the kitchen door and then sat back to receive the fish course and the meat.

I experimented with various combinations of wine and water, a pleasant pastime with endless opportunity for innovation. The level of wine in the bottle fell below the halfway mark.

The conversation moved on to families, homes, hobbies and politics. A selection of cheeses appeared followed by a delicate creme caramel. The level of wine in my bottle fell lower.

After two and a half hours I rose reluctantly with the other diners and navigated carefully through the doorway. Holding the bar firmly in both hands I enquired how early breakfast would be available.

"Any time you wish, Monsieur. We are open all night for the motorists."

I stumbled upstairs in a cloud of benevolence. Lovely people, as the man had said, and I could be off to a cool and early start next morning.

CHAPTER 4

DORDOGNE

The approaching cars still had their headlights on. The earth was dark. A distant airliner caught the sun and its vapour pencilled a silver line across the dawn sky. The eastern horizon became rose-tinted and changed its colouring minute by minute. I turned off onto the side road, twin metalled lines with grass growing in the centre running their pale course between indistinguishable rows of vines. The air was liquid joy, icy cool against my skin under the thin cotton shirt. It was as though the cool shower of the previous evening was still drenching me with delight.

The rays of the sun suddenly exploded upwards between distant cumulous clouds as it crept above the earth's rim and infused the whole world with colour. Happiness brimmed over. Thanks, Lord; it's beyond all my expectations. I really don't deserve it; its unbelievable.

The truck drivers had paused regularly at the traffic lights on their overnight journeys and motorists had stopped under my window for a quick refill. After a coffee and croissant on the bar stool I had set out and headed northeast for the Dordogne. The Dordogne! Now I was striking into the very heart of France.

I strode over the ground feeling bronzed and battle-hardened with a feather-weight pack. From a farmhouse just above the track a dog stood up and woofed at me, gently wagging his tail. I winked at him conspiratorially, agreeing to preserve the magic of this morning until the last possible moment. The GR6 abandoned the little road and switched onto an earth track after giving due warning with a double splash of white above red. Fields of maize blended into woodland and the track became a lacey tunnel with dew soaked grasses underfoot and wild flowers sunk in dark shadows. After a time it climbed back out of the trees and ran up to a substantial highway. The D17 had arrived on schedule. Eight-twenty and time for a rest.

I sat on a large rock dangling my feet in the ditch, extracted five postcards, and wrote lyrical reports to colleagues in the office; then had five minutes flat on my back while considering the choice of routes for the day. The GR6 did another north and south loop either side of the main road on its journey to St Foy-la-Grande but there was the option of breaking out of the northern loop and taking a shorter route up the valley of the Dureze to the Dordogne. We would see how the day went.

A short walk along the D17 disclosed the minor road off to the right as indicated on the map. I plunged down a couple of hairpin bends through woods towards an open cultivated plain and walked on to the next junction. This was fun. It was undisturbed walking in quiet country and I knew exactly where I was on the map. I waved cheerfully to a lady standing at her farmhouse door and admonishing her large woolly dog not to chase after me. It was now just a matter of picking up that track on the lefthand side which would appear immediately after the next junction on the right. It was a good thing they had taught map reading in the school cadet corp; one was able to put it to such good use later in life. Humming a merry little tune I swung past the junction on the right and marked the obvious spot for the footpath just by a clump of trees ahead on the left. There it was, easy as falling off a log.

The path curved into the trees and stopped at a rubbish tip. I shrugged my shoulders and withdrew in good order to the road. It must be just a bit further on. Yes, here we are, on the edge of this vineyard. Blast! The farmer had planted rows of vines at right angles to the route.

At that moment a well-weathered gentleman on a tractor trundled up the road. I waved him down to discover where the path had been diverted to. He pulled up, listened to my question and shrugged his shoulders.

"Route barré, Monsieur, " he exclaimed helpfully. Well, I could see the path was closed. That was obvious. You couldn't walk across a hundred rows of vines wired securely to their posts. I tried the point about a diversion again. He waved his hands expressively and repeated in a voice full of sympathy, "route barré, Monsieur. "

"I think I've met your sort in Cornwall," I muttered to him in English, fixing a courteous smile on my face and adding " merci, Monsieur."

He trundled off. Yes, the farmers in Cornwall were past masters at it. You began walking where the map clearly indicated a footpath and they suddenly popped out of the undergrowth full of polite firmness and assured you that there was no right of way, pointing at barbed wire fences guarding rows of cabbages.

O.K., it would have to be a quick flanking movement to get round his defences. Six attempts to rediscover the footpath behind the vineyard by stumbling along the edge of fields, skirting woods and walking in ditches resulted in exasperation and a pack which was getting heavier. Deciding to ignore the GR6 for a few miles and try again further on where the farmers might have retained some semblance of social conscience I headed direct for Cleyrac and followed the D672 for a while.

The game was repeated throughout the morning. A confident right jab past a white and red daub; follow through with a left hook while the momentum lasts; fail to connect with the next turning; try fancy footwork to find another opening; get caught off-balance by a farmhouse not shown on the map; saved by the bell as a white and red daub appears unexpectedly on a gatepost. At the conclusion of each round I sat down for a swig of water and looked at my watch with annoyance. By eleven o'clock I was utterly lost in a sea of vineyards with no habitation in sight. What I could really do with was a nice little road and a friendly motorist. I looked at the sun, consulted the map and set a course which must hit a road sometime. It did. I sat down again dripping in the shade of a lone poplar and calculated that St Antoine-du-Queyret must be just up there to the right. Loading up after a ten minute respite I paused to check with a motorist who came up behind me. No, he explained, St Antoine-du-Queyret was two kilometres behind us. He had just come from it.

I had lunch and reviewed the dismal progress. It had to be the shorter route today most definitely. At Listrac-le-Dureze the road slipped down into a narrow valley. I nodded farewell to the GR6 and headed due north in company with the D128 feeling pretty confident that it would not peter out on the edge of a vineyard and would eventually deliver me to the Dordogne.

My faith in the D128 was justified. It kept strictly to the valley of the Dureze climbing gently up the wooded escarpment on the shady western side and sinking down again to be met by another road crossing from the other bank. I reviewed the situation and was persuaded to cross the river and head for Gensac which, the map indicated, must be large enough to justify at least one bar. I hadn't tasted a panache all day and the urge was becoming irrestistible. If any further justification was needed the map also showed that the D18 ran in a straight line from Gensac to St Foy thus shortening two sides of a triangle.

Gensac offered a choice of two bar/restaurants in one of which the proprietor was busy with early preparations for dinner. I perched on a stool at the bar counter and waited. He acknowledged my presence briefly but there were priorities to be observed; the creative stream was running fast and his hands worked deftly at salads, vegetables and desserts. After a few minutes he paused with his head on one side and nodded with satisfaction. Then he rinsed his hands at the sink and came to serve me. The shade outside was restful and two panachés slipped down while the little town slumbered its way through the afternoon.

The D18 was certainly direct in its route across the plateau above the Dordogne valley but it was easy to underestimate the impact of those dark patches and thin blue streaks cutting across it on the map. Each one was a deep cleft channelling a minor stream northwards to the great river valley. One moment the road was bowling merrily across the undulating high country splashed with vineyards and orchards, and the next moment it was executing a double hairpin bend down an oak clad hillside and turning sharply across a bridge at the bottom. The urge to complete the day's journey grew steadily. This was the irritating thing about the late afternoon. Even with regular rests the legs would begin to put up growing resistance as the sun edged into the west. There were limits to what a year's training could achieve. The pack grew heavier, shoulder straps cut deeper, Pentax Zoom 70 bounced more irritatingly on my chest, and I looked forward increasingly to a shower and a laze on the bed before dinner. There had to be a striking change in the countryside if it was to draw any response from me at this time of day and even the orchards of ripe yellow plums were incapable of attracting more than a passing glance.

I topped a rise and stopped to gaze. A reach of the Dordogne river lay below me in the distance, wide and placid, overhung by woods on either side and backed by higher hills beyond the flood plain to the north. St Foy was now in view, almost within reach. I ate a Mars Bar for a final injection of energy and pressed on.

The road running the last two kilometres into St Foy should never have been allowed. It runs dead straight from Pont-de-la-Beauze to the edge of St Foy with an interfering jumble of houses and petty factories blocking out a decent view of the river. The toiling pedestrian is pitchforked from garage courtyard to unmade pavement, from steeply cambered roadway to derelict grass verge, and still the town remains obstinately distant in this disappointing arrival at the fabled Dordogne.

I plodded into the town in exasperation and looked around for hotels. A quiet side street drew me between old buildings towards the river and led to the door of a timbered inn labelled "La Vielle Auberge". That would do. The day had lasted long enough.

* * * * *

A large insect droned overhead. It was one of those heavy, fruit-laden days when every sensible creature takes a few hours lunch break, flat on its back if possible. The close mown grassy bank had drawn me off the road like a magnet. A faint breeze stirred the leaves overhead from time to time. I stretched in the shade with the rucksack as a pillow, contemplating the orchards in the wide valley of the Dordogne below; nothing to hurry for, no sound to disturb the warm air.

Another large insect passed overhead. Surely it would be less effort to do that sort of thing in the evening. Not that I was complaining; droning insects add another dimension to a summer day, a confirmation of warmth and wellbeing, a reassurance that old friends are around and may drop in at any moment and fold their wings for a chat or a brief stroll over the hairs on your leg.

Another one went overhead. I focused on him with difficulty against the blue infinity above. He homed in purposefully on a tree across the lane, alighted, and became invisible. He could not be a very discerning insect. The tree bore no fruit; it was old and gnarled, knotted, with bare patches on its flanks where the bark had fallen away over the years; its branches were the haphazard survivors of many winter gales. Any discerning insect would be busy in the orchards down below, nibbling a nectarine or a plum, giving a bullace the once over, grappling with a grape or two, or just keeping an eye on the apples.

There must be quite a family of them. They were arriving and departing as regularly as flights at Charles De Gaulle Airport. I pushed myself off the ground with some reluctance and got up to make a closer investigation. Eight feet above the ground where the stump of an old bough jutted out was a row of holes penetrating the twisted pattern of the trunk. I stood waiting to catch the next movement. Something buzzed by uncomfortably close and alighted at the edge of a hole. Its striped yellow and black body vanished from sight, all two-and-a-half inches of it. Before I had time to react another hornet appeared from a different hole and launched itself straight past my left ear. I threw myself out of the flight path, leapt for the safety of the far bank and began to stow things quickly in the rucksack; but hostilities developed no further and after a few moments I settled back once again to contemplate the orchards of the Dordogne at my feet.

The morning had started overcast with the only colour being provided by a few clumps of bright flowers along the path beside the river. It was a river with green weed trailing at its edges, green trees hanging low over the banks and green water gliding slowly. Occasional fishermen drooped in moored boats, hunched over their rods in inpenetrable thought, oblivious of the world beyond their reach. There had been stretches of path through close-packed saplings at the water's edge and long walks through maize fields; not the most direct route to Montbazillac but I had wanted to follow the river and it had curved quite a long way north before reaching the next bridge at Gardonne and permitting a change of direction south towards Montbazillac of the fabled chateau. And I had to admit that I was not totally sure where I was heading for. The problem was that the guide book for the GR6 mentioned no hotel at Montbazillac and Madame at La Vielle Auberge in St Foy did not think that there was one and could offer no advice. The tourist office had been long closed by the time dinner finished and I had strolled the streets pondering the problem uneasily; change the planned route or risk a night under the stars? The entrance to the four star Grand Hotel, decked out with credit cards and club cards of every description, had prompted a flash of inspiration.

The receptionist glanced respectfully at my spotless white shirt and neatly creased yellow trousers. Of course, he would be delighted to assist. One moment, sir, while he looked in the hotel guide book. Yes, the Relais de la Diligence was close to Montbazillac. Should he phone and make a reservation for me? It was done in a moment. The exact location? Well, it was only six kilometres from the village in a south-westerly direction. I thanked him profusely and stayed for a drink to repay the kind deed. The Grand Hotel did not have a bar; one took a seat at a wicker table in the floodlit courtyard under the vines and summoned a waiter while elegant couples strolled back and forth by the fountain.

I had retired to bed reassured and ready to sink into well earned instant oblivion but La Vielle Auberge had other plans. There was a fascinating plumbing system in the old quarter of the town by the river. Each house, and my bedroom window overlooked a score of old properties, had its own water storage tank which was replenished by its own electric pump at night. A symphony of sound grew out of the darkness as one after another the pumps switched into action. The performance began with a deep bass pump somewhere in the hotel itself; a french horn across the road joined in jauntily with a trombone hard on its heels. Then a chorus of flutes and piccolos edged their way in until a fully fledged orchestra beat the night air. With their tanks once again filled to the brim the participants ebbed away into silence once more and I turned over with a sigh to prepare for sleep. Then the first owl hooted.

I am not an ornithologist. Most birds look small and brown to me and it takes a distinctive call like that of the cuckoo or woodpecker to earn recognition from me. There were definitely different types of owl, but whether they were tawny, barn, short-eared or small I could not say. Whatever their family names they appeared content to share the hunting rights in this particular locality and egged each other on enthusiastically. I was thankful not to be a mouse or a water rat. At about one o'clock they had apparently cleared the town of vermin and moved off into the countryside. Then the mosquitoes arrived. I pulled the sheet up over my naked body, reached for the tube of insect repellant, anointed my face and neck, and shut my eyes firmly.

* * * * * *

The Relais de la Diligence, like the hornet's nest, had a commanding view over the valley. It had taken a long afternoon and several panachés in village bars to discover the hotel, but the food was good and it was well positioned for an early assault on the chateau. There had been an incredible number of little valleys to climb in and out of, sometimes on beautiful little roads and sometimes on dusty tracks which lost their way. One thing was clear; my loop round the river had taken a full day to cover a stretch of country which the GR6 covered in half a day and one of my legs was feeling slightly bitter.

My head nodded forward. A knife clattered to the floor. Madame smiled and shook her head; Monsieur must have walked a long way today.

* * * * *

"But how did you know that I was English?" I asked him. It wasn't fair. All I had said was the one word " ouverte " from the other side of the closed glass-panelled door and he had guessed that I was English. I mean, my accent wasn't that bad.

He continued to shift wine bottles on the floor behind the bar for a few moments and then looked up with a wicked grin. " Le phlegm, Monsieur . You are not French because you are not gesticulating. You are not German, because you are polite. You are not Dutch, because you are not speaking loudly. You stand there calmly waiting for me to come to the door; you must be English."

It sounded like a compliment. There was a moment's pause and then we both burst out laughing. I sipped my pastis and turned round on the bar stool as Madame emerged from the kitchen and placed a small black puppy with white paws on the floor.

"You are having dinner, Monsieur?"

"But of course, Madame".

"That is sensible of you. Everyone enjoys my cooking. Even people who stay at the other hotel come here to eat."

I could understand people selecting the other hotel for its accommodation. The rooms at the Hotel du Barrage were spartan to say the least, but I could not have walked one step further if I had wanted to. One leg was extremely painful. I had paused for a few minutes rest beside the long dam which spanned the river and had nearly missed the hotel altogether. The little sign had caught my eye just as I was about to trudge on.

The trouble must have started the previous day when my right boot had begun to feel tight around the ankle. I had stopped and loosened the lace a little, feeling slightly puzzled as this had never occurred before in seven months of walking in these boots. It had brought temporary relief and then the feeling of tightness had returned, so I had stopped again for a longer period. That was the lesson learned the hard way in a year's training at home: if it begins to hurt stop and relax at once; don't try and disregard it. That had solved the problem for a little while but another day of ups and downs among the hills around Montbazillac had done the damage and by the time I had circled back to the Dordogne a limp was developing.

The last stretch of the journey had been through the most peaceful scenery. The river and a canal ran along each side of a narrow road which must have been the towpath in years gone by. Tall lines of poplar and plane trees were reflected in the still water. Fishermen sat at intervals along the wide grassy banks and dozed in afternoon heat. A thin scattering of early autumn leaves lay unmoving on the ground, not daring to suggest openly that summer was coming to an end. Here and there a family group lazed quietly. As I approached one of them Pentax Zoom 70 made urgent representations.

'That's a perfect group to photograph.'

'Be quiet. I can't stop beside them and stand there taking pictures of them. It's rude.'

'Well, you can't walk by and miss that picture. You'll kick yourself for years if you don't grab the chance.'

'It's rude to take pictures of strangers. Anyway, we would disturb them.'

'Then stop and ask them if they mind.'

'I'm too shy.'

'Look. There's father fishing in a blue smock and blue hat, mother reading her book in a red dress and red hat, and that rather gorgeous daughter in very short shorts with beautiful short-cropped hair who is trying to pretend she hasn't noticed you. And you can catch the reflection of the trees in the water at the same time.'

'Oh, alright, if you think they won't mind.'

I removed my sunhat politely and stood smiling at them. "Pardon, Madame. C'est parfait! Puis-je prendre le picture ?"

Madame smiled back.

"Mais oui, Monsieur."

Pentax Zoom 70 clicked and wound on enthusiastically ready for another one. I closed the shutter firmly, thanked Madame and began to walk on.

"Good luck," said father looking up from his fishing. I spun round in embarrassment. Were they English? A quick check with the number plate of their camping van reassured me that they were French. Father was chuckling at my reaction and attempting to persuade his daughter to try out her English on me. She was blushing delightfully but declining to talk to a strange gentleman. Mother came to the rescue with questions about my journey. We chatted for a while before I moved on with one more little tableau of France etched in my mind.

The footpath wound its peaceful course beside the river and the canal for several more miles. A rugby match was in progress in Lalinde with an enthusiastic Sunday afternoon crowd cheering on the local lads who were perspiring bravely on the pitch. Small bands of cyclists gathered on the occasional bridges and refreshed themselves before stretching their muscles over another twenty kilometres.

It is a moment of the year which is so painfully beautiful. Summer heat threaded with a glint of autumn glory. Mown grass framing golden bracken. Trees moving majestically under full green sails in the last days before the storm. A whole year is dying quietly as the sun shortens its daily visits and the air is enriched with deep damp smells.

I moved on slowly and increasingly painfully through a late afternoon of beauty. Families of ducks nestling in the shade examined me one-eyed and concluded that I was harmless. Tremolet still lay on the far side of an enormous bend in the river. It was beyond reach that day. I would have to find somewhere closer. And so I had paused beside a dam and a railway bridge at the foot of the the great U-bend and heaved a sigh of relief when the hotel sign caught my eye fifty metres down the road. I could just about struggle that far.

The restaurant looked out across the road to the water. Its door was locked. I glanced around and saw that the accommodation was in a separate building; the door to that building was open and I investigated. A communal shower-room lay behind the first door and a rather bare corridor led past rows of bedroom doors. Well, at least it would be cheap. I returned to the main building and rapped sharply on the glass-plated restaurant door. There was no response. Peering inside I could just make out the figure of a man writing at a table. He looked up in irritation and waved me away. I rapped again.

"We are closed," he shouted.

"Ouverte ", I retorted firmly, pointing at the sign which hung above my head clearly indicating that they were open for business.

He shrugged in exasperation, got to his feet and walked towards the rear of the dining room calling out to a person unseen. "C'est un Anglais."

Blooming cheek! How did he know I was English? I stood there fuming quietly until Madame emerged with a bunch of keys and escorted me to a room in the other block.

Well, now I knew. It was the calm phlegmatic character of the Englishman which had given me away. Remind me to explain this to the Liverpool United Supporters Club one day.

I finished my pastis and was invited to take my seat at a table. There was no menu. Madame arrived with a basket of bread and a tureen of interesting soup which was left on the table for me to help myself. Something soft lodged itself against my foot. I peeped under the tablecloth and discovered Fidel, the little black puppy with white paws, looking up at me with appealing eyes. "You're too early, young man. I'm only on the soup course, even if I was thinking of giving you something," I advised him.

"Bon soir, René, " called out Madame as a casually dressed man entered and sat down at the table by the window nodding to me in a friendly manner. Bread and soup were delivered to him speedily. René dipped the ladle generously into the tureen a couple of times, then picked up a bottle of red wine and poured in a liberal dose. He stirred the mixture thoughtfully, sniffed it, and then got to work with loud sucking noises. This operation was repeated once more, after which he took a piece of bread and carefully wiped his bowl clean. He sat back in his chair and looked over to the kitchen with an expression which suggested that he was now ready to start dinner.

Madame returned to my table with a plate of heaped hors d'oeuvre; tomato, cucumber, beans, peppers, lettuce and over it all a delicious French dressing. Fidel was foolish enough to reveal his presence and was promptly summoned back to the kitchen. I waded in wondering how much room to leave for other courses and decided to play safe and not clear the entire plate.

Madame clucked when she came to collect the plate.

"You do not like it?"

"It's delicious, Madame, but....." I pointed to my stomach. "I'm only a small man."

She laughed and produced another plate with a large sea fish of some description resting in an exquisite sauce. My concern over the leg injury began to diminish. Clearly I might have landed in a worse place if I had to be immobilised for a day or two. First rate cuisine in an inexpensive hotel overlooking the river would do much to alleviate the frustration. I dutifully finished every morsel of the fish and was rewarded with cheese and fruit.

Madame and Monsieur then joined René at the large table by the window and recounted to each other the events of the day. I gleaned from the conversation that Rene was retired and took all his meals at the hotel, that Monsieur was a Professor of sorts about to return to University for the new term, and that Madame was Parisienne and had a low opinion of the social life of Mauzac.

I volunteered an observation from time to time.

"It is beautifully peaceful here."

"Peaceful!" snorted Madame. "Nothing happens here except in July and August." She related the story of a guest who came sometimes from Guernsey. He flew into Bergerac in his private plane, stayed for five days enjoying the " tranquillité " and departed with great reluctance. " Tranquillité !" exclaimed Madame with disdain. "This place is dead!" Rene and Monsieur chuckled good humouredly. They had heard it all before.

I noticed that Fidel had posted himself strategically beneath Rene's chair and was enjoying a steady supply of meat, fish, and cheese in spite of Madame's frequent demands that he should come and sit beside her quietly. A woolly and well-behaved adult dog had joined the party and was sitting obediently beside Madame casting disapproving glances at his young colleague. It looked as though Charles did his best to explain to Fidel that one must not pester the guests but was finding it an uphill task.

This evening's meal was of course only a light snack. On Sunday the French do their serious feeding at lunchtime. In fact they have two serious occupations on Sunday, feeding and hunting, the latter being known as " la chasse ". My first acquaintance with " la chasse " had been early that morning. The day had started with a fine drizzle which wrapped the whole valley of the Dordogne in a gentle grey cloak as I surveyed it from the walls of the chateau at Montbazillac. The world had not been in a hurry to rise. Scarcely a soul stirred in the village of Colombier as I trod quietly beneath dripping trees, but on rounding a corner I met a shining landrover parked in business-like fashion beside the road. Two men were propped against the bonnet attired in smart flash jackets, long green trousers tucked into elegant boots, and felt hats decorated with short colourful feathers. Ammunition belts added a purposeful touch. Sleek oiled shot guns were slung over their shoulders. I looked at them in some astonishment. Walking the footpaths of Suffolk through the seasons of the year I had become accustomed to startled pheasants taking off in indignation almost from under my boots and coveys of partridge hastening out of the way as I approached, the spoor of deer in the woods, rabbits in abundance, and hares racing over the skyline with

Wooster in hot pursuit. I had even come face to face on one occasion with a fox who had given way with great reluctance and had sat down in a meadow to watch me out of sight before continuing his daytime excursion to find out what the combine harvester might have disturbed from its home. By contrast in France I had seen nothing edible roaming the countryside in its natural state since the two deer in the maize field back in Aquitaine. "Bonjour, Messieurs . What are you after?" I had enquired.

"La chasse ", responded the more elegant one fingering his moustache; and with an air of determination, " Phaisans!"

I must have looked less than convinced for his assistant (I could see now that the other had more rugged features and a decidedly alcoholic nose) lowered one eyelid and murmured, "there is nothing much around today."

As the morning wore on there was an intermittent pop-popping of shotguns in the woods all around but no startled birds or woodland creatures broke cover in my direction. "La chasse" must rank equal as a pastime with mooring a yacht in a marina on the Orwell; good one-upmanship.

Later in the day after passing through Phenix I had sat down in sunshine for lunch beside the road and watched a more genuine local chasseur approaching me over the fields with a little terrier. He was clad in old clothes and a week's growth of beard. His accomplice, Sammy, accepted a cheese rind from me and we fell into conversation. Yes, he always went out with a gun on Sunday mornings. What for? Oh, anything that might be around; rabbit, pheasant, he was not fussy; but there was nothing around today. Never mind, it was enjoyable and his wife would have lunch ready by now.

Which brings me to Sunday lunch, that other great weekly tradition of the French. By three o'clock I had reached Lanquais after a magic walk through unspoiled wooded valleys and I was in a frame of mind to enjoy the picturesque bar/restaurant named "Les Marronniers". It waited inconspicuously at the end of the village facing into the hillside and enclosing a peaceful courtyard shaded by the chestnut trees from which it took its name. Old stone walls set off smart wooden shutters. Flowers stood in pots on the window sills and by the door.

Chairs and tables were arrayed invitingly in the courtyard. Not a soul was in sight as I came down the hill, but two doors stood open so they must be receiving customers. As I drew near the buzz of conversation reached my ears, the noise of many people talking earnestly with that lack of inhibition which is reflected in well loosened tongues. The bar was empty of customers and I was served swiftly by someone who appeared briefly from the dining room and left apologetically to return to the demands of the diners. I retired outside and stretched luxuriously in the shade marvelling at the determination of the diners. I had peeped inside at the packed tables and serious stomachs; it was clearly a solemn ritual for the families sitting close together under the heavy beams and white-washed ceilings.

Young mothers had emerged occasionally with squawling infants and fed them at the breast. Older children had come out in groups to escape the boredom of adult conversation and chased each other round the trees, eyeing with curiosity the dusty stranger who had failed to dress for the social event of the week.

I watched René consume a final peach and wondered what Madame's Sunday lunch had included. Judging by the quality of her dinner it must have been impressive. I rose to my feet, arranged a seven o'clock breakfast on the understanding that I might wish to stay for a further day if my leg was still painful in the morning, and retired to bed in the dormitory block.

* * * * *

"Winter has arrived," pronounced Madame Hilby in disgust as, with a coat thrown carelessly over her nightdress, she took Charles and Fidel for a brief airing on the most perfect of early autumn mornings. Mist almost hid the far bank of the river. The last arch of the stone railway bridge appeared to hang limbless between air and water. Ducks swam stealthily across the calm surface muttering quietly to each other. The air was heavy with river scents.

I had kept the rendezvous at seven o'clock but had been forced to admit that walking was out of the question and I would be staying for at least another day. Madame had been sympathetic and not in the least put out by rising unnecessarily early to provide breakfast. I explained that the muscle in my right leg which appeared to run from the instep up to the shin was tight and painful, and I enquired whether there was a chemist nearby. She said that she would consult Monsieur Hilby and see if they could arrange something. They would probably go into Lalinde at nine o'clock. I settled myself into a chair and sipped some hot coffee while Madame retreated upstairs again. A moment later she reappeared preceeded by a dog of majestic appearance. Tall and stately he descended the stairs with his head in the air, gave me not a glance and exited through the door to the outside world. A few moments later he returned with head still held high and padded swiftly back upstairs, again without acknowledging any other form of life. Madame smiled after his vanishing figure. "Pompom is Parisian," she explained. "He spends his days upstairs and does not mix with the locals." I nodded and wondered if he treated the guests with equal disdain.

After breakfast I retired to a wooden bench beside the river to ponder the position. A kingfisher sped across the river and perched in a flash of colour on a post not ten metres away, the most perfect view I had ever had of this striking bird. I contemplated the alternatives. Stay here in Mauzac until the leg recovered? It was certainly the most wonderful spot and I must count myself lucky to be here, but how long might I have to stay, and when would I know whether I was fit to walk unless I kept on trying? Anyway, it might be that walking gently was the only way to unstiffen the leg. I remembered John Hillaby's book "Journey Through Britain" in which he tells of his calf muscles seizing up when he reached Bristol and only unloosening as a result of further exercise. I could take one day's rest here and get transport to the Museum of Pre History at Les Eyzies so as not to waste the day and then move on tomorrow and see what happened.

The real problem was that there was only one free day in my itinerary. I had looked at the map the night before and it was impossible to shorten the route and still see the places which attracted me. It would also be extremely difficult to add a little bit to each day's march in order to gain another day's rest. The position of overnight stopping places determined whether it was possible to cover longer distances day by day. Perhaps it would be better to work out a completely different and shorter route to the Mediterranean.

I sat down and pondered. School children went past in ones and twos. A couple of fishermen arrived and set about their tasks with the serious concentration of anglers the world over. Ducks continued to glide over the still water in little groups. There was a rumbling sound from the far bank and a brightly coloured passenger train in smart red and blue livery emerged from the mists and thundered across the railway bridge vanishing quickly behind me. Very gently a breeze began to blow. I made up my mind. I would try and get a doctor's opinion.

At nine o'clock I returned to Madame and asked if there was a doctor nearby. Half and hour later with Monsieur Hilby at the wheel Madame and I, with Charles and Fidel, were in the car and driving to Lalinde. Madame and I were dropped at the surgery while Monsieur did some shopping. There was no queue in the waiting room. Madame explained my predicament to the receptionist and a moment later I was facing Dr. Leroy in the surgery. I removed boots and socks from both feet to demonstrate the extent of the swelling which had appeared, and asked whether I had strained a muscle. Dr. Leroy turned my feet at various angles, pulled, prodded and gauged the effect by my facial expressions. We struggled to understand each other with the nuances of French and English words. Eventually he grabbed the back of an ankle and enquired "what do you call this?"

Ankle?" I queried.

"No, no. This."

He pinched me firmly behind the ankle with his thumb and forefinger.

"Ouch! That's my Achilles tendon!" I squawked.

"Tendon!" he exclaimed with delight. " Oui, that is the word. You have a tendon inflammé. "

"Nothing strained? Nothing serious?" I asked with relief.

"No. I will give you something for it and you may have to rest for a little while. Some ointment for massage will be needed."

"Can I go on walking?" "It's up to you. You have some pain killers?"

I thought for a moment, passing before my mind's eye the contents of the tiny medical pack. Ah, yes. "Paracetamol," I declared. He sniffed. "I will prescribe something stronger for you."

I picked up the prescriptions from the local chemist and we all returned to the Hotel du Barrage after completing the shopping.

That afternoon Madame arranged a taxi to drive me in state the twenty kilometres to Les Eyzies. The Museum of Pre-History is a cultural necessity for those who are seeking earnestly to learn about the beginnings of civilisation in Europe. It is set in the very heart of countryside riddled with caves which were inhabited by prehistoric man and it is dotted with the overhanging cliff formations under which he sheltered. It holds a fascinating collection of artefacts and reproductions of stone carvings and cave paintings, some of the earliest recorded art of mankind. I am not a museum lover by nature but even I became enthusiastic as I toured the converted caves which housed this collection. Admittedly I had to overcome the initial shock of being asked at the ticket office whether I was an old age pensioner. I smiled politely and declined the opportunity of a cheap entry ticket, consoling myself with the thought that the painful climb up the steps must have made me look rather haggard.

The place was crawling with American tourists all telling each other how much better it was at such-and-such a place in Germany, or Spain, or Italy, or even Colorado. I tried to analyse why it was that they exasperated me, and concluded that it was not just their crude "collecting" of museums but also the crass comments which they were prone to utter when viewing these marvels of man's achievement. Perhaps, most of all, it was the irritation of hearing English spoken when I was doing my best to immerse myself in French. Somehow they seemed wholly out of place. Yanks in London and Stratford-upon-Avon, O.K. But Yanks in the heart of the Dordogne I would rather be spared.

I went round every section of the museum twice, re-examining spearheads, arrows, scraping tools, necklaces, skeletons, pictures carved in stone and reproductions of cave paintings depicting hunting scenes. Finally I returned reluctantly to my taxi driver who was sitting in the shade with a good novel.

"Where to next?" she enquired politely.

"I think there are some famous caves with stalagmites and stalactites nearby," I said, and that was where I made my big mistake. We drove two kilometres up the narrow gorge of the Vézère River and I hobbled again up flights of steps to an opening in the cliffside. We waited outside for a quarter of an hour in a group while another guided tour made its way round inside, then we trooped in one behind the other in a long snake. I had been hoping to move uninterrupted through the caves at my own speed pausing to examine what interested me. No such luck. I was pinned between a French family whose youngest member was distinctly unhappy at being led slowly along a dark dripping tunnel and a German who manoeuvred his camera over my shoulders and round my elbows. A French guide with a shrill voice permitted us to move in a series of short ten metre bursts which were punctuated by well rehearsed and lengthy statements on who had given that name to a particular limestone formation. Inevitably the centrepiece had been likened to the Virgin Mary with Child. Coloured lights flicked on and off to illuminate grottoes en route. We shuffled impatiently around a hundred metres of dripping caves, kept strictly one behind the other by a wire cage whenever a wider space occurred, captive audience to the tour guide, and stumbled thankfully out into the daylight at the far end.

I studied the map thoughtfully on the way back to Mauzac in the taxi wondering whether it was possible to slice a corner off the route of the GR6 by sticking to the Dordogne and avoiding a northward bulge round Les Eyzies. There was little point now in walking to Les Eyzies and I might be able to save a day by some careful re-routing. It depended partly upon whether one could cross the river close to the Hotel du Barrage. I consulted Madame the taxi driver as we drew into Mauzac. She looked at the map.

"There is no convenient road bridge. The only way across at this point is the railway bridge or the Barrage. One of the local fishermen would probably know if it is possible to get across the Barrage." She stopped obligingly and questioned a couple of fishermen but they had no opinions to offer. I thanked her for transporting me, handed over four hundred francs and stood on the bank surveying the

The place was crawling with American tourists …

Barrage. It was no good. There was indeed a walkway across it but it ran inside a wire cage which was interrupted at intervals by close fitting gates clearly intended to exclude trespassers. One would need a whole bunch of keys to get through that lot. I looked at the railway bridge a couple of hundred metres upstream. That had no obstacle to bar pedestrians but I remembered uneasily the little red and blue train which had flashed across that morning, and there had been others later in the day. It was quite a lengthy construction, needing eight arches to span the width of the river. I would consult Madame Hilby that evening after another session of massage on the tendon.

Madame listened to my plan of moving on gently the next day and following a course which would reduce the length of the journey and link up with the original route somewhere near Rocamadour. It all depended on crossing the river here at Mauzac.

"But we can take you a few kilometres in the car," she suggested. "No, no," I exclaimed. "The challenge is to get from coast to coast on foot the whole way in one month."

She shrugged her shoulders. "Very well, we will consult René about the train times. The men who work on the other side always walk across the bridge. It is just a matter of avoiding the trains."

René wiped his plate carefully with a piece of bread and gazed through the window at the bridge now scarcely visible in the dusk. "The first train runs at eight twenty," he announced. I relaxed into my chair and tickled Fidel behind the ear. That was alright. I could be across it shortly after seven o'clock with no problem at all. I arranged another seven o'clock breakfast with Madame Hilby and went back to my room for a last session of massage before giving the leg a good night's rest.

CHAPTER 5

RAILWAYS

I clambered stealthily up the embankment and looked round guiltily. Nothing was stirring, no-one was staring at me in horror; the village of Mauzac was ignoring this gross act of trespass.

Well, others had done it before me. That was obvious from the well worn path up the bank and the dip in the wire fence between two concrete posts.

I surveyed the railway bridge from this new angle. It was scarcely wider than the single line of track which ran over it. In which case there was virtually no room at all between the stone parapets for anything other than a fast moving SNCF wagon.

Hobbling carefully into the restaurant that morning at five minutes to seven and fending off Fidel's rapturous welcome I had frozen at the sound of a distant rumble. Madame and I looked at each other in horror and then rushed to the window to see a red and blue shape burst out of the gloom and hurtle across the bridge. She looked at me and shrugged one of those large and expressive shrugs at which the French excel. "René said..."

"I know what René said," I cut in. "You can tell him," I added in colourful but probably uncolloquial French, "where to put his railway timetable! What happens if I meet a train halfway across?"

"If you meet a train halfway across you will be back in Mauzac quicker than you left it," laughed Madame merrily as she departed to fetch coffee and croissant.

And now I was walking gingerly across the eight-span railway bridge in the September dawn with ducks quacking gently on the water below and still trees silhouetted in the waiting mists on the far bank.

I limped slowly out towards the middle and passed a little recess in the stone wall which was obviously designed as a safe retreat for maintenance engineers working on the bridge, always assuming they had enough time to get there. I passed the middle span and began to breathe more easily. That early train had probably been an unscheduled one which nobody could have predicted. I must not judge Rene too harshly.

A sudden rumble from behind stopped me in mid stride. Sweat broke out on my forehead. The safe recess was far behind me now. I glanced over the parapet and wondered how deep the water was. Was this going to be the inglorious end to a year's planning? Did they pay life insurance if you were killed trespassing on a railway bridge?

One hand was already fumbling with the buckles on my rucksack when I realised that the distant rumble had actually come from a juggernaut travelling along the road half a mile away. I took several deep breaths, wiped the sweat out of my eyes, and swore to observe all railway by-laws for the rest of my life.

The grassy embankment on the far side was infinitely welcoming. The dewy wildflowers gathered at the edge of the line seemed incredibly beautiful. I stood with hands on hips and looked back at the Hotel du Barrage. The mist made it indistinct but I felt sure that Madame was still watching me from the window with Fidel in her arms. And she was probably still chuckling.

"Thank you, Lord, for a safe arrival." I muttered. "Now I've got to get down this embankment, and getting down anything at the moment is extremely painful. Just hold on a moment, Lord, I may need a bit more help, please."

I slid down the embankment on my bottom and set off gingerly at a slow steady pace telling myself that pain was all in the mind. It was not enjoyable walking. I was developing a peculiar gait designed to avoid taking long strides with my right leg. The path met a metalled road which swung eastwards along the south bank of the river climbing into low hills.

Half an hour later I spotted a GB plate on a car in a layby just off the road and, feeling rather sorry for myself, broke my self-imposed rule of avoiding fellow countrymen and limped across for a chat. They were from Ilford, a friendly retired couple, apparently seasoned visitors to France.

"Have a nice cup of tea with us and rest that leg of yours for a bit," she said.

I took off the pack and sat down thankfully at a picnic table.

'We've got two weeks supply of bacon in the cool box.'

"I can't eat those French breakfasts. All that bread is bad for me."

I nodded politely thinking of warm croissant dunked in hot coffee.

"Jim and I make a cup of tea in the hotel bedroom and then stop somewhere in the country for a proper breakfast."

Jim was busy unearthing equipment from the boot of the car and pumping up a primus stove.

"We like our bacon and eggs each morning. We've got two weeks supply of bacon in the cool box."

Jim was putting rashers of bacon into a frying pan and hunting for the eggbox.

"We've got it all worked out now. Been coming over for years. Would you like some bacon and eggs? It's no trouble."

The smell from the frying pan was tantalising. They were so kind and homely. I nearly gave in but it would have been disloyal to all those people who had served me hot coffee and fresh baguette at the hotel bar in the early hours of the morning. I sipped a cup of hot tea gratefully but declined a full English breakfast.

They wished me the best of luck and I headed back towards the road feeling strengthened and encouraged. A cyclist in touring gear pulled off the road to take a swig from a plastic bottle.

"Bon ..." I began. "Morning," he cut in abruptly. "These bloody French roads aren't signposted properly and if you ask the way the silly idiots only send you in the wrong direction. Don't know why I keep coming back here. I shall miss my boat if I'm not careful. Where are you heading for?"

I explained rather hesitantly that I was heading for the Mediterranean but that I was handicapped by an inflamed tendon.

"You'll never make it," he stated helpfully, and sped off up the road legs pumping hard and bottom high in the air. I stared after him and decided that on balance I would, after all, avoid contact with my fellow nationals for the rest of the month.

There are parts of every holiday over which one draws a veil and which are by some kindly process eliminated from the memory. At some point I crossed back to the north bank of the river after short circuiting the base of the two enormous 'U' bends which bulged northward. I have no recollection whatever of the bridge which carried me back across the Dordogne. I was too busy putting one foot in front of the other in the least painful way. It was no good. I couldn't go much further in this state.

I began to pray for another nice little hotel to turn up. It had been daft to leave the Hotel du Barrage in this state. Nowhere else would be as comfortable and entertaining. A sign appeared advertising an hotel three kilometres further on at a place called Coux. Three kilometres! I gritted my teeth, kept my eyes fixed straight ahead and ground slowly on with rests every few hundred metres. Please, Lord, let it be a nice little place with friendly people. I shall just have to stay there for a day or two. It's only going to get worse if I push on like this.

The road went on and on. The river moved further away and disappeared beyond fields of maize. I checked the map for the twentieth time. Yes, I had passed that turning. The village must be getting closer now. Keep going. It really can't be far.

A group of buildings came in sight and drew towards me agonisingly slowly. I passed a cheerful looking primary school and came to a row of shops. This was promising. But where was the hotel? At the centre of the village the road dropped sharply down a little hill in the direction of the river. I eased myself slowly down it bit by bit and came in sight of a group of old stone buildings with bright window boxes and smart white-painted shutters. A sign announcing "La Cotte de Mailles" was surrounded by the usual assortment of hotel/bar and Kronenbourg notices. It looked promising. Please, Lord, a nice homely place with friendly people!

One door led straight into the dining room, which looked busy. I chose the other entrance with a bar sign above it and decided to order a drink and get the feel of the place first. A young man in a suit followed me in. I stood at the bar and pressed the bell for service. A little man appeared from the back regions and greeted me politely.

"Panaché, s'il vous plaît ," I requested, adding helpfully, " bière et limonade."

He took a bottle of ready-mixed shandy out of the fridge, flicked the top off and poured it into a glass; and then immediately filled another glass with a mixture of draught beer and lemonade. I looked at him in some puzzlement and explained that I had wanted only one drink. "But the other gentleman... Oh, pardon, Monsieur. I thought you were together!"

He gave a jovial laugh, took the money for one drink, and, after glancing nervously behind him, drank from the other glass. The young man behind me turned out to be a commercial traveller who had come to offer his wares and they fell into conversation while I retired to a table to observe the life of the hotel.

At intervals a rather fierce looking lady poked her head out of the kitchen quarters as if to check on the activities of the gentleman who had served us. On each occasion he hid his drink furtively and made soothing noises indicating that business was detaining him. The dragon withdrew looking unconvinced. When the commercial traveller finally departed Monsieur finished his shandy, washed the glass with a conspiratorial smile in my direction, shrugged his shoulders apologetically and returned to duties in the kitchen. I had taken a liking to him. He was helpful and had a good sense of humour.

I finished my drink, made up my mind and rang the bell at the counter. He reappeared.

"I would like a single room with a shower."

"But of course, Monsieur. For one night?"

I explained that I would be staying at least two nights because I had an injured leg and needed to rest it. His face at once registered concern and sympathy and he assured me that my stay would be made very comfortable. He took a key off its hook and led the way out of the front door and into a courtyard which separated the main building from outhouses. We passed the back door to the kitchen. A chicken stood on the doorstep on one leg and eyed us hopefully. An arch of vines created a shady area and hydrangeas bloomed in large clumps. We climbed a stairway to a room which looked out over old roofs towards the river. It was fine.

I took my picnic lunch downstairs and sat on a wide stone wall in the shade of flowering shrubs. The church was just across the road. Its enormous west end housed a bell which Monsieur had warned me struck every hour between eight o'clock in the morning and eight o'clock in the evening. The west wall of the church was scattered with deliberate recesses at which pigeons constantly alighted. I ate my baguette and cheese contentedly. This was perfect. If I had to be immobilised I was lucky to be here.

A slow stroll down to the river later that afternoon revealed a shingle beach by tree lined banks. The track down there had been well signposted from the village and it was obvious that "La Plage" was a good money spinner for the hotel during the season. A caravan was strategically sited for the sale of food, drink and ice creams, although it offered nothing for sale at the moment. Among the usual fields of maize there was a surprise crop of Kiwi fruit carefully shielded from the wind by an elaborate plastic fence at least eight feet high.

I returned to my room and lay on the bed. Occasional whiffs of cow dung wafted in through the window to add to the sense of rural peace. I dozed for an hour or two, returned to the beach with my swimming trunks for an evening dip and began to contemplate the idea of taking public transport for a limited distance, so as to give the leg time to recover, and thus catch up on my schedule.

Blast it! The first nine days had gone splendidly. Three hundred kilometres on the clock and going like a bomb. Why hadn't I been more careful on the downhill stretches? It had become almost impossible now to make the whole journey on foot. There just weren't enough days in the month and it would be pointless to try and extend the length of each day's march. This had to be a holiday as well as an adventure.

Dinner was enlightened by one of the less reputable locals who apparently came in regularly for the cheap menu. He arrived from the bar already warmed with pastis and steered a course towards the centre of the dining room. Madame despatched the waitress to head him off and he was persuaded reluctantly to take a corner table near the kitchen door where Madame could keep an eye on him. From there he kept up a running commentary in an accent which I found hard to follow but the topics he covered included discrimination against the poorer classes (whose money was as good as anyone else's, and he flourished a fistful of notes to demonstrate his point), the quality of the house wine, the slowness of the service, the preferential treatment given to foreigners (by which he meant Parisians), the Government, and Madame's cooking. The other locals regarded him with resignation and refused to respond to personal comments lobbed across the dining room. The intial embarrassment of visiting tourists diminished as their wine bottles emptied and they began to appreciate the entertainment value. The waitress expertly dodged the arm which would have encircled her and served him from the far side of his table. My friend the maitre did a round of the tables with apologetic murmurs and despairing gestures of the hands. He paused beside me and whispered, "During the winter our business is only with the local 'ouvriers'. It is difficult." I assured him that his hotel was delightful and that I had no complaints at all.

It had been a frustrating day. I retired to my room and massaged the tendon carefully. I had made no arrangements for an early breakfast. There was no point in getting up early.

* * * * * *

"Autocar ou train, Monsieur? "

I looked through the ticket office window with blank incomprehension. This was a railway station, so surely they sold tickets for trains.

"I want to get to Souillac."

"You can go by autocar or train. Which do you prefer?"

"Is it the same price?"

"Yes, Monsieur."

"Then I will go by the earlier one, please." "You catch the eight-ten to Le Buisson and change there, Monsieur."

I took the ticket in bewilderment. Le Buisson was in the opposite direction to Souillac.

I had spent most of the previous day on my bed resting the tendon and trying to come to a decision. I had pored over the map checking and re-checking the number of days and the distances to be covered, and had concluded that it was just possible if my leg recovered by the following morning to take a short cut and still reach the Mediterranean on foot by sacrificing the spare day at the end. Risky, but possible, and I would still have made it all the way on foot. But this

He arrived from the bar already warmed with *pastis* …

depended upon the leg being in full working order. What would happen if it wasn't? What was the fallback position? I had worked out that I must keep close to the railway line up the Dordogne valley so that if my leg packed up I could travel close to the planned route and rest again.

I had consulted my friend the maître d'hotel . He had referred me to the formidable Madame "who knows all about these things". Madame had indeed been most helpful. A telephone and a display screen had been produced from behind the bar and she had called up all the information on the screen. If I walked three kilometres to Siorac station I could catch a train to Souillac but if I wanted to arrive the same day I must catch the eight-twenty-eight train in the morning. It was only about a hundred kilometres to Souillac but she was adamant. There was no later connection out of Sarlat. So be it.

I don't know the record for unbroken prayer but I clocked up a solid three hours that morning lying on my back on the bed and running through all the stories of miraculous healing. Nothing spontaneous had occurred so I had decided to help matters along with a bit more massage. In the afternoon I could not face another three hours of prayer so I retired to the garden terrace and amused myself by starting to write a book about the journey. It helped to pass the hours.

I confided the plan to my friend who at once offered to drive me to Siorac station in his car but I explained that the three kilometre walk would be the test of whether I was able to walk on for the rest of the day. He understood and volunteered to wake me early the next morning.

And so he had tapped on my door at six-thirty while it was still dark and had seen me off anxiously after equipping me with bread, butter and cheese for lunch.

The walk to the station had been difficult. Not exactly painful, but slow and uncomfortable. I was not remotely capable of swinging along at forty kilometres per day and so I had reluctantly stopped at the railway station to buy a ticket. It was depressing. It was infuriating. I would never be able to say that I had walked across France from coast to coast. And I had done the first three hundred kilometres in blistering heat right on schedule before the trouble started. It was rotten bad luck.

In rural areas French railways have a cunning system of linking trains to coaches on the uneconomic stretches. A backwards journey to Le Buisson had been followed by a through run to Sarlat in another train, then by a frustrating wait for several hours, and finally a coach journey up the road to Souillac.

Now I was limping very carefully along the planned route once again, although sticking to minor roads and not venturing onto footpaths. In the little town of Pinsac they were celebrating the result of the local elections with a rash of little tricouleur signs in honour of the successful candidate. This seemed somewhat excessive to mark the election of a district councillor but perhaps local politics struck a deeper chord here than in the Babergh District of Suffolk. I stopped for a snack beside the upper reaches of the Dordogne and sat gazing at the Chateau La Treyne standing aloof amongst its woods. At least I was partially mobile which was something to be thankful for. I ought to be able to cover ten miles that day without upsetting the tendon too much. My spirits were rising partly as a result of an encounter on the road in the early afternoon. Another GB car parked beside the road had beckoned me in spite of my earlier resolutions, possibly because it contained a harassed young mum with a small child who looked as though she would welcome a temporary diversion. She had poured out her pent up frustrations. It was too hot. The children were bored and irritable. There was nowhere to buy a decent meal and there had been nowhere to stop for miles and miles. In the end they had just pulled off the road through hunger and exasperation. Her husband had taken the other child for a scramble down the bank to the river to get cool. It wasn't really the right sort of holiday for young children; they didn't seem to enjoy seeing places, and anyway the towns weren't terribly interesting.

I stood there making sympathetic noises and feeling sorry for her.

"How do you keep the children happy in the car?" I asked.

"We just pass them sweets and fizzy drinks." The interior of the car bore ample witness to this.

A pale faced young dad returned with the other offspring looking rather warm after the clamber back up the hillside.

"Where have you been visiting today?" I enquired politely.

"Rocamadour, and we might just as well have gone to Skegness. It was packed with people."

I wished them well and went on my way deeply thankful for my freedom, thinking of all the glorious places in which I had thrown myself down in the shade for a lunch of baguette and cheese, and remembering the impromptu wayside chats I had enjoyed each day and the magic peace of the early mornings. I might have a sore leg and I might have failed to walk all the way from the Atlantic to the Mediterranean, but thank goodness I was on my own two feet with nothing more burdensome than a rucksack.

The road had been climbing gently for some time and according to the map it was nearing a couple of villages known as Le Belcastel and La Cave. I was gambling on their size and their location close to the river to produce a hotel. Le Belcastel turned out to be a private chateau poised on the brink of a rocky outcrop with a sheer drop of hundreds of feet down to the river bed. The village of La Cave nestled at the foot of half a dozen hairpin bends. I gazed with horror at the sharply descending road, and the tendon winced in anticipation.

Half an hour later I was at the bottom and tottering towards an elegant hotel set in large grounds. I had earned one night of luxury in a well carpetted room. I had earned a dinner cooked by a chef of renown.

"Tout plein, Monsieur."

I explained my painful predicament. It had no effect. They were still full. However, they kindly telephoned the other hotel one kilometre further down the road near the famous caves and reserved a room for me. I hobbled on.

The village of La Cave is a down market tourist trap with trinket shops, a cave stuffed with the usual collection of stalagmites and stalactites (which I studiously avoided) and one cheap hotel with a large bar. I was allocated a room with a balcony on which I hung out my washing. The telephone did not work. Breakfast the next morning would not be served until eight thirty. After dinner I settled the bill and retired early to bed. Some days are better kept brief.

* * * * * *

The track wound beside a little tributary of the Dordogne which had cut its way down through a deep valley from Rocamadour. It was shrouded in dense early morning mist. Trees appeared singly, one by one, out of the gloom dripping moisture into their own little enclaves. A silent grey-green world was reflected in the river.

A breakfast of Mars Bar and water had sent me on my anxious way at a quarter past seven determined to allow plenty of time for rest periods while I tried a first tentative full day of walking. The track was good. It was old and well compressed and smooth, free of loose stones and sudden ruts. The road had vanished from sight and the only sound was my own muffled footfalls. Purple autumn crocuses grew in the fields, in the hedgerows and in the track itself. The track rose and fell gently as it followed the course of the little river into the narrowing valley, riding over a spur of hillside and dropping back again. There was little soil above the floor of the valley, and the vegetation on the hillside seemed to survive on a diet of gravel and slipping boulders.

The track narrowed to a footpath which forced its way through tall lush grasses and long-stemmed flowers at the edge of the river. An old water mill loomed out of the mist. Its tall stone walls stood intact but the water chutes and equipment had long ago fallen into disrepair. A sign announced "Gite d'etap" as I walked into a courtyard and discovered evidence of occupation, but the residents were not yet stirring so I moved on another hundred metres before stopping for a snack.

The sky was getting lighter with the sharp outline of treetops now clearly reflected on the surface of the river. Pentax Zoom 70 amused himself capturing these reflections and blending pale greens with autumn browns and yellows. A woodpecker felt the brightening of the morning and laughed merrily somewhere on the far bank. He was right; it would soon be warming up. I had better get on my feet again.

Enormous snails glided in leisurely fashion across the path in front of me risking capture or more speedy death by crushing. A bag full might have been traded in part exchange for dinner that evening but they looked so content and trusting that it would have been discourteous to disturb them. The valley narrowed again and the river became a tumbling stream. The footpath climbed away steadily to one side, just wide enough for one person to walk on comfortably, a narrow ledge cut into the slope, snaking its way carefully between bushes and scrub oak. The sky lightened again. Damp leaves began to sparkle in the sunshine, and the rocks turned from uniform grey to white and orange. The air was unbelievably delicious to breathe. It was perfect, so perfect that when I emerged from the valley half an hour later into a world basking under a cloudless sky I suddenly realised that I had quite forgotten about my tendon. I took off the pack and stretched luxuriously. It was going to be all right. I would soon be swinging along again at the proper speed. The path widened once more to become a track and briefly took on a metalled surface as it passed close to some scattered farm buildings. Then it changed direction abruptly and entered another valley two hundred metres wide between high vertical walls of limestone pockmarked with caves. In some bygone age the high plateau had been cut by a fast flowing river which had now dwindled to a thin stream flowing under trees at one side of the valley. The floor was flat as a pancake and bright green with grass for haymaking.

Rocamadour caught me unawares. It was clinging precariously to the walls of the valley high above. Tall houses grew out of the rocks and sat like lizards in the sun, blinking their shuttered windows in the heat. This was an obligatory stop for tourists. But tourists normally arrived in their cars at the top and gazed downwards. I was standing at the bottom gazing upwards. "We might as well have gone to Skegness" echoed in my head but that was a wholly inadequate comment. I could imagine the tiny streets creeping up and down the steep hill between the perched houses and precarious trees. Pentax Zoom 70 was itching to get up there but I was not going to risk the thudding descent which would follow the climb upwards. The tendon was doing remarkably well and it would be stupid to upset it again so I sat on a bridge at the bottom and admired the town from a distance.

An hour later the valley was just a narrow tree-lined gash in the surface of the plateau, and the stream was no more than a series of pools. Sunlight could scarcely penetrate the interlacing branches overhead, and welcome coolness had turned to damp gloom. Dappled sunlight changed to a dense depressing shade. The track reverted to a narrow path with thin saplings springing out of it, and the path merged with the bed of the dried up stream to become a painful obstacle course strewn with slippery boulders and overhanging branches. Occasional wide pools required an agile leap. I clambered in and out of three historic mills whose elaborate stone water channels suggested a glorious past when a rushing river must have driven wheels the whole year round to grind the harvest from the fields above. Today a layer of moss covered everything and the leaf mould of centuries filled the once busy channels. What geographical disturbance had diverted the water and robbed this valley of its life? I guessed that the river had simply gone underground for not far away there was the incredible Gouffre de Padirac, an underground river system on which tourists travelled by boat. It had been on my original itinerary but I had reluctantly struck it out in order to shorten the distances for the next two days.

   The footpath finally left the valley and made its way to the little town of Gramat where I sampled the panache and cashed two thousand francs of travellers cheques. The red and white daubs were inconspicuous on the far side of the town and instead of diverting into little farm tracks I found myself plodding down the dead straight line of the N140. It was noisy and uninteresting and scattered with rubbish. I cursed myself for missing the turning but decided to keep going as it provided the most direct route to the day's destination. Large trucks did their best to edge me off the road and fast cars scowled at me. I ignored them both and studied the lizards which rustled in every patch of dry leaves. If I had been less interested in the lizards I might have noticed the little circle of wire left on the verge by a careless farmer. My right foot landed on the one side of the circle and tilted the other side slightly into the air, my left foot slid straight into the trap, I tripped forward, got both feet firmly inside the ring, staggered forward for three more desperate steps and toppled with a crash onto the loose tarmac chippings at the side of the road. The palm of one hand and the knees of both legs trickled blood as I disentangled myself from the pack and struggled to a sitting position. I wiped my hand on the grass and diverted the streams of blood away from my socks. Blast all untidy farmers! Why couldn't they clear up their mess? The gash in my hand looked nasty. I wrapped a handkerchief around it while I dug into the rucksack for the first aid kit. What had been her instructions? "It's no use putting on TCP or stuff like that; you just wash a cut with water and make sure it's absolutely clean."

I reached into the side pocket and took out the precious remaining water bottle. Oh well, better to be thirsty than suffer infection. I poured water over the cut in my palm. Ouch! There was still dirt in there. I held back the flap of loose skin with one finger and doused the angry gash again. Ow! That was agony! But at least it looked clean. I dried around it gingerly, applied a large plaster, and emptied the rest of the precious water over my knees. Drat that farmer. I picked up the offending circle of wire and flung it over the hedge towards the farm buildings with a string of imprecations.

The village of Themines lies just off the N140 and boasts a gîte and restaurant, both of which had been highly recommended to me by other travellers. The gîte was part of a group of old farm buildings sitting in the evening sunshine. It was securely locked. I approached two elderly gentlemen leaning on their bicycles and enquired the whereabouts of the owner.

"At the Chateau, Monsieur", they assured me pointing across the road to a magnificent building which dominated the village and stood amongst imposing lawns and ornamental gardens. It seemed an unlikely combination but there was no doubt about their directions. I crossed the road, pushed open one of the enormous wrought iron gates, walked across a gravelled drive and ascended a flight of broad steps which brought me to the front door. Did one ring at the front door or enquire at some side entrance? I began to walk uncertainly along the imposing frontage and glancing in through the large windows became aware that I was looking into a virtually empty house. There was almost no furniture and the floors were bare boards. I stopped and suddenly found myself looking at three people sitting round a rough kitchen table with glasses of wine. I gestured apologetically but a lady jumped to her feet and waved in the direction of the front door.

It was obviously a stately home which had fallen on hard times and was eking out a bare existence. Madame was a pleasant practical lady who escorted me to the gite with a key and introduced me to the hot water system, the outside loo, the bedding store, the kitchen and the shower. There was a spacious dormitory upstairs but as I was the only occupant that night Madame suggested using the comfortable couch in the downstairs dining area. I thanked her and paid the thirty franc charge.

Leaving my washing to dry in the last rays of the evening sun I made my way back into the village and called in at the bar for a drink before dinner.

"Is the public telephone working?" I enquired of the barmaid, remembering that the one at La Cave had been out of order and it was three nights since I had reported back to base.

"It works very well," she replied emphasising the word 'very' and giving me a peculiar look as she passed a panaché across the counter. I pondered her reply as I sat at a table. One spoke of a knife being very sharp, or a car travelling very fast, but not usually of a telephone working very well. It was odd, but it was too early to telephone home yet so I dismissed it from my mind and went to find the highly recommended restaurant.

While I sipped a pastis and talked to the proprietor the son of the house was despatched into the garden to find salad and vegetables and Madame got to work in the kitchen. It was a pleasantly relaxed meal with heaped dishes left on the table for self-service and a carafe of local wine. I studied the map and wrote up the diary as the daylight faded and electric lamps were switched on in the low beamed restaurant. The total bill was only fifty francs. That made an overnight stay totalling eighty francs or eight pounds. Not bad. I could even afford to spend an extra few francs on a longer telephone call.

A car was parked beside the kiosk and a man was engaged in earnest conversation with a pile of papers propped beside him. I settled myself some distance away so that he could see I was there but would not feel hustled. He finished his call and immediately dialled another, entering into further intense discussions and scribbling busily. After a few minutes he replaced the receiver and I got to my feet expectantly but he was already busy dialling yet another number. I strolled up and down in a rather pointed manner consulting my watch and peering in at him. He was impervious. The next time the receiver was replaced I was at the door before his fingers started to hit the buttons again.

"Monsieur, I have to telephone home to my wife in England..." I began indignantly. He came out full of apologies and waving a one franc coin.

"Listen carefully," he said. "You need only put in one franc piece and you can talk for as long as you like. I will wait until you have finished." Saying which he withdrew to his car in good humour and settled down to read a newspaper.

So that was why the telephone worked very well! I fished in my pocket for a one franc piece and dialled delightedly. Nothing happened. Oh well, maybe it didn't work for overseas calls. Perhaps that would have been too much to hope for. I dug out a handful of coins, slipped a five franc piece into the meter and dialled again. A bleep-bleep sounded and a familiar voice answered.

"Darling, how's the leg? Where have you been?"

I recounted the story of the last few days at some length and made confident noises about my return to mobility. She was reassured.

"Better not talk too long, darling. You'll use up all your francs! Oh, by the way, a letter came for you from Marks and Spencer, and I thought you would want me to open it."

The day before leaving home I had written to the director in charge of buying clothing for Marks and Spencer and told him that their thick woolly ski-socks had given me a year's walking free of blisters without showing the slightest sign of wear, and suggesting that they also market them as hiking socks. The letter had finished with an explanation of the planned journey and a suggestion that, if the marketing idea was of any use to them, they might like to join in sponsoring the walk as I was using it to raise funds for repair of the village church. It was a long shot, but every little contribution helps when you are saving up for a new lead roof.

"What did it say?" "You'll never guess, darling. There was a cheque for two hundred pounds enclosed!"

"No! Aren't they a super company. They really are great. We might make a thousand pounds altogether with that!"

My delight at their generosity obliterated the slight trace of guilt experienced in reminding my benefactor that I had met him personally at a conference two years earlier.

I glanced at the meter. It still registered five francs to go. A few minutes later I replaced the receiver, recovered my five franc piece from the returns tray and waved my accomplice back into the kiosk to continue his business calls.

The whole evening had really been very good value from every point of view.

CHAPTER 6

HIGH TOPS

The resident spider in the outside loo was large and malevolent, and I was at a psychological disadvantage. The gîte was self catering and although there were facilities for boiling water I was carrying no tea or coffee in my pack so breakfast had been a drink of cold water, not the best preparation for facing sudden danger; and the loo was one of those squat-over-a-hole-in-the- floor ones which, even behind the privacy of a closed door, make me feel self conscious and undignified. In this enfeebled state I found myself gazing into the eyes of the creature which crouched in the low ceiling just inches above me. I hurried about my business and escaped breathlessly before it decided to leap down and attack me with my shorts around my ankles.

The gîte must have seen many merry evenings during the high holiday season when the dormitory was packed, with a log fire in the spacious dining room and a crowd of people at the wooden table. I had slept curled up on the couch with an extra rug to keep me warm and I would have welcomed a blazing fire to take the chill off the old stone walls. But it had been comfortable and different. The building lay directly on the GR6 which ran literally through the old farmyard. I tucked the key back in its hidy-hole and went down the grassy slope to a stream at the bottom, crossed a couple of narrow foot bridges and worked my way up an uneven path through the trees on the far side. Within a few minutes the track was running along hedgerows through peaceful fields and pastures. It was a Saturday morning but one of the local chasseurs had decided to steal a march on the Sunday Brigade and was already out with a little terrier which had a bell on its collar, presumably to ensure that its master did not mistake it in the undergrowth for a rabbit. As I was carrying no warning bells myself I took the precaution of calling out a loud greeting and enquiring whether he had seen me, having no wish to be mistaken for an early morning deer grazing behind a clump of blackberry bushes. He waved to me absent-mindedly and continued to urge the little dog into investigating the bushes. I hurried on out of range of his gun.

It was well farmed countryside and nature was busily going about its own affairs. All day long the woods echoed with the laughter of woodpeckers. Butterfies in yellow and blue and stone-coloured finery fluttered and darted everywhere in their tireless search for nectar. Grasshoppers of different kinds sprang off the path ahead of me filling the air with the chizzling, sizzling sound of their vibrations. Acorns fell to the ground beneath the heavy-leafed trees and lay waiting for whatever winged or furry creature might need them. Rambling blackberry bushes spanned the seasons with pink flowers still in bloom, red berries swelling rapidly and dark ripe berries glistening in the sun. I paused frequently to gather a handful in compensation for the missing breakfast; they were sweet and delicious and addictive. The first chestnuts lay on the ground peeping through slits in their prickly sheaths and promising roasted delights in the months to come. And everywhere along the tracks the lizards scuttled out of the way. Amazingly camouflaged they lay still and invisible until I was within three paces and then shot away into the dry leaves or grass or under a ledge or rock to become once more invisible. I slowed my pace and concentrated fiercely on trying to see them before they moved; it was almost impossible; their colours blended so perfectly with the dull browns and greys and greens of the track itself. Pentax Zoom 70 challenged me to get a picture of one of them. I loosened him from the restraining strap across my chest, extended the zoom to the fullest extent and moved even more quietly. I got closer to my prey but there was nothing which would be recognisable in a picture. I was about to give up when I spotted a sizeable fellow basking on the edge of a white-washed slab of concrete marking the side of a small lane at an intersection. I crept up to him, knelt painfully on the loose chippings, raised Pentax Zoom 70 and took careful aim while he snoozed in the sun unawares. A quiet click and the purr of the film winding forward startled him into life and he shot across the slab and vanished.

Down the little lane came two Amazonian figures as I rose to my feet. Their brief shorts revealed thighs which were the circumference of my, admittedly reduced, waistline. Rolled sleeping bags topped enormous packs which hung from their massive shoulders. Thick soled boots crunched the gravel in unison as they strode towards me each carrying a walking stick. They did not look French but I dared not risk offending them by chancing any other language.

"Bonjour, Mesdemoiselles " I called out.

"Bonjour, Monsieur. "

We paused, eyeing each other uncertainly, and enquired each other's destinations. On learning that I was bound for Figeac they recommended it highly. Their accent was gutteral but they were very friendly.

"You are Dutch?" I enquired tentatively. They laughed. "And you are English?" they replied accusingly.

"Could you please do me a favour? I am under instructions from my wife to get some pictures of myself on the walk and so far I have not got a single one."

"But of course. That is no trouble!" I handed over Pentax Zoom 70, withdrew a short way up a lane and was snapped striding towards them. We parted with mutual expressions of encouragement.

An afternoon of sandy tracks and scented pine forests led to the village of Cardaillac, its single street slumbering in the shade of plane trees. The Rustic Bar was obviously hospitable by nature; it had gaily coloured flags draped between the trees above the pavement to attract customers and cheerful yellow plastic chairs were set around tables outside its doors. This was the quiet hour of the day. Three young men and a girl chatted intermittently at one of the tables while the proprietor read his newspaper at another. I took off the rucksack, stood it beside a vacant table and strode into the bar. The proprietor followed me in. We exchanged a few words and I re-emerged with a panache and seated myself at the table. It was that hour of the day when one was quietly polite and did not disturb others with unnecessary conversation. I reclined in the comfortably shaped chair and closed my eyes.

The motor cycle, like all small motor cycles, made a shattering noise. I opened one eye reluctantly and the proprietor looked up resignedly from his paper. The three youths at the other table showed more interest as the new arrival skidded to a halt, leapt off his machine and, depositing it against a tree before the engine had died, strode across to join them. The girl showed more interest than anyone else. She was an attractive girl with a mass of long blonde hair which lay across her shoulders and glinted in the sun when she tilted her chair back out of the shade. She was dressed casually in pale blue set off strikingly by a red kerchief. The young man went straight up to her, bent over and kissed her on the cheek once, twice, a third time and, I opened both eyes wide, a fourth time! That I had never seen before; three was the previous record. Did this denote an engagement? In France there is this carefully graded scale of kissing when you meet and part. It is a ritual worth studying. The solitary peck on the cheek used by the reserved Englishman would be rated an insult in France. Admittedly it is more a question of two parties brushing cheeks together (rather than leading with the lips) first on one side and then on the other, but even a 'double' is considered pretty formal and a 'triple' is needed if you wish to demonstrate warmth and intimacy. A 'quadruple' had broken new ground for me.

    The young group broke into an animated discussion around the new arrival. As far as I could make out it was gossip on the activity of friends and reports of entertainment in the local towns, the conversational material of youth the world over. A quarter of an hour later Romeo departed after another affectionate 'quadruple' and I too rose from my table sensing that the afternoon's entertainment had come to an end.

    A gently undulating landscape drew me towards Figeac. The upper slopes were wooded and the woods gave way to pasture land which then merged with fields of grain in the shallow valleys. The last of the harvest was being taken in. A young mother and her little daughter waited at the edge of a field while father drove the combine down the very last strip of standing maize. The footpath led into a deeper valley more densely wooded than the rest with a surfaced road running down its length. Two young boys came cycling up it on shining new bicycles. I wiped the perspiration from my face and looked at them in astonishment. They wore track suits. Surely shorts and cotton shirts would have been sufficient to keep them warm today. I smiled at them and resisted the temptation to suggest that they got their knees tanned. Two minutes later there were loud whoops behind me as they came swooping down the long gentle incline of the road with the air rushing past their faces in the shady tunnel beneath the trees which ran on downhill for nearly three kilometres and explained why they were more concerned with keeping warm than getting a sun tan.

* * * * * *

"Ninety francs," I offered as he approached the last row of clothing still on display on the market stall.

"Ninety-nine francs, Monsieur," he replied firmly, pointing at the card displayed above the row of shirts on their hangers. It is not in my nature to haggle over purchases; I prefer to live in the comfortable certainty that the vendor is a gentleman who is charging the right price. But I had thought that he might be willing to make a quick cut price sale at the last moment before close of business on a Saturday evening. Evidently not. I fished in my pocket for a hundred franc note.

The weather demanded light weight shirts and my only other reasonably respectable one had collected a colourful assortment of stains which stoutly resisted all my efforts in hotel hand basins with frugal squirts of concentrated washing liquid. Squashed blackberries and tar were the most persistent stains collected whilst resting flat on my back in the shade. Monsieur unhooked the shirt and slipped it into a plastic bag. I collected one franc in change and set off to explore the big city. Well, it seemed a big city. Anything with a shopping centre extending to a whole street of shops looked like a fair sized metropolis after villages which had been proud to boast one boulangerie and a bar.

I had fallen for Figeac the moment I walked into it that evening. The little narrow streets twisted their way between tall elderly buildings and were lined with tantalising displays of fruit, vegetables, cakes, chocolates, books, clothing, jewellery, footwear and anything which you might care to eat or wear. Doors stood wide open. The populace strolled unhurriedly along the shady streets enjoying their evening shopping while making their way down to the river's edge. Every town needs a river at its heart, a living pulse to carry its history, a space to reflect the sky and the seasons, a place for social gathering. Figeac has the Cele, a tributary of the Lot, and along its banks there are tree-lined promenades. Parked cars do their best to nose their way into the long vistas but they are dwarfed by the overhanging trees. The houses of the old town climb the hillside further back from the river and balconies packed with flower boxes extend over steep cobbled streets. Old stone walls enclose fruit trees within their gardens. Everything is well established and settled and confident of its place in the general plan of life. I felt that I could live in Figeac.

The attractive hotel overlooking the river was full. I removed my socks from the top of the rucksack before trying the next hotel and found that they had one vacant room which I took even though it was above my usual tariff. They were packed out with a wedding party and I looked forward to an entertaining evening with impromtu speeches and flowing rivers of wine into which I might be invited to dip my glass. It was not to be. This must have been the hotel where the staid aunts and uncles and the married sisters with families had been deposited while the young blood celebrated elsewhere. However, I derived a certain amount of pleasure from sitting in the foyer with a drink and pretending to write my diary whilst covertly examining the latest fashion in wedding clothes and guessing the relationship between guests who greeted one another warily, effusively, cooly or not at all. Cousins in their forties sized each other up and wondered who had the larger car; their wives eyed each other's jewellery and adjusted their hats minutely in the mirrors around the walls. My sympathy was reserved for two small boys who were decked out in a hideous form of sailor suit which included shorts that dangled far below their knees. I wanted to take them one in each hand and lead them to the ice-cream stall where I had paused an hour earlier and where you could choose from twelve different flavours to form a triple cone of your own design. The colours would have dripped devastatingly down the front of their spotless sailor suits.

* * * * * *

That was the second smartly dressed middle-aged lady who had passed me walking along down the road into the town and responded warmly to my greeting. Of course, it was Sunday; they must be going to the eight o'clock service at the church.

The porter had proved a good ally and had provided coffee and croissant half an hour before the official breakfast time so that I could get off to an early start in an attempt to do two days journey in one and thus regain the option of taking the longer route to the Mediterranean. It was worth a try, but I must treat the tendon with respect. It was still being massaged carefully every morning and evening.

I had noticed the GR6 quite by chance on my way out of town. The double daubs of red and white had indicated a turning to the right which had turned out to be an excellent short cut across a long bend in the main road even if it was rather steep. It was dull   and overcast after a night of rain but pleasantly cool for walking and I was gaining height rapidly. The night's sleep had been severely disrupted by a dog belonging to one of the wedding party which had barked monotonously for two hours so it had been a relief to get on my way shortly after daylight.

The road climbed steadily for a whole hour and it was still cool when I stopped for the first break of the day, but by the time I was on my feet again the sky had cleared and promised another fine day. The GR6 was following a small D road to St Jean Mirabel but scarcely a vehicle had appeared. The world was my own on this Sunday morning and I followed the spine of the hills with no sound other than birdsong to break the silence. The village of St Jean Mirabel looked so attractive grouped around its church that I was lured off course to inspect its stone buildings with spacious first floor balconies, its dovecotes in their towers and its bright flowers crowding the narrow street. From there I decided to take a short cut across one side of a triangle and promptly set off in the wrong direction.

It was exquisite countryside and it led me to the only friendly alsatian in France. I had walked into a private world of miniature hills and valleys with steep sloping pastures and grazing cows. I had met a couple of friendly chasseurs with dogs of indeterminate breed, ginger and white with enormous bloodhound ears, who had posed for me as an affectionate hunting group. I had passed road signs which bore not the slightest resemblance to names on the map and I was totally lost by the time I came to a little hamlet which seemed to be the end of the road. I paused uncertainly outside a farmhouse, conscious that it was still rather early on a Sunday morning, but the distant sound of voices encouraged me to knock tentatively on the door. A large black alsatian appeared round the corner of the building and I froze in horror. It was not on a chain and it had found me standing suspiciously by the half opened door. To my astonishment it stood still and wagged its tail without even bothering to bark.

"Bonjour, Monsieur, " said a woman's pleasant voice behind me. I turned round with a start to find a lady in an apron standing in the doorway and began to explain that I wanted to get to Montredon.

"Oh, you are going in the wrong direction, Monsieur," she explained, coming out of the farmhouse and pointing back down the road. "You must go to St Jean Mirabel first."

"But is there no footpath across country to Montredon, Madame?" I persisted, looking at the map in puzzlement.

"Non, Monsieur, " she gestured. "You must go that way."

I thanked her and set off unhappily to retrace the journey of the last forty five minutes. Something warm and moist nudged my hand. It was the alsatian offering his commiserations and volunteering to come with me. I stopped and patted him on the shoulder. His tail wagged again enthusiastically.

"You had better stay here," I said. "You are supposed to look after this place." For an answer he hurried off ahead of me ignoring my calls to come back. I turned round but Madame had vanished from sight so there was nothing to be done but follow him.

Everyone knew him. The chickens looked up as he passed, clucked unconcernedly, and went on scratching at the roadside. When he stopped and thrust his muzzle between the barbed wire strands beside the field the nearest cow would saunter over and sniff at him. But his real friends were the birds. On the second occasion I realised that it was a well rehearsed game. He spotted a gang of noisy starlings chattering in the hedgerow down the road and rushed up to them barking delightedly; they immediately took off just out of his reach, flew fifty metres down the road and set up another racket. He pursued them again with the same result. After three or four repeat performances the starlings retired to a nearby wood in high spirits and my friend sat in the middle of the road panting and looking pleased with himself. Ten minutes later the game was played again.

I was becoming very attached to this engaging character but equally concerned that he was straying further and further from home. Every minute or two I would stop, stroke his head, point back in the direction of the farm and say firmly, 'Right, off you go now. Time to go home or you'll be in trouble.' Each time he would look at me in gentle reproof and trot off in front once more. I began to have visions of arriving at a hotel that evening with a large black alsatian at my heels and asking for a room with a dog basket.

We arrived together at a crossroads and I stopped to consult the map and see if it was really necessary to go all the way back to St. Jean Mirabel. A battered blue Citroen came along the road and I waved it down to consult the driver. Yes, it was necessary to go to St Jean and he would be happy to give me a lift. As I was simply retracing my steps I felt I could accept the offer and I took off the haversack and stowed it on the back seat.

"And the dog, Monsieur?" he gestured to the back of the car indicating that there was plenty of room.

"He's not mine," I said firmly, giving my friend a last pat and closing the door resolutely before he could leap in and join us. He sat beside the road panting happily and watched us depart.

* * * * * *

It was a perfect day in the depths of farming countryside somewhere in the middle of France. The GR6 had left the minor roads and was following a series of farm tracks which ran on and on through a deep solitude under avenues of trees beneath a cloudless sky. Sometimes I arrived at junctions with other tracks and there was no indication where to go next. A farmhand came out of the dim recesses of a cowshed carrying a pail of milk and gave directions. An old man leaning on a rake at the end of his allotment raised his hand to me. A flock of turkeys, some black and some white, emerged from a barn and scuttled noisily across my path. A warm breeze began to blow in my face as I strode on and on along leafy tracks in supreme contentment with the sound of woodpeckers never absent for more than a minute or two.

The countryside opened out to rolling hilltops with long hazy vistas in every direction. The breeze had turned into a strong wind which blew steadily in my face. The world was green and blue and warm, with rolling waves of hills spread out below. My feet danced over the ground. It was utterly exhilarating.

Four people with packs were approaching me and we met on a smooth rounded hilltop which dominated the country for miles around. I waved my arms above my head in joy and shouted a greeting into the wind. They laughed with me and swept their arms around the view.

"Have you come from Conques today?" I enquired hopefully as that was my destination if I was to catch up one of the lost days.

They shook their heads. "No, we have only come from Decazeville today. But Conques is a lovely place. The gîte is wonderful and there are some excellent restaurants."

We exchanged details of our journeys. They were Swiss, although they had not walked all the way from Switzerland, and were interested in my route.

The path began to descend with panoramic views over an enormous horseshoe bend in the river Lot. I stopped and consulted the map in an effort to identify on the ground the route to Decazeville. A short cut might be needed to make Conques by nightfall. The piers of a long vanished bridge which would have given me a straight line to Decazeville were confirmed by the road pattern on the map but it was no longer possible to cross at that point. The next best route was over one of two other bridges which lay strangely close together. I set off down the hill with a growing feeling that Conques was out of reach that day. The first of the two bridges at Livinhac was a suspension bridge which had been pensioned off before it succumbed to heavy traffic. It was wide enough for only one vehicle and had now been by-passed by a much larger construction. A concrete tub of bright red flowers prevented anything wider than a motor cycle from crossing it. I stopped at the bar at the near end of this bridge and ate an early lunch with a panache while reviewing the day's progress. It was not good. The tendon was creaking ever so gently. It would be fine as far as Decazeville but distinctly risky to go beyond that point today. Stopping in mid-afternoon would be frustrating but there was no intermediate point to head for.

Decazeville had been worrying me; that was one reason for attempting to avoid spending a night there. It wasn't mentioned in any guide book and there was something jarring about the name. It sounded more like a mining town in the Congo than a part of rural France. My fears were confirmed on reaching the top of the escarpment above the town and looking down. In the distance ran the scars of an immense opencast mine which had removed a large part of several hillsides. Below was a rash of highrise flats creeping up the green valleys away from the town. They were bright and clean and only about six storeys high but at the end of such a perfect walk they came like a blow in the face.

I descended reluctantly into the old part of the town with derelict corners cut off by new roads, an abandoned canal in the process of being filled in, a dusty railway servicing the mine, and a town centre wrapped in the depressing inactivity of a Sunday afternoon. There was nothing beautiful to admire. I went to investigate the church but it was a depressing church of dark towering columns and uncomfortable wooden chairs so I retreated to the sunshine outside and began to investigate the hotels.

* * * * * *

The waiter conducted me through the dining room with pride and ushered me to a small table in the upper section which overlooked the main area. It was really rather amazing. The fittings had literally been removed from railway dining cars and I was sitting on the plush velvet of a high backed seat in a little cubicle which was lit by an antique sphere dangling from a brass chain. Old sepia photographs hung on the walls depicting scenes from a frontier town of the nineteenth century. Apparently a Duc de Decaze had started the mining industry in the early days of the railway and had prospered.

The town was a dump of the first order and was the last place in France in which to have spent half a Sunday afternoon, but I had washed my clothes, waxed my boots and relaxed. And the meal was decent; I should not complain.

* * * * *

If I had approached Decazeville with some foreboding on account of its peculiar name I set off towards Conques with equal misgivings. It was not the name that worried me in this case; it was the image projected by every piece of literature which I had read about the place. Without exception the commentators concentrated upon its impressive Romanesque church. Pictures in leaflets and books featured this massive building stuck on a hillside with a small group of stone houses drawn tightly around it like a protective skirt. Its inhabitants would be fifty per cent black-robed priests walking silently along stone cloisters ringing bells every hour and swinging incense inside their musty building. However, it lay firmly across my intended route and was not to be avoided.

I left Decazeville without regret, crossing the railway and joining the footpath at a point which I had reconnoitered the previous evening where it left the main road and departed up a semi-vertical lane by a row of old cottages. It was a speedy escape and got me warmed up within minutes, and I was just congratulating myself on this convenient exit from dusty streets when I ran into a brand new housing estate which had cunningly crept up another slope of the same hillside. The ancient wooden poles which had carried a mixed assortment of cables, and had borne the vital red and white daubs, were replaced without warning by modern metal lamp posts and superior telegraph poles which were devoid of all markings. The old lane had been obliterated and replaced by a web of new residential roads which gave no hint of the whereabouts of the GR6. I was drawn reluctantly down the hillside along the main artery of this development with a mounting conviction that I was running off course. A young mother taking two children to school in the back of the car and pausing at a road junction was sympathetic but unable to advise me; she knew of no footpath in the area. A motor cyclist emerging from his garage was less sympathetic and equally unproductive. An elderly pedestrian recalled that there had once been a footpath but had no knowledge of its whereabouts; he waved a hand at the tide of housing creeping up the slopes amongst the trees and commented that the world was changing.

I consulted the map. Two things were clear. I had to progress eastwards and I had to gain height. I took the only route which appeared to satisfy both these requirements and set off without further delay up a little road plentifully endowed with cow dung to which I have no objection since it epitomizes rural life. Two minutes later I met the animals coming towards me on their morning ramble to new pastures, splendid brown creatures with long curling horns and little cream coloured calves trotting beside them, a different breed altogether from the black and white milk factories which congregate in vast herds further north. I climbed the bank to a safe distance and nodded benevolently to both the cows and the attractive young lady in a red anorak who was brandishing a stick and making encouraging noises at the rear. Reaching the first crest of the hill I paused beside a modern bungalow in the hope of convincing myself that I was on course. As if in response to my questioning gaze a man came out and enquired whether he could help me. I explained that I wanted to be on the footpath which followed the little road through the village of La Combe. He replied that he and his wife had only just retired to this spot and summoned her to provide assistance.

La Combe? Yes, it was that group of buildings over there, she assured us. I followed her pointing finger. On the next ridge to the south was a little hamlet; between it and me lay a deep wooded valley, the inevitable penalty of getting two or three degrees off course at the start of the day. I thanked them for their help. They seemed to welcome this visit from the outside world and I had a strong suspicion that they were already experiencing the classic feelings of those who retire to the country; a magnificent view and no-one to talk to. They listened eagerly to the usual description of my journey which was becoming more fluent as the days went by and made the usual gratifying comments. I tucked the map back into my belt and set off down the road into the wooded valley with ' bon courage ' ringing in my ears.

From the crest of a hillside everything looks easy. The route is obvious. The relationship of one place to another is beyond doubt. At the bottom of a densely wooded valley ten minutes later the world looks entirely different. All that can be seen is identical wooded slopes crowding in upon you with no distinguishing features and no far horizons. The sun still shines and provides a rough indication of the compass points but La Combe has vanished from sight and might lie anywhere within a quadrant of forty five degrees.

A cemetery lay at the bottom of this valley. It was not attached to a church but on sound business principles had a stone mason's yard and his house established beside it. Monsieur was standing in dusty overalls surrounded by a tasteful display of monumental stones awaiting only the name and personal details of his next customer. He waved a large chisel at me and I enquired how to get to La Combe. He wrinkled his brow. La Combe? It was as though he was searching his childhood memories for some echo of a name once heard long ago. He called out to someone unseen and his wife emerged from the office clutching a handful of invoices. La Combe? Yes, it was over there; or was it over there? Her hand wavered in a wide arc from roughly east to southeast. They entered into an animated discussion on which of their customers lived, or had lived, at La Combe. Their daughter, drawn by the sound of voices, arrived with a tea towel in her hand and asked what all the excitement was about. I repeated that I was heading for Conques via La Combe. Without a moment's hesitation she pointed. "La Combe is that way, Monsieur," she stated. "Up this way?" I enquired, indicating a little road which departed from the cemetery not quite in the same direction as she had pointed. She brushed aside this small discrepancy. " Montez, Monsieur. Toujours, Montez! " she exclaimed waving at the hillside.

Her mother questioned these directions and her father then suggested another alternative. All of this was brushed aside. She looked at me imploringly. It was so simple.

"Montez, Monsieur. Toujours Montez!"

I thanked all three of them profusely for their help and set off once more. She was absolutely right. It was very simple. You just had to climb, and go on climbing, and climb a little further, and then do some more climbing. I was soon gasping for breath but I was rewarded by the sight of red and white daubs on a post. They led up roads, up earth tracks and up tiny paths which brushed between overhanging branches. Always on one side there were steep valleys covered in oak and chestnut with scarcely a trace of habitation. After an hour and a half the path crept up a narrow ravine over a rocky outcrop and deposited me on the final broad ridge of the hills. The open tops were pasture land and fields of maize. The strong warm wind of the previous day blew in my face again. Range upon range of hills marched in from the misty distances on both sides. I screwed up my eyes and peered to the south. There were eight separate ranges of hills distinguishable before definition became lost in the wavering heat haze. Woodpeckers laughed in the woods immediately below and cows grazed on the open grassland which rose from the trees and spread across the high tops. The wind sang through a cluster of pine and birch trees standing on lookout beside the road. It was just like the previous day, only more so; more liberating, more exhilarating, more utterly perfect. Red clover and yellow daisies lay in occasional drifts beside the road where a protective strand of wire had held the cows at bay. Drooping bushes of blackberries swelled every hedgerow. Gleaming red rosehips shone on thorny branches. And the feathery tops of the maize leaned over uniformly in the wind.

The high tops undulated gently and reached a point of lonely perfection. A rise of ground in front cut off all vision beyond it. The cropped grass of the pasture swept smoothly to the skyline; unbroken green met unbroken blue; the open road at my feet curved up to converge on this line with a single row of posts beside it. Land and sky met in utter simplicity. It was a moment in life, whose horizon is always just ahead of us hiding the future.

I stood for minutes unwilling to break the spell, but was drawn on to discover what lay beyond. It was a landscape of further rolling hills, but these were clothed in heather and birch and bracken and they rose higher in the distance.

'Montez, Monsieur! Toujours montez!'

Lunch was lingering and supplemented liberally with blackberries. Somewhere ahead the GR6 was going to leave the road which ran along the high tops and descend eastwards to Conques.

The sign appeared in the right place and the path forked off through waist-high bracken across a heather covered slope dotted with scrub birch trees. It was a drier landscape, too steep and sandy to be worth converting to pasture. Warm scents filled the air and there was a drone of insects bumbling over the dense undergrowth. The path switched suddenly to the right and plunged without warning straight down the contours of the hillside. It took more effort to hold back than to go with it so I descended at a fast trot swooping from one hand hold to another, leaping fallen branches and loose rocks, down and down to lower levels. The air became moister and the sparse birches gave way to close packed sweet chestnut with a carpet of leaf mould. I skidded to a halt where the path shot out unexpectedly onto a road. The map confirmed this meeting place but urged me to cross straight over and continue the descent. A gap in the trees gave the first glimpse of Conques. I paused and examined it perched halfway up the far side of the deep cleft into which I was plunging. There was no easy way; one had to get to the bottom first. But at least the place looked more friendly than I had been fearing. The church was clearly visible and did not appear to wholly dominate the town. I slithered on down through the woods and came to a breathless halt at the bottom. A river!

Well, of course, I ought to have guessed. I ought also to have studied the map more carefully. But I had so convinced myself that Conques was stuck on a bare hillside, grouped in glum penitence around its Romanesque and gloomy centrepiece, that I had missed the fact that it stood just above the river Lot.

A notice on the riverbank announced that bathing was permitted although not ' surveillé ', which I took to mean that there was no lifeguard standing by to rescue over-adventurous swimmers. I could not believe that anyone could seriously need a lifeguard. It was an idyllic spot. The crystal clear water drifted slowly between steep woods and was spanned by a narrow stone bridge which led across to the foot of the town on the far bank. The town began as a thin line of houses climbing between the trees towards a larger grouping higher up. One part of the bridge was covered with scaffolding for repairs but activity was not what you would call frenetic; in fact it looked like the French equivalent of a Youth Training Scheme. Three young men stripped to the waist were wandering thoughtfully over an exposed bank of loose rocks apparently looking for material with which to effect the repairs. They carried plastic buckets into which they occasionally dropped a small rock. Sometimes a rock was rejected and flung into the river to the delight of a black labrador which seemed to be part of the gang. I walked out onto a spit of fine shingle and looked into the cool water. A few yards away a deep pool had been formed beneath the overhang of a large rock on the outside of a bend. Within moments my boots, socks, shirt and shorts were strewn along the water's edge and I had rummaged into the haversack for my trunks.

It was blissful; plunging into the depths of the pool below the overhanging rock and floating on my back in the sunlight. The labrador gave up looking for stones and paddled over to inspect me. We circled each other lazily and exchanged a few words. I began to feel that Conques had hidden rewards which had escaped the attention of the brochure writers who presumably arrived in their cars from another direction and made a beeline for the church. The silence was broken only by the occasional clunk of a rock being dropped into a plastic bucket.

No traffic had crossed the bridge, which was not surprising since it was wide enough for only one vehicle and the young lads had parked their car on it; but nobody had even attempted to force an entry to the town from this direction. Enormous stone slabs formed the roadway of the bridge. It was the most beautiful approach to a town which I had yet come across, running straight into a narrow street between pink washed timber framed houses on one side and buildings with clean white stucco walls on the other. More delightful houses peeped out behind them, all with well kept roofs of stone tiles. The little street crossed a road which ran parallel to the river and turned into a wide stone flagged pathway climbing steeply up the hill past one exquisite stone building after another. Pentax Zoom 70 stopped me at every second step to catch the angle of a roof, a line of steps or the creeper on a wall. It was a slow progress of utter delight. A wooden sign lay on the road with two rusty screws protruding; it had fallen from the wall of one of the very few buildings which was not occupied and well cared for. I turned it over casually with my foot and found the word ' gîte ' with an arrow. Of course! The Swiss had told me that the gîte at Conques was wonderful. It was difficult to guess in which direction the sign had pointed so I left it on the ground and continued up towards the centre of the town past enchanting side streets with views of flower boxes and carefully tended gardens. It was a photographic paradise; angles and shadows and flashes of colour, pictures which framed themselves between old walls; and the hillside faced west into a sun which was just beginning to sink.

There were plenty of hotels and restaurants and numerous trinket shops for tourists but they had all been kept firmly under control and made to fit discreetly into the old buildings. There were no flashy shop windows or garish neon signs. I studied the tariffs of the hotels carefully and finding them all reasonable abandoned the idea of the gite. Even the church was not as bad as I had feared, in fact its stone tiled roof viewed from slightly higher up was an exquisite piece of craftsmanship. I edged inside one of the little doors at the west end and took a closer look. Well, it was too big and it had those ghastly pillars everywhere but it was actually quite well lit by the sun through a large west window; it could have been a lot worse. I sat down on a small uncomfortable wooden chair for a little while and said thank you for some fantastic walks. Was it really only a week since I had hobbled across that railway bridge? I thought of how I had come down the hillside that afternoon, and offered more heartfelt thanks.

Outside a coachload of German tourists had arrived and was spreading out around the streets. I selected a gentleman in a felt hat who had a couple of cameras slung over his shoulder and looked as though he might be able to frame a decent picture. He willingly took Pentax Zoom 70 while I poised with bronzed knees against a background of curving streets and timber framed buildings. Then I headed for the Auberge St Jacques.

* * * * * *

The proprietor of the Auberge St Jacques in Conques was a man determined to promote the happiness of his guests. My slight disagreement with the booking clerk on arrival was swept aside; if Monsieur desired breakfast at seven o'clock the next morning because he would be walking forty kilometres to Estaing there was no problem at all, and indeed he was waiting for me personally at six fifty-five am with coffee and croissant poised on the bar counter.

He also took a personal interest in ensuring that his guests had a convivial dinner in the evening. The staff were not permitted to dot people at isolated tables around the dining room in order to protect them from the embarrassment of conversation with strangers. He himself escorted me to a place on the padded seat which ran round one wall of the dining room and placed me at a single table between a French couple and a young French woman. Let's be clear about this; on my scale thirty years is young. She had a pleasant look of competence and wholesomeness, if you know what I mean. Her face would not have launched a thousand ships but she was quite capable of quickening the pulse. You cannot ignore a person whose elbow is almost touching yours and I gave her a quick sideways glance and addressed her in French.

"Bon soir, Mademoiselle . You are keeping a diary too?" I enquired, indicating the notebook in which she was writing, and placing on the table my usual collection of maps, diary, dictionary and biro.
She smiled back pleasantly. "My diary and some arithmetic," she replied. "I am working out what I have spent."

"Are you staying in the hotel?"

"No, Monsieur. I am staying in the gîte ." I cursed myself for a fool. Why had I not persevered a little longer in looking for the gite before settling on the hotel? I liked my comforts too much; that was the truth of the matter. The Swiss people had said it was a superb gite . I should have made the effort to find it.

"I am the only person staying there," she added.

Oh, no! That was rubbing salt in the wound! To think that we could have been sharing the gite together. Life is incredibly unfair at times.

"You are on holiday?" I ventured.

"Yes, I am on a walking tour."

Ah. The situation might yet be retrieved if we were heading in the same direction. "And where are you going?"

"I am doing the Compostella Route."

"I beg your pardon." This had me mystified.

"The route of St Jacques de Compostella, from France down into Spain. You know it?"

The light dawned. I had seen a large diagram on the wall of the cathedral cloister that afternoon showing a long route from northern France across the Pyrennes and into Spain. It was a sizeable journey and unfortunately it cut across my route at right angles.

"And how long will it take you?" I enquired with interest. "It sounds much longer than my journey."

"Oh. I am doing it in stages. I come back each year from my job in Strasbourg and do a little bit more. But are you walking as well?"

I explained my own route, adding that I had the month of September in which to complete it. Her eyebrows shot up in a delightful and most gratifying way.

"How far do you walk each day?"

"About forty kilometres on average." She looked at me in admiration. "That's a long distance to do day after day. You must be very fit."

She was an intelligent and charming lady. I was beginning to enjoy myself. And the handful of other diners, although not overtly watching us, were obviously enjoying the exchange between this oddly matched couple one of whom spoke an entertaining version of the French language. My half bottle of vin ordinaire had arrived. I glanced at her table, saw that she was near the end of the single glass of wine which she had ordered, and offered her some from my bottle. She hesitated for a moment and then declined politely. I did not press her.

It appeared that she was a secretary to a Professor of Medicine at Strasbourg University and was able to take fairly generous holidays.

"And have you a family?" she enquired. I listed the four of them explaining that one had actually achieved financial independence but that the other three were still students, and added that they went their own way for holidays nowadays.

"Your wife does not enjoy walking?" she enquired with a twinkle in her eye, determined to discover why this ageing Englishman had deserted his family and was roaming France on the loose.

"She is not well," I began, and then wondered how on earth to describe M.E. in French. It was difficult enough to explain it in English without the added hazards of translation. And then I remembered that Mademoiselle was secretary to a Professor of Medicine. "In English it is sometimes known as post-viral syndrome" I said, pronouncing the last three words very slowly and clearly, and hoping that their latin root would find common ground.

She understood at once and a look of concern clouded her face. "Oh, that is bad. It must be very difficult for you both."

"The doctor recommended her three weeks in the sun as a tonic back in February before he diagnosed post-viral syndrome so we packed her off to New Zealand for a month to stay with a school friend. That's how I have been able to take a month's holiday on my own," I explained. She appeared to accept this as a proper explanation and told me about the farm which was worked by her father and two brothers.

"But what does your mother think about you wandering round France on your own?" I counter-attacked in an attempt to discover why this very presentable young female should be travelling unescorted.

She spread her hands and rolled her eyes to the ceiling. "My mother!" she exclaimed. "My mother is awful! She forgets that I am thirty years old and tries to treat me like a schoolgirl still. I have terrible arguments with her."

"Don't worry. My mother is eighty-seven and she still worries about me walking on my own!" We chuckled together over the foibles of mothers.

"And how do you like France?"

"France is beautiful," I assured her. "I am enjoying myself immensely. But I have one complaint. French dogs." I had struck another chord.

"Oh, our dogs! They are terrible. Have you been bitten?" She turned to face me in consternation. "I have been bitten twice. They have drawn blood."

This was more than I could lay claim to. I quoted the alsatian which had buried its teeth in the heel of my boot at Grammat and another beast which had grabbed my hand without breaking the skin. "They are so noisy. You cannot possibly need all those dogs to protect your homes."

"It is stupid," she agreed. "We have far too many and most of them are left alone all day. I hate walking past barking dogs when I pass houses. It is so unfriendly."

We sat in silence for a moment or two. There was something I wanted to ask her but it was difficult to frame the question. Was she lonely travelling on her own as a woman and unable to engage in casual conversation in the way which is so easy for a man? I was intrigued to know what it was like for a young woman braving the footpaths alone, and yet it would be disastrous to ask her outright if she was lonely. She would be bound to regard it as a rather clumsy pass. I had a bright idea and thumbed through the dictionary to check the French for 'lonely'.

"I am travelling alone, but I am never lonely," I stated tentatively.

"That's right!" she exclaimed. "That's just how it is with me. I stop and talk to people when I want to, and," she smiled with a charming directness, "it is such fun to talk to people in the evenings. I am never lonely either; it is so nice to find contentment on your own at times. And are you going to write a book about your journey when you get home?" she added, eyeing the diary in which I had been making a few jottings.

"I would like to. I tried once to write a book about a year I spent in Kenya but I got only halfway through. There were too many other things to do in life."

This led to a discussion of the importance of travel for young people and the need for nations to see each other face to face and build up friendships. She had been to Brazil and wanted to see more of the world. It was good. We shared many feelings and found it easy to talk.

"And what will you call your book?" she enquired, returning to the subject of my diary.

"Well," I confessed, "I have been giving some thought to that point while I have been walking. It might be simply 'September Sun' because the sun has never stopped shining since I arrived." She nodded. "Or it might be ' Montez, Toujours Montez '". I explained my encounter at the stonemason's yard.

She chuckled. "I like that. It's good."

"But I have another idea," I said, warming to the theme. My socks came from Marks & Spencer, so did my shirts and my shorts, and these trousers and these shoes. Practically everything in my rucksack came from Marks & Spencer and," I added, "they are a most generous firm." And I related the story of the £200 cheque. "So I think perhaps I shall call my story ' En France, avec Marks & Spencer'. "

She clapped her hands and laughed in delight. "That would be lovely. I am sure they would appreciate the advertising!"

"But I think perhaps the fourth alternative is my favourite. You French have such a lovely way of saying farewell and wishing a person good luck for a journey. I would like to call my book ' Bon Courage! '"

She turned round and looked at me with her eyes sparkling. "Isn't it lovely," she said, "when people say that to you. It makes me feel so warm inside. They really understand that you are doing something special."

Now I understood that even if she wasn't lonely on her journey she knew the risks and was grateful to those who gave her encouragement. She might walk only fifteen kilometres a day but in human terms it was far more of an undertaking than mine and required much greater trust in other people.

Yes, I like that," she said. "I would like to read your book when you have written it."

"If I ever get round to it."

"Oh, but you must," she pressed.

We sat in warm companionship for a while over the coffee. I offered her a liqueur. She paused for a moment but again politely declined. I had to admire her. She had firmly resolved never on her journey to accept any form of hospitality from men in order to avoid the embarrassment of becoming indebted to them in any way. It was very sensible, and also very difficult to adhere to at times when it might have given offence. It led me to consider how I should bring the evening to a close. At all costs we must end the encounter in the same warm atmosphere of trust and understanding. I had the feeling that she would not offer her cheek. The dangers of an embrace of any kind at this time of night after an intimate meal were too great to risk. And yet it would need some bodily gesture to confirm and put a seal upon the pleasure of the evening. She was clearly in no hurry to break up the party since she had made no move to leave the table and we were now alone apart from the late drinking locals at the bar.

She broke the silence. "Have you seen the relics in the Cathedral?"

I explained that relics were not in my line of country and that I found French cathedrals oppressive. In my opinion they were grim buildings, dominated by dark towering columns, musty with incense, and wholly depressing. For me, God was not there.

She agreed fervently, "God is not there for me either, but" she added, "you should look inside some of the little village churches. They are absolute gems." I was to remember that advice a day or two later.

The locals at the bar said their farewells to the Maitre, and Mademoiselle reluctantly gathered her belongings together and looked at me.

"I have enjoyed our talk."

"So have I, Mademoiselle. May I walk with you back to the gîte ?"

"There is no need. It is only a short distance..." she relaxed her guard almost imperceptibly.

"I will come with you," I said, quietly but firmly.

We walked to the door together and the Maitre gave me a wicked smile behind Mademoiselle's back. His guests had discovered each other, which was what he liked to see, and now they were departing together...

"I will be back," I said pointedly, indicating that the door had better not be locked behind us.

We strolled through the deserted town under a full moon reluctant to reach our destination. The dark shadow of the cathedral passed us.

It's not as bad as some of them," she murmured.

"No, I must admit that the sun does push its way in through a few windows."

She chuckled.

"Our church at home is full of light," I added. "I help to take some of the services because our priest has four churches to look after."

"Oh, we do the same in my church at home. There are not nearly enough priests for all our villages."

We turned up a little side street not more than four metres wide and came to a tall three storey building of old stone with a long flight of steps running up the side of it in shadow to the first floor.

"This is the gîte, and that's the dortoir up there." There must have been a twinkle in her eye but it was too dark in the narrow street to be sure. We stopped and turned to face each other squarely for the first time in the whole evening.

"Mademoiselle," I said taking her hand, "I have been delighted to make your acquaintance." I raised her hand to my lips.

"And I have been delighted too, Monsieur."

"Bon Voyage, et bon courage!"

"Bon voyage, et bon courage!" she echoed.

She turned and ran lightly up the steps. I turned too and walked down the street without looking back feeling very lonely and yet very happy.

I reached the main street and chuckled quietly. It might have been so very different if I had discovered the gîte. It might have been quite embarrassing to find ourselves alone together. We might not even have dined together and I don't suppose I would have slept a wink feeling so fit and young as I did at that moment.

Lord, You are as cunning as a serpent. You really managed this evening very cleverly.

CHAPTER 7

WINGS OF THE MORNING

The stairway was in total darkness when I crept down the next morning and, pushing open the restaurant door, I was just steeling myself to start the day on an empty stomach when I discovered the Maitre, true to his word, awaiting me behind the bar. A large steaming cup of coffee appeared. I hitched myself onto a bar stool and began dunking a croissant.

"That was a very pleasant dinner last night."

"I am so glad you enjoyed it, Monsieur."

"If Mademoiselle should happen to call in today would you please give her this." I handed him a piece of paper with my name, home address, and an invitation to visit us if she was ever in England. It was ridiculous but we hadn't even discovered each other's names the previous evening.

"She is a delightful young lady."

"Yes, indeed, Monsieur. I will watch out for her."

I settled the bill, thanked him for rising early to see me off and walked out into another day. The sky was overcast and the road was already wet from an overnight shower. I climbed up the hill past the turning to the gîte, past the cathedral and up to the new Mairie and the silversmith. I was alone in the world as usual at this hour.

Goodbye, Conques. You are a most beautiful place and I shall remember my evening with you for a long, long time. Stay just as you are with the cool river below you, the high hills above and a warm welcome for travellers.

I climbed on steadily up the hill out of the town. It began to spit with rain but I kept under the trees and ignored it, overcome by a strong reluctance to take the anorak out of the rucksack when it had remained unused for the last four hundred and fifty kilometres. The spitting turned to a steady fall of rain, not heavy but wetting. I stopped, stowed Pentax Zoom 70 in the rucksack and extracted the large green anorak lined with teflon which had set me back £75. I would have been more than happy to carry it all the way across France without using it once but fate had decreed otherwise. It was voluminous, falling just below my knees. I fiddled with the substantial zip but it just would not zip up. This was ridiculous. It had worked fine back in February when horizontal rain had caught me on the way home across the fields below the Royal Hospital School. I fiddled and pulled in exasperation but the zip simply would not zip up. Realising that the rain had stopped I thankfully stuffed the anorak back into its place and carried on.

The morning remained overcast but I made good progress across the high plateau towards Espeyrac. At mid-morning a crowd of walkers appeared coming towards me in the opposite direction. They were well kitted out with waterproofs but appeared to be carrying little in the way of baggage. Two vigorous middle-aged ladies led the pack. "Bonjour, Mesdames, " I called out cheerfully. "The weather is not good."

"Where are you heading for, Monsieur?"

"I am making for Estaing today, and on to the Mediterranean."

"You are English," said one of them accusingly and turned to address her friend in German. They had penetrated my pitiful disguise with ease and now spoke in perfect English.

"You are brown. You have come far?" enquired a well-built blonde who had joined us, eyeing my tanned knees and coming within an ace of fingering my chest. I edged away cautiously and asked where they were bound for.

"Oh, I don't know where we are going today. Ask our leader. She knows everything," answered the first lady.

They tramped on, all two dozen of them, with an authoritative lady expounding loudly in their midst and brandishing a map. I looked after them and pinched myself. It couldn't be true.

Now just stop type-casting people, I admonished myself. That lady with the map was not in the least like Hitler; she was just a well organised, informative tour leader. I walked on along the road musing deeply on the character of the German nation and reminding myself of the delightful party of youngsters from Dortmund who had come to our village some years earlier and spent several weeks of their summer repairing churches and looking after the younger children. I told myself to stop building theories out of nothing. If I was on a walking tour with a group of other people I wouldn't be worrying about the route; I would be relaxing and leaving it to someone else. Even so...

I stopped in horror. When had I last seen a red and white daub? Returning to my own affairs with a jerk I began searching the hedgerows anxiously for an indication that I was still on the GR6. Half an hour later after a lengthy detour I was back with the red and white daubs and telling myself it was just what I deserved for thinking libellous thoughts of fellow walkers.

It began to rain again, steadily, heavily, in earnest. I retired to the shelter of a large pine tree on the edge of a wood and yanked out the anorak once more. The downpour became a solid deluge beating through the branches above and threatening to drench any part of me which was left exposed. Now think calmly. The zip worked in February so it must work now. And then it dawned on me, of course. There were two little runners which worked together. Sure enough, the second one was up by my neck. I ran it down to join the other one. They linked neatly together and in a moment I was watertight.

Or was I? My socks were beginning to get damp where the water cascaded off the anorak at knee height and streamed down my legs. I dived into the rucksack again and extracted the long waterproof spats which Eleanor and Geoff had given me for Christmas two years ago. Within moments they were in place protecting the upper parts of my boots and the whole of my legs up to the knee. Snug as a bug!

I adjusted the wired rim of the hood so that it stuck out over my face like the edge of an alpine roof. Perfect. Not a drop was coming in. Behind me the earthen track had turned into a raging torrent of brown water. The branches overhead were useless. Cascades of water fell all around me. I might just as well move on. Bless Lyndie for telling me to wrap everything separately in a plastic bag inside the rucksack and put the whole lot inside a bin liner. My belongings were going to need every bit of that protection today. I hoisted up the rucksack, adjusted the straps for my extended girth and plodded out into the open.

It was exhilarating. The elements blasted me with sheets of water but I was bone dry and cool inside my armour. Water drummed on my head, poured down the smooth green exterior of the anorak and bounced off the spats. I looked out through a tight little circle in the hood and laughed at the world. I couldn't see sideways; it was like being a blinkered horse, but I strode on defying the elements gleefully, splashing through long puddles, feeling impregnable. A figure clad in similar fashion danced towards me down the main street of a little village. We paused and laughed at each other, little circular faces peering out at each other. She was jet black with a row of gleaming white teeth and a pack half as big again as mine. I wished we could have sat down for a chat but it wasn't chatting weather.

A steep hill led down to the little town of Espeyrac nestling at the confluence of three tributaries of the Lot. In a side street hung a welcoming bar/restaurant sign and I realised that it was time for a bite of lunch. I pushed open the door and walked in spraying about two litres of water over the stone floor. Fortunately no-one was within range. In fact there was no-one to be seen. I took off the anorak and shook it vigorously adding a few more rivulets to the ones making their way under the tables. Then I stamped both boots sharply to dislodge any further lurking raindrops. This had the effect of summoning Madame from the kitchen where she was busy feeding the family.

"Bonjour, Madame . Some coffee please."

"White coffee, Monsieur?"

"Yes please."

"A large cup?"

"Very large and very hot please, Madame." She made no comment on the flood creeping across the floor and cheerfully gave permission for me to eat my packed lunch at one of the tables, retiring to the kitchen once more to attend to the family. I munched baguette , cheese and Mars Bar while I studied the map. It was not a day to get lost and walk an extra five miles. The coffee went down well; I had been on the verge of feeling chilled and the hot mouthfuls surged through me chasing the red corpuscles into life again.

A local came in for a glass of wine and stood chatting to Madame. I got up feeling refreshed, stowed my lunchbox and zipped myself back into the anorak. They looked out at the weather and enquired how far I was walking that day. Conques to Estaing? But that was a long way. Where was I going after that? The Mediterranean!

Mon dieu! They demanded to know the route in detail and followed me mentally through the mountains with gratifying exclamations.

The rain still fell in drenching vertical rods as I left them and splashed my way a hundred metres to the outskirts of the village where a GR sign pointed me on the way. I strode past it before something registered in my consciousness. GR416? What on earth was that? I was supposed to be on the GR6 for days yet. I was turning back to study the sign when I heard a cry behind me and saw the figure of Madame running towards me through the downpour in her apron.

"That is the wrong way, Monsieur," she panted. "The road to Estaing is over there. I will show you."

She had rushed out after realising that I had turned in the wrong direction on leaving them. We retraced our steps together in the pelting rain to a point at the other end of the village where another sign announced 'GR6' and pointed in the opposite direction. I thanked her profusely. She waved away my thanks and ran back to the shelter of the restaurant.

A little act of kindness, but the whole of life is made up of little acts. Madame, the reputation of France will always be safe in your hands.

The GR6 left the road and wound its way up into wooded hills. The clouds clamped down firmly and obscured any view. It was the first day on which Pentax Zoom 70 had been confined to the rucksack. I explained patiently that it was for his own good and that it hurt me more than it hurt him but he mumbled something about his automatic flash and retired in a huff.

Without a view to gaze upon one's thoughts have to turn to other things. My thoughts inevitably moved two days ahead to ponder once again the wisdom of planning a day's journey which the Topo Guide clearly described as eleven and a half hours walking without allowing for rests; and a lot of that was up and down work, not swinging along on the level. It had been causing ripples of unease in the pool of my sub-consciousness ever since I had worked out the route during the Christmas holiday. Try as I might I had found no way of avoiding this day's march if I was to cover the chosen route in one brief month. It would take me up the side of the Monts d'Aubrac, turn south for twenty eight kilometres along the high ridges and then plunge into a narrow gorge in preparation for the assault on the limestone plateau. I had already discovered that the authors of the Topo Guide were athletes whose words were to be taken seriously, and my apprehension was growing as the fatal day drew closer.

* * * * * * * * *

"But where is the shower and the toilet?" I demanded. The tariff displayed outside the hotel had definitely included these facilities and although the room was beautifully appointed with new cupboards and fittings I did not intend to be put off with sharing a communal bathroom.

"Ah, let me show you, Monsieur. We are very proud of this design."

He took hold of what looked like an ordinary handle to the wardrobe and pulled steadily. The whole wardrobe swung mysteriously into the room like one of those revolving stages in a modern theatre and revealed a complete bathroom with shower, basin, bidet, mirrors, clothes hooks and electric shaver socket; it was all purpose-built into a scheme of cream shaded plastic walls. I gazed in amazement.

"Please go in. And let me show you how the door works". He demonstrated.

I took a step up into the neat hygenic plastic world and swung the pivoting section fully into place. The bedroom vanished. An electric fan whirred discreetly. I was alone in a plastic capsule with no windows or any visible connection with the outside world. A moment of panic seized me. I grabbed the handle and pulled. Nothing happened. Help! Locked in the loo for days with only water to sustain me! I wrestled vainly with the handle again and then calmed down sufficiently to look at the arrows plainly indicating how guests should extract themselves. The panel swung back again to disclose the smiling Maitre.

"Incredible," I commented. "Most ingenious."

"The rooms are so small in this old hotel," he explained. "We had to make good use of the space."

He departed and I tackled the normal evening chores. It had stopped raining in late afternoon and I had finished the journey to Estaing with a long walk beside the lake under grey skies, reaching the town as an early dusk began to descend. The hallway of the hotel had been stacked with luggage. A tour party was in residence and I had been lucky to get a room.

Practically everything had survived the rain intact. The Marks & Spencer yellow evening trousers were slightly damp where they had poked out of one end of the plastic bag and one side pocket of the rucksack had let in a little rain, but that was all. I washed the day's socks and shirt and hung them out in the window, although they would be lucky to get much drier before daybreak.

There was a loud buzz of conversation from behind one of the doors leading out of the bar. I picked up my pastis and peeped through the door at the tour party. They were English and were being addressed by a stalwart lady who appeared to be the unofficial poet because she was reading rhyming couplets describing the day's events amidst a barrage of bantering interruptions. It was all very jolly and hearty. I withdrew quietly and went to the other dining room for a chat with the Maitre and a French couple. He apologised that breakfast was not available until eight o'clock since none of the staff slept on the premises, but assured me that the front door was left open all night.

* * * * * * * * *

The clouds had vanished but it was misty over the river and a few street lights still shone brightly in the gloom. The cockerels wake early in Estaing, in fact I strongly suspect that they only sleep in shifts round the clock and provide a chatty twenty-four hour service for anyone who wants to listen in. The one on the hillside facing my bedroom window came on duty sharp at five thirty with a clarion call to his mate somewhere higher up the valley; his mate needed a bit of prompting and didn't really join in the dialogue enthusiastically until six o'clock. By six thirty the darkness was vibrant with cockerels in various stages of wakefulness so I got up and examined my boots. They had dried out reasonably well after their soaking of the previous day and I sat on the bed and gave them a thorough waxing. There was no coffee and croissant today so I took a pristine Mars Bar out of its wrapper and chewed it thoughtfully with an occasional swig of cold water. I must jettison the last bits of surplus weight before the great test tomorrow. That would be easy because I would reach Espalion by mid-morning and on the map it looked big enough to support a major Post Office. Every surplus item in the pack would be ruthlessly ejected. I had earmarked maps, another shirt, the string vest, and even a pair of small disreputable chamois leather gloves which were to have been my last protection against icy blasts in the high mountains. I was under no illusion about the rigours of walking for eleven and a half hours during the twelve and a half hours of daylight which would be available the next day.

Estaing lies at the heart of a network of footpaths. On my reconnaissance the previous evening I had found a battery of signs on the far side of the river and had made a careful selection. The main objective today must be to arrive at St Chely in time to find a comfortable hotel and ensure a good night's rest.

I was swinging along in the comfortable knowledge that I was off to an early start on the right road when a telegraph post suddenly brandished a double band of red and white as advance warning of a change of direction. That's odd. I could have sworn the footpath followed the road for the first few kilometres. I looked at the map in the grey light and was forced to admit that the red dashes were not actually on top of the road all the way but they definitely joined it later on so this was probably an entirely unnecessary diversion. I tucked the map back under my belt and walked on down the road past the place where the path vanished up into the woods. Fifty metres later I stopped. It would be foolish to lose the waymarks this early in the day. I went back to where the path diverged and peered into the woods. It was just light enough to see that the path sloped up the hillside at a slight angle to the road. I started up it with some reluctance, brushing aside damp undergrowth and watching out for loose rocks. It wasn't too bad a surface and the route rose slowly to give occasional views through gaps in the trees, but it was slow progress compared with the road. Fifteen minutes later it returned to the road once more. I brushed the leaves away from my ears and pulled an assortment of cobwebs out of my hair. The spiders in this part of the world live on a special diet which enables them to produce high tensile webs. You don't brush your way casually through them; you grab them with both hands and wrench them apart praying that the owner is not a hairy monster with carnivorous tendencies. I muttered a few comments about useless diversions and set off once more.

The village of Verrieres does not wish to be associated with modern France. It has tucked itself away inconspicuously in a triangle between two roads in the hope that tourists, house hunters, tax gatherers and other plagues will pass by harmlessly without settling on it. I was amazed that the inhabitants had not erased the old red and white daubs in an attempt to divert walkers, but perhaps this species of intruder was considered harmless. I was accosted by several chickens who were patrolling the village street. They passed the news of my arrival to some dogs who got up and peered out of their kennels, shook their chains and gave half-hearted woofs. It was too early to be aggressive. The only sign of human life was the cowman busy milking by hand in the byre under one of the farmhouses. The street meandered gently between stone houses, crossed a miniature square, dodged a few barns and turned itself into an earth track running out into the fields.

I walked into a luminous white mist, the sort which reveals your surroundings bit by bit as you penetrate it and holds a definite promise of sunshine and blue sky somewhere just above. A store cage for maize cobs, some grazing heiffers, a blackberry hedge, and old wooden gateways loomed out of the mist around me. No sound of cars, no barking dogs; absolute peace.

The ground sloped upwards towards a church and the mist thinned out. The walls of the church took on a warm glow in the early sunlight, their towers rising like battlements above the surrounding pastures and thrusting slated pinnacles into the sky. A small packed churchyard was wrapped tightly round one side of the buildings.

French churchyards give me the creeps. Most civilised nations are nowadays content to bury their dead six feet underground and leave a discreet stone marker with a name and a date, but the French are creating increasingly elaborate memorials which include permanent plastic flowers, polished marble slabs, stainless steel angels and photographs of the deceased. Far from being places of rest their churchyards are a surging sea of shapes and colours, a motly of materials and a museum of faces. Personally I would prefer to be incinerated and have my details recorded in the parish register.

As if in league with the bedlam of the churchyard the footpath ran steeply up the side of the hill over a chaos of loose rocks which demanded slow and painful walking. It was nothing more than a dried stream bed. I stumbled up it composing a letter of complaint to the Minister of Tourism with a copy to the Minister for the Environment. I informed them that La France was neglecting her glorious heritage of footpaths, that greedy landowners were incorporating them into vineyards or letting them decay and disappear, and that the day of reckoning would come when the world's oil supplies ran out and the Greens demanded action.

The path escaped from its stony course into open country in full sunshine. The valley of the Lot lay like a scooped out hollow below me, filled with pure white pockets of mist. Trees beside the path were black outlines against the low morning light with sunbeams streaming through their branches, and every ecstatic drop of moisture sparkled with life. Lord, You've done it again. I don't deserve this. It's far too beautiful to absorb in a few moments. I am overflowing with joy.

Pentax Zoom 70 cleared his throat and enquired whether I might like to keep a permanent record if I was that much impressed with what I saw. He added that it was getting a bit stuffy inside his leather case. I apologised for this oversight and we enjoyed ourselves together for a while lurking behind trees to capture lighting effects and hunting for good vantage points from which to frame the pools of mist below us. It was hungry work and finished with a late breakfast snack of stale baguette and cheese.

It was one of those mornings when you wonder what you have done to deserve such an experience of beauty. I walked along murmuring thanks to a Creator who felt extraordinarily close, and gazed round me with scarcely believing eyes. All right, so it was only hills and trees and green grass scattered with wild flowers, but the light was pure and magical and breathtaking. The silence was enchanting and intoxicating. This was how the world must have looked and smelled when it was first created.

I came reluctantly down to Espalion, not because Espalion was objectionable but because it is always difficult to descend from the heights and rejoin the common stream of life. Espalion has a friendly Post Office, excellent coffee served at tables in the shade, delightful red-stone buildings, a couple of pleasing bridges and some exquisite reaches of the Lot running beside beech woods.

The Monts d'Aubrac now dominated the skyline ahead and filled the map across which I was walking. I recrossed the Lot at St Come-d'Olt and swung up north towards St Chely d'Aubrac. The path ran briefly through a few fields and then took off abruptly across the packed contour lines on the map. I was gasping for breath within moments. It felt like a frontal attack on a forty-five degree slope. Thankfully the hillside was wooded and the ground was firm.

Twenty paces up, pause, and breathe deeply. Twenty paces up, pause, and breathe deeply. What the blazes was I carrying in that rucksack? I had just chucked out all the surplus weight. Twenty paces up, pause, and ... The sweat stung my eyes. It ran down the small of my back and drenched my shorts. Every pore of my skin oozed moisture. Why hadn't I trained on hills like these? It was steady grinding murder. The beauty of the morning was obliterated in a moment by moment fight to gain height, to get to the day's destination and collapse. Gaps in the trees showed that the world was falling away sharply to the left into a deep valley. I climbed on step by step with hands on knees, hands on hips, hands dangling relaxed, anything to ease the strain and help my legs lever me up the little path between the overhanging branches.

The incline eased at last and the path broke out into a clearing and headed across open slopes to the village of Lestrade. I straightened up and breathed more easily as the old steady rhythm returned. The path skirted the village and ran behind a little cultivated field where a man and a woman were clearing the tops of the potatoes and digging them up. I stopped and leaned against the fence.

"You look busy."

They paused willingly and leant on their implements in a way which welcomed the interruption.

"You going far?" he asked.

"Just up to St Chely today."

"Where have you come from?"

"Estaing this morning." He whistled.

"That's moving!"

I admired their spuds and asked what else they produced. She proudly listed all the vegetables they were growing.

"Where are you from?"

"England."

"You've walked all the way!" They moved closer with warming interest.

"I started from Arcachon, over near Bordeaux."

"How far are you going then?"

"Well, I'm aiming to go through the Cévennes and down to the Mediterranean at Sète."

They exclaimed simultaneously and he blew on the tips of his fingers, then shook them vigorously in the air as if he had touched something too hot to hold; a delightfully French gesture indicating that one has been deeply impressed.

"Mon Dieu! How long will that take you?"

"Just one month. I have until the end of September."

They questioned me closely on my route and expressed total disbelief at my intended journey on the following day, which was flattering, if rather unnerving.

"You are doing that in one day!"

"I hope so. It's about forty kilometres I think."

"But it is over the mountains!" They shook their heads in admiration and then enquired how I liked the countryside.

"Oh, La Belle France! " I exclaimed with a sweeping gesture of the hand. They seemed delighted and on that high note I took my departure.

"Bon voyage, Monsieur. Et bon courage!"

The rucksack was suddenly featherweight. I bounced on my way with the glorious phrase ringing in my ears, revitalised by their admiration and encouragement. A few moments like that could put a sparkle into a whole day of sweat and fatigue.

The GR6 joined a road which ran across a plateau to a final ridge of the Monts d'Aubrac some miles away. It was high walking with open views, always an exhiliarating combination and now with a tingle of trepidation added as the testing ground came into view ahead.

St Chely lay in a cup of the hills well sheltered on three sides, which was a nuisance because it meant losing height that would have to be gained once more the following day, but it was worth it. The GR left the road and ran down the hill through a wood of ancient beech trees on a track which must have carried horse-drawn vehicles for centuries. The sun just penetrated the leaves to give an evening glow to the deep leaf mould which deadened all sound. Even the birds called in muted song in the cavern below the high branches. What stories would the old track tell if it could speak? It was beautifully engineered, running in broad sweeps round the contours of the land and descending steadily all the way. Snapshot views of St Chely appeared, and then the track abruptly rejoined the road. I emerged into the open once more and to my delight spotted the very point where the next day's route left the road and disappeared up into the woods on the far side.

It was a quiet village street. There would be no traffic there that night. I stopped at the first hotel.

"A single room with a shower, please."

"But of course, Monsieur."

It was a lovely little room with a deep window facing west into the setting sun over a little back street. I stretched out on the bed contentedly for a few minutes before taking a shower.

* * * * * *

As I left the hotel in the last minutes before daylight the mountains were a towering black mass ahead of me, capped with a rim of bright light. Overhead stretched the palest of dawn skies with a hint of pastel blue and no trace of a cloud.

The gentle breeze which had blown all night rattling the clothes hangers which displayed my washing at the bedroom window had fallen away, and the village had returned to silence after the departure of the school bus. The local children of secondary age had congregated like a flock of migrating starlings outside the hotel door, clambered into the bus with duffle bags and satchels and vanished into the dark. What a life! And it was nowhere near winter yet; autumn was only just beginning. Vivid memories of childhood yearnings had returned while I sipped coffee and watched them. The yearning to grow up into adult freedom and no longer suffer the daily pressgang hustle to school for hours of drudgery. Ah, the myths of childhood! If we had known what lay ahead we might have staged a classroom sit-in which would have made the TUC look like a bunch of bumbling amateurs. And then there were those early mornings on the parade ground at 4 Training Regiment in Catterick Camp gazing across the frosted world to the distant Hambledon Hills, the 'hills of freedom' as I had dubbed them in my mind, a paradise where civilians were free to wander at will while we were drilled endlessly in the art of opening ranks and sloping arms. Was future freedom always an illusion? I had only once been able to grab a brief hour while driving north on a balmy May afternoon to walk over those hills, and it had taken me thirty four long years to escape the treadmill of work for a whole month.

  I followed the road round the cleft of the valley to the place where the footpath climbed steeply away up through the woods. Muttering a brief 'into your hands, Lord' I hoisted myself off the road and into the gloom of the trees. It was now just light enough to distinguish the surface of the footpath in this leafy tunnel. An ankle turned over on an unseen rock would not have been clever, but the timing was perfect; not a minute of daylight wasted.

  Over a pre-dinner pastis the previous evening the maitre d'hotel had given an optimistic weather forecast when I had confided my plan to him, but he had been decidedly non-commital on the timing of breakfast. That was a matter for Madame and breakfast was not usually served before seven thirty at the earliest. I had not pushed the matter then but had thought it over carefully during dinner while I studied the map and jotted in the diary. I definitely needed an early start after a hot breakfast if I was going to make la Mothe by nightfall. Over the cheese course I decided on my tactics.

"Madame," I said with a smile of devastating charm, as she brought the coffee, "your cooking is delicious. I have much enjoyed my dinner. That sauce with the veal was exquisite."

This appeared to take her by surprise, as though guests were not usually so effusive over her cuisine, and she raised her eyebrows fractionally while thanking me.

"I have a long journey tomorrow," I continued quickly, "and I was wondering what time I could have breakfast."

She eyed me then with a ghost of a smile, having already been briefed by her husband.

"Would seven o'clock be all right, Monsieur?"

"Seven o'clock would be perfect, Madame," I replied, forcing myself to keep a straight face.

It was a good path with a firm surface but it made no bones about gaining height. I lectured myself severely to remember all the lessons of the past year and of the last two and a half weeks. Take it steady; you were away in good time and there's no need to rush; don't push your legs too hard; you're going to need those muscles in good trim for several hours yet; stop when they start to ache, and take a breather; if a foot begins to rub inside the boot stop and get rid of the rub immediately; and most of all, don't let those red and white daubs out of your sight for too long!

A wrong turning early today would be an absolute disaster and it would be impossible to make up even half an hour wasted in re-tracing steps or attempting to cut across country. I double checked at every conceivable point where the GR might sneak away from the obvious path. If there was a gateway into a terraced pasture I checked it suspiciously and only breathed freely when I found the next marker along the path. It was blessedly cool. The postcards in a shop window in the village had pictured winter sports as a local attraction, and indeed my feet had almost felt cold on the bedroom floor. Every minute or so I paused and breathed deeply with hands on hips, easing first one leg and then the other. If I wasn't fit enough now I never would be.

The slope eased and the path wound through ancient fields with a mixture of old and not so old red and white daubs. I back-tracked patiently three times and forced my way along an abandoned pathway in the clutches of a hedge rather than take an easy route over open ground. I was not going to let those marks out of my sight. They led through the deserted farm of les Enfrux and into the tiny hamlet of Mas Nouvel where a rabbit, almost the first I had seen in France, flicked his ears at me and squeezed quickly under the door of a barn. Cunning little blighter; if you want to stay hidden, stand under the light. No gun-toting chasseur was going to spot him on a Sunday morning. I swung the haversack off and reached for a water bottle. There were no bars along the route today so every drop of liquid was precious. Take a sip, rinse it round the mouth thoroughly and then swallow slowly. Not yet eight o'clock. That's fine. I could enjoy a ten minute break before tackling the slope above Mas Nouvel on something which the map described cryptically as 'Ancienne Voie Romaine'.

I rounded the elbow of the hill above the hamlet and stood stock still. The track ahead of me sped straight as an arrow traversing the hillside at a constant gradient as far as the eye could see. I knew intuitively after twenty days on my feet that this was a gradient which I could climb for hours at a short steady stride without my legs collapsing, my lungs bursting or my heart complaining. At that precise moment the sun lifted itself above the brow of the hill and shone with sudden brilliance straight down the line of the highway into my eyes. I was dazzled, stunned. My feet moved forward involuntarily breaking into a steady, rhythmical stride and carrying me up the hill without any bidding.

The Roman Legionary on my left grunted with satisfaction. "Them engineers done a good job on this stretch, didn't they, mate?"

"Damn good job, I reckon", replied the Legionary on my right. "Cunning bastards ain't they? They know just what a bloke can manage when he's got his equipment on his back."

"Of course, them Gauls done a lot of the hard graft; shifting rocks, clearing trees and such like."

"Blinking right too, I say. They got all the benefits of us blokes being around to keep the peace. About time they lifted a hand to help us."

"You reckon they want us here?"

'Them engineers done a good job on this stretch …'

"Course they do. We're civilization, mate. Roads, water, proper housing. Its all happening. Course they want us. Stands to reason."

"Can't understand why we have to dig in every night then. Surely if they want us here they ain't going to attack us in the night, are they?"

"That's just the regulations. Standing orders. Anywhere between Tuscany and Hadrian's Wall you dig in at night, just in case. Anyway, Big Nose wouldn't be happy if he couldn't shout at us every evening to get fell in with our shovels."

The Centurion's horse clattered up behind us. "Stop talking in the ranks there! You'll need all of your breath before the day's out. We are doing an extra ten miles today to get us over the mountains fast."

My companions groaned in unison. After a while the one on the right inquired, "Where are you from, mate?"

The question was clearly addressed to me. I gulped. Should I reply in Latin, French or English? I took a gamble and blurted "Angleterre."

The Centurion's horse clattered up again noisily behind us and, fearing further chastisement, I turned round to explain......

A battered Renault was climbing the hill noisily behind me. I moved hurriedly to one side giving a friendly wave. As it passed me the driver raised a hand in acknowledgement. Ten minutes later I caught up with him sitting in his car at the brow of the hill where the road changed direction by a few degrees to the next vantage point. He was gazing over the early morning mountains with obvious enjoyment. As I approached he emerged with two blocks of salt for the cattle. We greeted each other cheerfully.

"Roman Road?" I inquired. He nodded.

"The Romans knew how to build roads," I said.

He spread his hands in a wide gesture in each direction and nodded in a way which expressed profound respect for the men who had carved their way through forests and over mountains to establish the first European Community long before that name was ever dreamed of.

The track shifted five degrees south and sped straight to the next vantage point. How many legions had tramped this very road at dawn two thousand years ago? They would have joked amongst themselves, the old sweats telling tall stories about blue-painted women out on the fringes of the Empire way beyond civilisation. Some of them would certainly have seen the Hambledon hills on a frosty morning. Nothing was new. It had all been done before. Well, that might be true but nobody seemed to have done it recently, which was what gave it a touch of excitement.

An hour-and-a-half further on I was flat on my stomach wriggling under a barbed-wired fence after crossing a stretch of open grassland. The high tops were beginning. Another long stretch of well-maintained Roman road lay ahead. Everything was going fine. I had prayed for a comfortable hotel for the previous night's rest, an early breakfast to launch me on my way and make full use of the daylight, a blue sky to walk beneath, and no wrong turnings; and it had all been granted to me.

I had also requested a gentle breeze blowing in my face to keep me cool. As a new stretch of track led up to the top of a ridge I was met by the full blast of a force six wind hurling itself gleefully over the mountain tops. I leaned into it and started down the far side laughing for joy. I was going to make it to la Mothe today. Nothing on earth would stop me now.

I searched my mind for a song or a hymn which I could shout to the world in triumph but nothing could match my elation, my mood, or the rhythm of my march. I stopped trying, and the words came to me at once unsought. 'If I take the wings of the morning and dwell in the uttermost parts of the sea; even there shall thy right hand lead me...'. There it was in a nutshell! I had taken the wings of the morning and flown to uttermost parts. And although my God lived everywhere and was always ready for a chat I found Him most easily in open spaces on mountain tops. There was nothing to do but go on laughing for sheer joy.

A tractor driver bowling along with a load of hay bales looked incredulously at a short, tanned, balding man who strode towards him. The man carried a large pack with various articles of clothing flapping wildly on top of it. His hair, what was left of it, blew straight back in the strong wind and he was apparently laughing to himself over some huge joke. He waved both arms in hilarious greeting and gave a double thumbs up sign. The tractor driver burst out laughing too and waved back with equal abandon.

* * * * * * * * *

I was walking due south. For nineteen days I had been heading east into the rising sun and into the heart of France. Now my steps were pointing to the midday sun and to the Mediterranean. The road undulated across a vast open landscape which was the roof of France under the infinite dome of the sky. Distant cattle grazed the short grasses from one horizon to another. Occasional clumps of trees clustered on the rounded slopes of rocky hills which tried to thrust above the immense sweep of land. Greens and greys merged and separated in flowing bands of colour, sun-dried passive colours which emphasized the smoothness of everything. The only brightness came from a sky of clinical morning blue, blown clear of every vestige of cloud before the heat of the day could generate an enveloping haze.

The GR6 swung onto a stretch of track no longer in regular use. I settled myself on a grassy bank below the Col de Maihebieu and contemplated the view with satisfaction. A valley was beginning to cut its way down from the plateau but the GR6 would stay on the high ground for a long way yet. A haze began to form to the disgust of Pentax Zoom 70 but I assured him that we would keep a full record of the day's proceedings even if the results were not products of great beauty. It was not wild country. Man had been in control for a long time even if he was not there in person at the moment. Cattle roamed freely over vast fenced areas and ancient dry stone walls ran for miles. An occasional deserted farmhouse looked down from a ridge.

The track turned a corner below one of these farm houses and forked. I followed the GR6 to the left over a low rise and abruptly walked into autumn. The sea of bracken had taken on a golden look and the valley which ran down to one side was now a streak of bright colour. The change was uncanny. I strode on for miles marvelling at the spectacle of orange, yellow and brown until the track terminated without warning at a tarmac road.

This was ridiculous. I had studied the map countless times and today's route went nowhere near a surfaced road until the very last stage. I pulled the map out of my waistband indignantly and opened it up. Just above the hamlet of Trelans the red dashes of the GR merged with the most minimal of minor roads where it began its existence and ran briefly down to the D56. I followed it somewhat reluctantly down to Trelans and left it before it began to produce motor vehicles.

The path dipped into a valley and then began to climb again. I groaned. This wasn't fair. I had done all the uphill bit in the morning and this unexpected demand took my legs by surprise. I nursed them patiently uphill again murmuring encouragement and, in my blissful ignorance, assuring them that this was positively the last ascent of the day.

It was worth the effort. The GR emerged onto the last spine of the Monts D'Aubrac running southwards. The late afternoon sun shone from the west at a low angle bringing out all the rich autumn colours in the valley to the east. The track ran gently downwards along the ridge with a view on all sides. It was an old track, smooth and firm, ideal for tired legs which had lost interest in lifting their boots over obstacles. I swung along contentedly ticking off features on the map and watching the horizon change ahead until a scruffy little sign announced 'Detour'. Blast it! Any detour would be sure to take me away from the GR signs and that always spelt trouble. Sure enough the red and white daubs ceased as the track turned into a newly bulldozed slash across the hillside, elbowed off the old route by the activities of a local farmer, who was clearing scrub and bracken. Another barley baron wreaking havoc on the environment, probably with the aid of a fat EEC subsidy. I picked my way cautiously along this raw new track to the point where it joined the old route again and found two men wielding mattocks as they unearthed a potato crop. They were going at the task with such savage energy that I stopped and shouted encouragement, brandishing an imaginary whip to urge them on. Like my acquaintances of the previous evening they gladly seized the opportunity of a break and walked over for a chat.

I suggested jovially that they ought to have painted some new GR signs on the detour. They misunderstood me and expressed concern that I had lost my way.

"No, no" I assured them. "I am heading down there to la Mothe." I admired their potatoes and enquired whether it was not too dry to grow them up here.

"Oh, it is very healthy up here; there is never any fog. We have had English visitors this summer in the village of St-Pierre-de-Nogaret over there. They loved the climate. They were very nice people."

Our conversation ranged over a multitude of topics including the Channel tunnel. They were an interesting pair. One of them, the more weathered and red-faced of the two, was clearly a labourer working for the other one who owned four hectares of land on the hillside. The former spoke volubly and, to me, incomprehensibly but the latter at once grasped my linguistic limitations and spoke slowly and distinctly. The weathered one listened carefully as his companion explained that I had started from the Atlantic coast.

"Mon Dieu ! But that is a long way!" He gazed at me as though I had arrived from China. "You have got good boots for that?"

They examined my boots with approval. The better part of a thousand miles had given them a tough and battle-hardened appearance.

They obligingly went back to work so that I could satisfy the demands of Pentax Zoom 70 and take a picture before I departed.

"Au revoir, Monsieur. Bon voyage. " A pause, ..." et bon courage!"

* * * * * *

Out of the haze in which the far horizons had been lost since midday there began to emerge the dark outline of the next mountain ranges. They were not the usual style of mountains which begin with polite foothills as an introduction and lead you gradually into greater things. They rose sheer from the valley floor to an impressive height and then abruptly levelled off like an extended Table Mountain. The Causses. I watched their outline sharpen as the heat haze lifted in the evening, and it began to dawn on me that I was going to descend to the very bottom of the gorge which lay between us. That still looked a long way down, and it would look a long, long way up the next morning.

It was a long way down. I went through the village of Mogardel, met the D56 and went on down towards the bottom of the gorge, knees bending, pack bouncing, thighs stretching at every step. Going steeply downhill is not effortless. Going steeply downhill with a large pack is hard work. Every step is an act of braking, a cushioning of forces. I reached the bottom and threw myself flat on my back in the long grass under an oak tree. It was six o'clock. I had been walking with only brief respites for the last eleven hours. My legs felt like jelly, not strained or sore, just lifeless, utterly limp; the signals from my brain were no longer getting through and yet there was still another hour of steady walking along the valley.

I took a swig of warm water and began to wonder how I was going to make it before dark. After a few minutes of deep breathing I nodded off and woke again with a start as a car sped past. The energy pills! It came to me in a flash. I unbuckled the haversack and reached inside for the plastic screwtop container which had started its life holding ground coffee beans and now held all the little oddments which might otherwise get lost; nail scissors, miniature torch, finger plasters, paracetamol, and energy pills. This was the first time I had resorted to them, but I rated it an emergency. After all, I might miss dinner if I arrived too late in the evening. The little white tablets tasted quite nice. I ate four and settled down to relax again for a few minutes while I checked the map.

There was a choice. Go on down to the main road and turn east beside the river and the railway or turn off east now and follow the footpath through the countryside on a parallel course. The main road was coloured red on the map indicating that it was a trunk road; I couldn't face that after a day on the roof of the world. And yet the route of the footpath looked ominously like a scramble back up into the foothills; that was equally impossible in my present enfeebled state. I decided to compromise and try the minor road which ran between these two routes after the point where the GR left it and wandered across a few haphazard contours.

Things began well. Within minutes I was feeling the benefit of the tablets as sucrose seeped into the blood stream and stirred the muscles back into action. The GR followed a shady earth track which forded a stream and continued between giant blackberry bushes. I kept up a steady pace without pushing myself since there was no sense in worrying over the last little bit of the journey. The GR vanished up the hillside to the north and I was left on the minor road which continued for a time between fields below a railway embankment. Yes, I had chosen well; it was peaceful and direct and a fitting end to the longest day.

A little group of houses known, according to the map, as le Viala appeared ahead perched just above the valley floor and looking attractive in the setting sun. To my horror the minor road suddenly swung off towards them at an incline of about one in five. I muttered nasty things beneath my breath and plodded slowly up consoling myself with the thought that there would be a nice little view. No sooner had the road squeezed past half a dozen houses than it dived down once again to the level of the flat fields.

I fell for the same lousy trick at ten minute intervals at the hamlets of Pratnau, les Salelles, le Segala and la Blaquiere. My knees turned to jelly again and my thighs found places to ache which had never been revealed before. I became rebellious. I was damn well going to get to la Mothe before it was dark even if I had to get out the compass and barge through half a dozen hedges. The thought was no sooner in my mind than the GR6 reappreared and a change-of-direction sign waved me through a gate and straight across the middle of a sloping pasture. No-one had walked this part of the GR6 for the last five years judging by the array of nettles, bracken, muddy streams and brambles which I forced my way through. Finally the path descended by a series of hairpin bends to the railway track and.... la Mothe! I paused at the last hairpin bend and beamed happily at the hotel below me. It was a large old building tastefully renovated, with brand new shutters and bright paintwork. It promised a hot shower, a comfortable bed, good food and a choice of wine.

I galloped merrily down the last incline, trotted over the railway track and crossed the road to the hotel. Bowls of flowers stood outside the door. I grasped the handle. The door was locked! I rattled the door with a sickening feeling in the pit of my stomach. Then a man appeared and my spirits rose. He came and unlocked the door.

"We are closed, Monsieur."

"But I have walked forty kilometres," I insisted. "I must have a room tonight even if you cannot provide a meal."

"I am very sorry, Monsieur. But there is another hotel three...."

"I screamed silently. My legs went rigid. My shoulders bent under the weight of the pack. I couldn't. I just couldn't walk another three kilometres. There was no stuffing left in me.

"... hundred metres down the road beside the railway station," he finished politely, pointing down the road.

I raised my eyes wearily and looked down the road. I might just manage three hundred metres with a bit of luck and a following wind. I nodded and set off.

* * * * * *

The one advantage of an old railway hotel is that it has an old style bathroom; and old style bathrooms have real baths, the things you can lie in. Showers are all very well; they are economical on water and they don't form dirty rims round the side; but they can't compete with baths when you are totally, utterly and completely knackered.

I ran a generous amount of hot water, peeled off sweat-soaked and dusty garments, heaved a sigh of immense satisfaction, stepped in and sat down.

Ouch! What had I sat on? I stood up, rubbed my posterior and examined the bath. It was smooth enamel without a fault. I sat down again gingerly and the truth dawned on me. I had walked and climbed and sweltered for the best part of three weeks and there was no padding left. My buttocks had vanished.

My buttocks had vanished.

CHAPTER 8

MOUNTAIN RANGES

Life is an emotional switch-back which tosses us genially from the heights to the depths and back again without a great deal of warning, and I suppose it would be incredibly dull if we were always sitting pretty up on top. I mean, can you be really happy unless you know what it is like to be utterly miserable? But I am in danger of becoming philosophical. It was just that my days seemed to alternate between delightful experiences and routine interludes. The Dune du Pilat and the Lac de Cazaux had been followed by a slog across the desert of Aquitaine, an evening with Mademoiselle at the Auberge St Jaques had been followed by a day in the rain, and now an intoxicating day across the wind swept roof of France was being followed by a dull overcast day labouring across the Causse de Sauveterre.

And the geographical peaks and valleys sharpened the emotional experience. From the bottom of the Lot valley to the plateau of the Causse was at least seven contour lines on the map or three hundred and fifty metres which, in plain English, is a thousand feet. The GR6 wasted no time in niceties of approach. In one brief kilometre it ascended the cliff above la Canourgue, offering occasional handholds of roots and branches to help the hapless traveller up thirty degree slopes strewn with loose boulders.

The view up on top was not encouraging. The term 'causse' has become dangerously over-worked. It is suffering the same fate as costa, riviera, vale, gorge, and a host of other once meaningful words. Causse must originally have been intended to depict a rocky vastness open to the wide heavens with distant views carrying the eyes across 'sauvage' countryside high above the polluted plains of civilisation. Consequently I had looked forward to crossing the Causse de Sauveterre from the valley of the Lot to the valley of the Tarn but geographers had now scattered the term carelessly over the map applying it to any fairly flat area over a few hundred metres high. This particular causse was almost smothered in boring conifers planted over endless boring little hills whose main purpose appeared to be to obscure the view.

The one moment of excitement came when I spotted the print of small walking boots in soft stretches of the path. A recent local shower had left patches of mud and the prints showed clearly. They must be female and they were moving in the same direction as me. I quickened my pace at the prospect of female company.

Two hours later near the village of Soulages I passed a young woman sitting in a pasture below the road amongst the tinkling bells of a flock of sheep. Her rucksack was beside her on the ground. She was a severe looking young woman with swept back hair and spectacles, studying a book on her lap. Her brief glance in my direction could not be interpreted as welcoming. I continued on my way disappointed.

By contrast the village of St-Georges-de-Levejac offered a warm welcome. It was Friday lunchtime and the little restaurant was crammed with a mixture of businessmen hastening the end of the week and local pensioners on a spree. The sprawl of cars parked carelessly in the narrow road augured well even before the hum of conversation reached my ears. Two men emerged from the door of the restaurant onto a terrace at first floor level and helped each other down the steps.

"Marche bien là, " they volunteered expansively without waiting for an enquiry on my part, indicating that Madame's cooking was worthy of investigation.

I helped one of them carefully off the bottom step and went up. Rich smells wafted from the restaurant into the little bar just inside the door. Madame was attentive to the stomachs of her customers but her husband sought my eye through the throng of earnest talkers and came up promptly with a panache . I turned round with difficulty nudging a few glasses with my rucksack and retreated to the terrace where there were vacant chairs and a view. People passed in and out nodding warmly in my direction, the flow of voices enveloped me companionably, and I gazed out from the terrace over a foreground of moss-covered stone roofs.

The son of the establishment was concerned that I should be sitting alone outside and he came to converse with me. After a minute or two he pointed at the darkening sky to the west and murmured something about thunderstorms. I followed the line of his gaze and decided not to linger too long in spite of the attractions.

I was following the GR sign through the village when my eye was caught by the roof of a little church and I remembered the words of Mademoiselle at Conques, that some of the little village churches were 'gems'.

Right, I thought, I will take Mademoiselle at her word and investigate. Rounding a corner, the first thing I noticed was the bell tower, a separate and exposed framework for most French churches, not an integral part of the church as in England. The timber frame was new and the metalwork shone with fresh black paint. This bell was rung regularly. I walked round the church hoping to find a door unlocked. Pushing open a wrought iron gate I found the door of the church standing wide open. Splendid! I entered quietly and turned to face the altar.

An ancient crone shuffled down the aisle leaning on a broom for support. She stopped and eyed me with penetrating disapproval. I was suddenly acutely conscious of my dusty boots, socks down round my ankles, disordered hair, and bulky pack topped off with last night's washing fastened there to dry in the sun. She pointed at a stone receptacle just inside the door and gabbled something which I could not catch but took to be an instruction to make a contribution to the fabric fund.

"Oui, madame, " I responded gravely. She tottered out of the church after another riveting glare and banged the wrought iron gate emphatically behind her.

I walked up the aisle. The little south transept held the organ topped with a gorgeous spray of flowers. The north transept, also lovingly decorated with flowers, held an altar. I turned and looked back down the nave with the sunlight streaming in from the south windows. Every single pew was brand new. Solid timber polished to perfection.
Round the walls hung a set of wooden carvings depicting the stations of the cross; they were clearly very old but in excellent repair and were highlighted with fresh colours.

I stood basking in the glow of the accumulated warmth and beauty. Then a nasty thought niggled at the back of my mind. Was this

She stopped and eyed me with penetrating disapproval.

one of the national religious monuments which the state had decided to preserve for reasons of history or tourism? The French Government is known to be doing this in Val D'Isere in preparation for the influx of the next winter Olympics. That question could be answered easily enough. I walked back down the nave to examine the congregation's books of worship. A neat stack of modern service books stood on a table and I picked up a few of them. They were supple and well thumbed. The notices and the leaflets were up to date. This was no hollow showpiece; it was the meeting place of a regularly worshipping community which took immense pride in its church.

I fished in my pocket for a coin to drop into the place which the ancient one had indicated and found to my astonishment that it was a hollow scooped in a chunk of stone and filled with water. Lord, she must have thought me an ignorant tramp! She had been waiting for me to dip my fingers in the water and sign myself with the cross before entering her church. I put the coin back in my pocket, unbuttoned my shirt hoping fervently that she would not reappear at the critical moment, extracted a note from my money belt and stuffed it through the slot in the fabric fund box which I could now see was firmly embedded in the wall. Maybe they too had a diocesan loan to repay.

Mademoiselle, you were right. It was a gem.

* * * * * *

Pointe Sublime, as you might guess from its name, is a vantage point with breathtaking views. It teeters on the edge of the Tarn Gorge not far from Les Vignes which was my objective for the night, and it overlooks a chasm which makes the Lot valley look like a railway cutting. The hazy atmosphere with shafts of sunlight breaking here and there through ominous banks of dark cloud produced a Tolkein effect in this great gash in the earth's surface. Pinnacles of rock grew out of the mists; dark clumps of trees lurked within recesses of the cliffs; the river swirled between banks of sand and shingle at an infinite distance below.

Shadows rolled across the opposite mountains. Pentax Zoom 70 polished off a twenty-four exposure film in minutes and demanded more. I stuffed in another one to keep him quiet and he busied himself in all directions before we began the laborious descent to les Vignes. It was a matter of fine judgement whether to take the road which tacked carefully across the contours with the aid of ten hairpin bends or to plunge recklessly down the shortcuts which descended precipitously from one arm of the road to the next. I chickened out and took the longer route justifying my choice by the damage which my shorts might have suffered had I slithered down shortcuts on my bottom.

Les Vignes on a grey evening was rather depressing, although dinner was enlivened by a Dutch couple who had deserted their caravan for an evening on the town. I lay in bed later listening to pounding rain driven against the windows by a howling wind.

* * * * * *

Madame was a motherly sort who liked to launch her guests well-prepared into the rigours of a new day. Heated croissant and baguette, butter, jams, and a large steaming bowl of coffee were placed in front of me with loving care. She would have been horrified had I slipped out of the door early on a Mars Bar and a glass of water, and looking at the sky outside I was thankful that I had sacrificed half-an-hour for the sake of a good breakfast.

I crossed the bridge under grey clouds and walked through the houses to where the footpath started at the side of the gorge. It was going to be another of those calf-stretching, lung-bursting, heart-pumping scrambles to gain height. There was a road which rose to the top by a series of long lateral runs and hairpin bends but it would have taken a long time and it lacked the macho image which we long distance professionals like to assume. Did I hear you murmur 'inflamed tendon'? That, may I remind you, is a downhill hazard. Uphill may be exhausting but it's safe.

Where the path was stony the stones skidded downhill underfoot, where it was smooth earth it had turned to mud overnight, and where it was grass-covered or overgrown everything showered raindrops when it was touched. After twenty minutes I broke out onto one leg of the road at an encouragingly high point. The footpath signs directed me to follow the road for a while which seemed quite a good idea since my legs had passed their first flush of enthusiasm and were muttering about taking a break. I was examining a spot where someone had built a new retaining wall to stop rocks rolling down onto the road when I suddenly realised that the red and white daubs were directing me to leave the road at this point and start scrambling again. They must be joking! I studied the hillside. Some convenient steps mounted the retaining wall itself and the path then vanished into a sort of grey crevice between chunks of rock. In fact, not so far above was a veritable cliff face with stack-like features towering over me. I hesitated, then reluctantly followed the signs; there was no point in losing the GR at this early stage in the day.

Ten minutes of heaving, groaning, and sweating, of straining knees and grabbing handholes, and I was staggering through a gap into an eyrie with breath-taking views, views which had been seen by men centuries before me judging by the remains of massive stone walls which linked sections of the natural rock. The group of stacks formed the pillars of a regular fortress which leaned out from the mountainside and dominated the road below to the north. To the south the Tarn Gorge ran for miles, a massive slash deep into the earth's crust with sheer cliffs falling vertically from the limestone plateau on each side and, below them, sweeping tree-covered slopes tumbling down at a steep angle to grip the slim river winding its tortuous way thousands of feet below. The ochre-grey of the cliffs contrasted savagely with the deep green of the trees and the silver patches of distant water, and the whole vista lay under a grey cloak of cloud which here and there spilled menacingly over the rim of the cliffs. Man was an intruder. This was where the elements fought out their battles over centuries and earth gave way grudgingly to wind and water in a ceaseless struggle.

I stood there appalled, an insignificant creature who might be crushed in a minor rockfall which would not alter this panorama in any discernible way. How could man ever have lived up here? How had a garrison been fed and supplied? It was all very well to be inpregnable but they must have had to come out and join the world some time. The inaccessibility of the site was confirmed by the absence of any attempt by the authorities to maintain and preserve the original fortification. I scrambled back to the footpath and continued upwards in thoughtful mood, ascending literally into the clouds which held the plateau in a still embrace.

It was chilly sitting in the clouds but I had to stop and rest my legs. I pulled out the red wind jammer and snuggled into it before taking a swig of cold water. Feeling even colder after this spell of uncomfortable relaxation I extracted the green anorak and zipped myself into it, then started off at a brisk pace along the little road which ran between stunted pines. It was uninspiring country but I suppose most country looks pretty uninspiring under a blanket of cloud.

The church at St Pierre des Triniere lit by a sudden shaft of sunlight looked like freshly washed Cotswold stone in perfect repair. A beautiful double arched entrance led into a right-angled corner of the cluster of buildings. I thought of Mademoiselle's comment again and went hopefully to the door, but it was locked.

Deeper into the plateau the sky lightened and the low ridged hills became more entertaining. A tuneful tinkling of bells announced a flock of sheep long before I came across them firmly occupying fifty metres of the path and not in the least inclined to give way to me. Pentax Zoom 70 thought it was unnecessary to waste exposures on such stupid creatures but we compromised on a couple of quick shots as I struggled through a variety of bushes and brambles beside the path. Shortly afterwards I was forced to give way again. The sound of voices from above broke the stillness as a female of impressive proportions and muscular legs came into sight descending the path at a brisk trot. Her boots thudded down the track bouncing from one rock to another and a line of other hikers trod confidently behind her. The onrush was so sudden that I leapt to the safety of a large boulder to escape being rolled backwards by this human avalanche.

"Bonjour, " I called courteously, realising in the same instant that the flaxen haired bulldozer at their head could only be German.

"Bonjour, " she responded as she swept passed followed in close formation by a string of young men and women.

I waited a few moments and then exclaimed in English "Crikey, how many of you are there?"

"Goot morning," replied a young man politely.

"There must be thousands of you!"

"How many? No. I am zer last von," commented the rearguard precisely as he strode past me.

I looked after them. They were so close together that they must have been marching in step. I burst out into a lusty rendering of my favourite Bavarian folk song:

> "I love to go a-wandering
> Along some mountain track,
> And as I go I love to sing
> My rucksack on my back..."

but they had already vanished from sight and my rendition was wasted, which was perhaps just as well since they out numbered me and I might have been treated to a swift journey downhill.

"Now that would have been a picture worth taking," said Pentax Zoom 70.

"I know, but I had to leap up here to avoid us both getting trampled to death, didn't I?"

"You've got to be faster on the draw. That blonde would have made a fantastic shot."

"She was almost on top of me. There wasn't time."

"Well, you could have got the whole line of them from behind."

"I had to hang on with one hand to stop falling over."

"That's a pretty weak excuse. You've got to be prepared all the time. That's why I spend whole days bouncing up and down on your chest."

"Oh, shut up! I've taken some jolly good shots already today."

"I was only pointing out...."

"Look," I said, playing my trump card, "do you want to come on the next long walk or shall I leave you resting comfortably in a nice drawer at home?" That shut him up alright.

The top of the next rise revealed another deep gash in the ground, the Gorge de la Jonte, somewhere at the bottom of which lay Meyrueis where I planned to spend the night. I paused to look around and found to my delight that bright blue sky was racing up behind, the picturesque sort of blue sky with featherweight bundles of cumulous bowling harmlessly across it to provide the perfect backdrop for every view. I quickened my pace. I knew what was coming shortly; those breathtaking distances seen from le Pic Houren which we had shared on the previous year's holiday after a night in Meyrueis. A telephone kiosk stood beside the road in Hyelzas. I headed towards it groping in my back pocket for the plastic bag of coins and pouring them into my hand, looking forward to sharing the moment and letting her know that all was well. But the miserable collection of one franc and fifty centime pieces was utterly inadequate. I cursed myself for not keeping some fives and twos ready for a phone call and walked on feeling suddenly crestfallen. No, I must stop and get some change, right now. A hundred metres away two young mothers were deep in conversation after collecting their young children from Saturday morning school. I extracted a hundred franc note discreetly from my money belt, ran a comb through my hair and approached them trying to look like a respectable married man, which is not easy when you are on your own with several weeks' suntan and a large pack.

"Excuse me, but could you possibly change this note for some coins?" I said courteously; and added wistfully, "I need to phone my wife in England."

"Your wife in England? Oh, mais oui! "

I had touched the right chord. Any husband abroad who was so dutiful as to phone his wife at home on a Saturday morning must of course be assisted.

"I will have a look indoors at once." She emerged a moment later with her bag but it yielded nothing but centimes and large notes, so her friend took me at once under her wing and we went to the other house, but that produced little more. Two minutes later I was in the grandparents' house and the entire family were pooling their resources in the good cause. I thanked them profusely and returned with bulging pockets to the kiosk where I was able to exchange a few minutes of excited reminiscence on the phone, recalling the day of the lunchtime rendezvous at which I had arrived three hours late after getting rather off course on a glorious walk.

For a few kilometres now I could follow the route of that brief day's outing the previous year. Starting from Meyrueis I had set out to climb up from the gorge and meet her at a little place called Drigas. It had been a splendid walk, even if somewhat longer than intended, and had been one of the determining factors in plotting this year's route. The Causse Mejean was not to be missed and it provided a marvellous approach to the Cevennes mountains.

The familiar hamlets of les Hortes and les Herans came into view with the very path up which I had walked so joyfully fifteen months earlier, then the entrance to the caves at Aven Amand looking like a NATO Headquarters with the flags of a dozen nations fluttering from tall flagpoles; and there was le Pic Houren, a gently rounded hilltop not all that high in itself but with views in every direction. I looked fondly at all these names on the map and my eye was caught, as it had been on the previous occasion, by the words 'Tomb of the Giant' with a little diagram of one horizontal rock slab resting across two vertical slabs. It had baffled me last year that such an obvious feature should be so difficult to find but half an hour of searching the open hillside had failed to reveal it. I decided suddenly that I would search until I found it this year for, according to the map, it lay right in my path. I stopped at a small vantage point beside the road close to the spot indicated on the map, unbuckled the haversack, and dumped it beside me on a convenient patch of bare rock. Then, spreading the map over the rock, I studied it carefully as I ate my lunch. The bearings all checked out ok. There was le Pic Houren south-south-east with the road to Drigas running across the bare plateau to the north-east. Behind me to the north was a patch of woodland. It all fitted exactly. But where was the tomb? It must be visible somewhere or no-one would have bothered to show it on the map. I stretched and lay back for a few minutes on the smooth rock pondering where to begin the search. The hot sun and warm wind were welcome after the cold of the early morning cloud. Raising myself to a sitting position after a few minutes I sat puzzling why the road engineers should have constructed a water gully above the level of the road which sloped quite steeply at that point. Clearly a bit of drainage would be helpful but I could not see how they expected water to run uphill off the road at this particular point. Then a creeping suspicion began to dawn on me. Engineers did not expect water to run uphill off a road. The 'gully' must have another explanation. I leaped off the convenient smooth rock, the only large chunk for miles around in a landscape of thin earth and higgledy-piggeldy rough stones, walked round and peered underneath my resting place. The 'gully' ran into a little man-made cavern with two solid vertical slabs of stone forming its walls and my convenient smooth rock resting squarely across them as the roof. I stood there chuckling at the sudden recollection that I had paused at just this same place in my search the year before. Mind you, he could not have been all that big for a giant because, even after removing the litter of empty beer cans and pink toilet paper which lay in the bottom of the tomb, you would have been pushed to fit in anybody over six foot tall. Perhaps giants in those days had enormous girth; they could have stacked six people of my size in there comfortably one on top of the other. Or maybe they buried people in the womb position with knees up under the chin to indicate rebirth into another world. You can see how anthropologists build up tremendous theories about races who lived several centuries ago; its just a question of letting your imagination run riot when you find something inexplicable. In a few years time someone would explain to us that it wasn't a tomb at all; that it was just the earliest example of an ice-box to keep food cool during the long hot summers.

    I carried on triumphantly to the top of le Pic Houren to enjoy one of the unique vistas in Europe. The Causse Méjean is practically bare apart from man-made conifer plantations which, thank goodness, are relegated to small clumps here and there. The majority of the plateau is a rolling open plain of thin rocky soil with patches of scrub and a few stunted crops. In spring it has drifts of wild flowers but by September it has become a patchwork of dry browns and greys. On a day like this the banks of fleecy cumulous drift their shadows across mile after mile of the plateau in an awe-inspiring parade. Other mountain ranges ring the hazy distance and infinity becomes a reality. It is a land for sheep to wander over, a land of occasional eagles rising above inaccessible cliffs on the edge of gorges, a land of extreme seasons, a land of vast silences.

    I stood there once again lost in awe and admiration, painting a picture in my mind to carry with me, feeling the air around me, lost in the distances. Lord, thank you. It is just as beautiful as last time; I didn't dream it.

I walked on reluctantly along the stony track. One cannot linger forever on the heights.

* * * * * *

From the edge of the escarpment Meyrueis looks insignificant. When one arrives it has the bustle of a lively town with everything one could possibly need; films, lens cloth, butter, St Nectaire cheese, Mars Bars, and even a comb to replace the one which had slipped out of my pocket. A comb is essential for a long distance walker who seeks accommodation at respectable hotels. Sweat-stained, dusty, weathered and laden with baggage one may be, but my theory is that neatly combed hair offsets all these faults in the eyes of the discerning Madame. She sees through the outer crust to the inner man, the orderly man who will emerge from his rough crysallis and come down to dinner in his true colours.

Madame at the Hotel la Renaissance was suitably discerning and allowed me into room number 11 after a brief inspection over the top of her spectacles.

* * * * * *

My cheek was still glowing from that final kiss as I crossed the road and turned to give a farewell wave. She waved back vigorously and there was a chorus of farewells as they made off down the road....

Farewells were one of the great features of this journey. They ranged from the helpful to the hilarious, from the happy to the heartwarming. The warmth of the last one had taken me by surprise.

Indeed, it had been a day of surprises. I had descended from my room at seven thirty in the expectation of a welcome in the dining room but had found the door into the main hotel area still firmly locked. Residents could use a side door to the street at any time and emerging through this I found the basement entrance to the store rooms and kitchens open with one light on. Picking my way warily through a dimly lit maze of boxes and laundry baskets I ascended a flight of stairs into the heart of the hotel feeling more like a burglar than a paying customer. No sign of life; not a soul stirring. This was too bad. Madame had promised breakfast at seven thirty and it was now well past that without even a kettle on the boil in the kitchen. I pulled open the dining room door, switched on the light and settled down to study my maps.

The sound of voices drew me to another door which opened directly onto the street. It sounded like the casual chatter of employees waiting outside their place of work so I drew back the bolt and opened the door cautiously. Two chambermaids and a waitress looked at me in astonishment.

"Bonjour, Mesdames, " I said throwing wide the door with an expansive gesture.

"Bonjour, Monsieur, " they chorused politely as they trooped past me. Clearly they were not used to being admitted to work by one of the guests.

I returned to my seat in the dining room formulating in my mind a stern rebuke about the laxness of timekeeping in this establishment and a stiff complaint to Madame, but the speed and friendliness of the service pre-empted any assault. Dusting crumbs of croissant off my shirt I rose from the table and enquired if Madame had arrived as I wished to pay the bill.

"Madame will be here at seven thirty, Monsieur."

I consulted my watch and indicated to the waitress politely that it was almost eight fifteen. "No, no, Monsieur" she responded with comprehension dawning on her face. "It is only seven fifteen! The clocks were changed last night."

Within minutes I was on the move, still chuckling. It had been a fortunate mistake. The valley was wrapped in mist and for the first time in three weeks I started out wearing the red and white wind jammer over my cotton shirt to keep warm. A narrow path climbed southwards out of the Gorge de la Jont through a valley of natural pine and chestnut straight into the heart of the Cévennes. The mist thinned and lightened as I walked upwards. It was exquisitely beautiful as the hillside gradually took shape around me and every leaf and spider's web sparkled when the moisture was touched by the rays of the sun. Rocks, thorn bushes, briars and gorse emerged suddenly twenty metres ahead and retreated into the void behind me. Gradually the sky turned blue overhead and there were breathtaking moments as I climbed slowly out of the mist and looked down on a vapour filled valley below. My memory did a sudden flashback across thirty years and I was in the Cotswolds gasping my way up the little path known as 'The Nap' in the Nailsworth valley from Amberley to Minchinhampton Common; it was another autumn morning cloaked in mist with the smell of decaying leaves; I had passed the memorial to Queen Victoria and had just emerged into the sun on the edge of the common when the children in the primary school below broke into a joyful morning hymn; it had been utterly impossible to absorb the whole beauty of the moment; the peace, the pungent air, the pure children's voices, the depth of the valley hidden below; at such moments I feel utterly inadequate and simply stand there murmuring 'thank you' over and over again.

  Part of the beauty was the path itself. It was smooth, just wide enough for one person, ascending steadily at a gradient of which a Roman engineer would have approved , twisting with the contours of the hillside and offering frequent window views. It was too good to last. The underlying rocks decided to break through in awkward ridges. Loose six inch rocks spread themselves carelessly and drifts of smaller stones ganged up and lay in ambush at corners. I was forced to stop for a breather which caused me to glance behind. One of the traps into which the long distance walker can easily fall is to keep looking ahead and forget to look behind since he unconsciously assumes that he has seen what is behind him having already walked through it. To look at a landscape first from the north and then from the south or from the east and then from the west is to look at different faces of the same coin; the view is totally different.

  Behind me was a distant vista of the Causse Méjean. Ramparts of rock rose above the great pool of mist and the low rays of the sun lit every detail of the vertical walls throwing into sharp relief dark entrances to caves, sheer vertical slabs of rock and the tumbling lower slopes. A mountain mass whose northern face two evenings before had loomed mysteriously in late afternoon shadow was now revealed with startling clarity on its southern side, and each of these experiences was quite different to standing on top of the plateau itself and feeling the cloud shadows sweeping across its undulating crown. I marvelled for the hundredth time at the way my legs could carry me from one world to another in a few hours.

The sound of barking dogs shattered these peaceful reflections. Surely there were no houses to be patrolled up here. Of course not, it was Sunday morning and every true Frenchman was out with a gun and a dog chasing the few miserable specimens of edible wildlife which might still be lurking in the woods. Five minutes later two dogs of spaniel appearance came bounding down the path, their barks echoing up and down the valley and effectively alerting every living creature within a radius of five kilometres. They did not appear to be on the trail of anything in particular since they paused for a chat before rampaging off again. As no armed and camouflaged chasseur accompanied them I concluded that they had become bored with seeking non-existent deer, rabbits, wild boar or pheasant and had decided to take a day off.

The rock-strewn path came out briefly into open rolling country and was almost immediately swallowed up in a belt of forestry. The views vanished and I walked along a wide track between walls of conifers until it reached a bowl in the mountains at a place where the trees had been recently cleared. An even better panorama lay behind me. I was now looking down onto the Causse from a higher vantage point. The view extended right across the distant plateau to further ranges beyond and the early morning air was clear for scores of miles. The rucksack came off for the official hourly break and I had several swigs of cool water while I studied the map. Good Lord! Half the day's journey was already done. I remembered now; it was one of those awkward sections of the route which meant that you either had to do a rather short day or a very long day, and I had opted for the former on the basis that there would be plenty of ups and downs on the way. Ah well, relax and see what the day brings forth.

I flagged down a passing chasseur in his Citroen and had my photograph taken against a backdrop of the Causse Méjean. Pentax Zoom 70 agreed that was a good one for the record and we pottered about for a little while searching for dramatic compositions.

An hour later I had paused once more to refresh myself and feed another film into Pentax Zoom 70 when a group of people topped the horizon a quarter of a mile ahead and moving in the same direction. In the distance they looked like a mixed bunch of male and female walkers proceeding at a fairly leisurely pace. I sprang to my feet and decided to investigate. The opportunity of fellow walkers going in the same direction was too rare to miss.

I closed on them bit by bit wishing that I had a pair of binoculars. Undoubtedly there was a mixture of generations. A school party? Two or three families out together? Certainly some of the younger ones were female. I pressed on hopefully, losing sight of them for a while after they entered a belt of forestry. The path suddenly ended at what appeared to be a wide earth road recently bulldozed through the trees. A series of signs indicated that it must be a ski run. The group was now in full view just a hundred and fifty metres in front and it had a predominantly female cast. I put on a final spurt to catch them up and then drifted in casually amongst them engaging two young ladies in conversation. They were from the Montpellier hiking club, a group of three retired couples and eight single ladies in their twenties out for the day together. When the party halted at a junction I was introduced to their president, a bronzed retired bank manager of fifty-five, and in a flash of inspiration I explained to him that I was under instructions to obtain photographs of myself during the journey. Would he be kind enough to photograph me with the young ladies? He immediately grasped my intention and called out to the ladies sitting on the bank to make room for me. An attractive brunette with a blue ribbon gathering her long hair immediately patted the ground next to her and beckoned to me. I seated myself beside her while Yves, the president, experimented with Pentax Zoom 70 and issued instructions to the group. He took one exposure. The brunette's leg was pressed firmly against mine. He moved in for a closer shot. Suddenly I found myself in a close embrace being kissed firmly on the cheek. Pentax Zoom 70 caught the moment deftly amid enthusiastic applause.

"Would you like to join us for the day?" enquired Yves with promptings from the ladies.

"Enchanté, Monsieur, " I replied with enthusiasm, conscious of the pressure of an elegant tanned leg. "Where are you heading today?"

"We will have lunch somewhere," he replied firmly as though that was the whole purpose of their excursion, and I was reminded that it was Sunday in France. A debate ensued between those who preferred to lunch gently in the shade and those who were intent upon improving their already impressive sun tan. The outcome was indecisive but Yves led off purposefully down one of the tracks which took us on sweeping curves through mature beech woods. The ladies were concerned at the size of my pack and enquired anxiously whether I could enjoy walking with it. They were reassured when I explained that I had carried it happily from the Atlantic coast. We reached a point where Yves climbed off the track and invited people to select their own picnic places. He had chosen well. There was a grassy glade in the midst of tall trees on a slope covered with the warm soft leaf mould of centuries. Sun worshippers and shade seekers could both be satisfied within a few feet of one another and all could recline in comfort.

The club stripped off their haversacks and settled to the serious business of the day. Plastic boxes, cutlery, paper plates and glasses appeared. Napkins were spread. Cooked meats, green salads, mixed dressed salads, loaves, pastries, cheeses, and cruets were spread on the ground. Bottles and hip flasks were placed reverently in safe positions. With a brave face I took out a plastic water bottle, the stub end of a baguette from the previous day, one tomatoe, a distinctly messy butter container and the remains of some St Nectaire cheese. Yves's wife threw up her hands in horror.

"You must have some of this," she insisted, and a chorus of offers echoed under the trees. I tried to explain that my midday meal was always modest but the excuse fell upon deaf ears. It was Sunday lunchtime, not the moment for half-hearted gestures. One after another the members of the Montpellier hiking club pressed offerings on me and ignored all protests. I settled back encircled by delicacies and Yves planted a glass of pastis in my hand and urged me to empty it speedily so that it could be re-charged with red wine. I judged it best to surrender gracefully and to trust that the effects of the alcohol would wear off before we attempted any more walking.

I had positioned myself strategically on the edge of the senior citizens group but within conversational range of the friendly brunette, trying not to make my preference too obvious. I need not have worried. She was clearly the acknowledged raconteur and live wire of the gathering. After accusing the other young ladies of frightening off a group of four eligible young Frenchmen whom we had met en route she switched to a series of indirect comments on long distance walkers which drew chuckles from her audience and finally she enquired my name. I offered her a choice of Guillaume, easily translated from William, or Rodney, for which I could produce no French equivalent. We settled on Bill.

"And your name, Madamoiselle?" I enquired. "Bernadette," replied the other ladies in unison, as though they were used to explaining their companion to strangers.

I was conscious that I had so far been on the receiving end of the general food exchange and this concerned me until I remembered my strategic reserve of Mars Bars. Of course, something recognisably English! I extracted the four bars from the recesses of my haversack, carefully sliced each one of them into three parts and proceeded to offer an English dessert which was well received as a final course to round things off. There was a general stretching and yawning as people settled into comfortable nooks in the leaf mould, and presently silence reigned. Even Bernadette curled up and closed her eyes. Pentax Zoom 70 coughed in a meaningful manner and I rose carefully to my feet for a couple of quick snaps before nodding off amidst a true ' entente cordiale' .

"Where are we going now?" was the general demand as people stretched once more, vanished discreetly behind trees and gathered up the residue of the meal. The wives were looking at their watches and calculating the time it would take to get home. The young ladies were examining a map and suggesting a variety of mountain peaks within a radius of twenty kilometres. Yves shepherded them skillfully onto the track and explained that a decision could be taken when we reached a certain junction.

I found myself walking beside Bernadette in the dappled sunlight. "What is your work?" I enquired.

"I'm an accountant technician with a firm in Montpellier."

"Really? I'm an accountant too."

"But you must be an expert comptable ," she insisted.

"Yes, but we are both accountants," I replied, anxious not to introduce class distinctions. "And why do you choose to go walking on Sundays?" I added.

"It is nice to get out and take exercise; and on Sundays my little boy goes to stay with his father for the day."

She and her husband had separated, and our discussions edged gently into family relationships, care of children, financial problems and the need for friends. She was an attractive person in many ways.

The party came to a halt at the junction. Senior citizens other than Yves headed for home. The rest of us voted to climb Mont Aigoual, the highest peak in the Cévennes.

As we started off I expected to mount through woods to a final rampart of rock with some wind blown pinnacle from which one could view the world below with a feeling of supremacy. The footpath, still the faithful GR6, led us indeed steadily upwards through alternating woodland and forestry, gaining height relentlessly but without open views to prove that we were rising above the rest of the Cévennes. At four o'clock I looked in horror at the metalled highway which suddenly confronted us as we broke out of the woods to high open country. The D118 took us up the final stretch to the peak of the Cévennes in company with pale-faced families gawping out of the windows of large Renaults, coach tours gazing from their elevated seats as they effortlessly ascended the last few hundred metres and cyclists who pumped past us in their elasticated leggings. On the beautiful open dome of Mont Aigoual was a large car park, an ugly grey communications station with a forest of aerials, and a lookout post with a cafeteria for tourists.

"Come on up and see the view," called the ladies as they led the way up the stone steps to join the queue for the lookout point.

I told myself curtly to stop feeling aggrieved. Why should I expect everyone else to make a six hour trek on foot in order to enjoy a view for fifty kilometres in all directions? I could be a masochist if I wished but I had no right to inflict my daft ideas on others. It was just that mountain tops were so special. They seemed to deserve an effort from those who came to look down on the world from above. They seemed to be devalued by such ease of access. I wanted to put this point to Yves but my French was inadequate for the task and none of the others appeared to resent sharing their achievement with several hundred motorists.

Anyway, the view was great. Range upon range of tree covered Cevenne mountains rolled beneath our feet into the hazy distance. Greens and browns merged into a purple horizon. On a clear day, the well-informed maintained, you should be able to see the Mediterranean. I sat on the parapet and gazed. It was worth it.

* * * * * *

Bernadette stopped with one hand over her eye in obvious discomfort. We had outstripped the others and were on our own. She turned to me apologetically.

"Bill, there is something in my eye."

For three weeks and six hundred and seventy five kilometres I had made sure that there was always a clean handkerchief in the left pocket of my shorts in case of sudden emergency. I whipped it out in a moment and shook out the careful creases. Tilting back her head gently I leaned closely over her and drew back the eyelid. We stood close together in breathless concentration for a few seconds while I edged the offending fly to the corner of her eye, oblivious of the approach of the rest of the party round a bend in the track a short distance away. The fly was drawn out gently. We parted and smiled at each other.

"Oh, thank you! That is much better."

"It was a pleasure."

Only then did we become aware of the merriment of our companions. Yves arrived first, half concerned that one of his young ladies might have been receiving unwanted attention and half amused that the confident Bernadette might have been in another predicament. In answer to a volley of comment which was too fast for me to catch she protested, "but I had a fly in my eye. It was painful. He is very kind and gentle. He got it out for me." I waved the clean handkerchief in confirmation but this drew only further delighted accusations from her companions.

Yves glanced at his watch and got the chattering party once more on the move. We arrived at some crossroads where l'Esperou, my destination, lay in one direction and their cars lay in another direction. There was a pause while water bottles came out and various members vanished into the washrooms next to the restaurant. We were standing symbolically beside a sign which proclaimed this spot to be the watershed between the Atlantic Ocean and the Mediterranean. The party stowed its refreshments and hoisted on rucksacks. Yves did a final count to check that all his charges were present. We were one short; Bernadette. There were guffaws of laughter and shouts in the direction of the washrooms.

"Bernadette, there is no need to have a shower."

"Bernadette, you need not put on your make-up just to say goodbye."

"Bernadette, shall we leave you both behind?"

She emerged unruffled and brushed off their comments with a few choice rejoinders.

I turned to Yves and thanked him for his hospitality, congratulating him on his choice of lady members. "Very pretty, very kind, very ' sympathique ' - very French!" I said. This went down well. I shook hands all round offering my hand last to Bernadette. She drew me towards her; we brushed cheeks once, twice, and then a warm full kiss landed on my cheek.

.... and I paused there happily with my cheek still glowing, while back up the road there floated cries of " bon voyage, et bon courage!"

'But I had a fly in my eye ... he was very kind and gentle.'

CHAPTER 9

DESCENT

The grass was stiff with frost and it crunched under each footfall. The sun had at first been visible as a low red presence behind the dark skyline of triangular pine tops but it had vanished as soon as I turned off the road onto a track running down a valley beside the woods. My hands were cold and I thrust them into the pockets of my red wind jammer; it was not really a morning to be wearing shorts.

The linoleum on the bedroom floor had felt positively icy the evening before. I had come out of a hot shower and hopped hastily across to a minute bedside mat before towelling myself vigorously. It had been a novel sensation to snuggle up to a radiator in the dining room and enjoy the warmth of a bowl of soup. L'Esperou was primarily a winter resort; that was obvious from the style of the hotels and the view of surrounding ski runs, but even so the cold had taken me by surprise after the heat-hazed view from the top of Mont Aigoual.

The young couple running the hotel had been courteous but were clearly ticking over gently in a between-the-seasons mood. My fellow diners and I had been edged out of the dining room with our third cups of coffee in our hands and had retired to their room to continue our chat. They were an entertaining Dutch couple who, after listening to my exchanges in French with the proprietor, had enquired politely whether I spoke English. He was a young but bald-headed policeman engaged in anti-drug work and she was a well-built swimming instructor assisting the more serious Dutch citizens in their latest craze of a three-part decathlon (tri-cathlon?) embracing swimming, walking and cycling. Apparently everyone aspiring to fitness in Holland these days must face the challenge of a fifteen kilometre walk, followed by a brisk fifteen hundred metres in the pool, topped up with a quick fifty kilometre dash on a bicycle. I had expressed the view that a lethargic forty kilometres a day on foot would probably keep me from running to fat.

The sun was rising higher and lighting the autumn colours on the far hillside. I blew on my fingers and wished that the last parcel despatched home had not included the pair of ancient chamois leather gloves; they would have been a welcome protection in the freezing temperature down in the shadows at the bottom of the valley. The footpath came to an icy stream spanned by a frost covered telegraph pole anchored in a cairn of rocks each side. With the aid of a handrail I might have attempted it, but without such assistance the odds against a dry passage were overwhelming. I had a sudden recollection of a similar pole across a water-filled ditch at the end of an assault course at Catterick camp; it had been a March morning and an inch of snow had just covered the revolting collection of obstacles arranged to greet us after the ritual run round 'Suicide Hill' and through the marsh.

I had been lucky. I was the first one round and I got to the pole before the snow had been compressed to ice; a careful balancing act with a rifle had got me across unscathed. Lacking a rifle with which to balance myself on this September morning I willingly made a short detour and wobbled across a group of large boulders which stood in the water.

The track wound on through deep woods of pine, oak, beech and chestnut; a time of green silence broken only by the song of unseen birds and the buzzing of umpteen insects which appeared to be tucking into all sorts of autumn goodies in the higher branches of the trees. A gang of wasps buzzed me menacingly in a glade when I stopped to check my directions and I hurried on before they decided to investigate the mixed aroma of St Nectaire cheese and tomatoe. Pausing for a few minutes at a point where recent tree felling had provided a view I was joined by the woodsman who arrived in his landrover to start work.

"It's not very warm," he commented as he got out, and I was just acknowledging his remark when I paused in apprehension as a large alsatian bounded up a track and flopped down beside him panting heavily.

"His morning exercise?" I enquired.

"Yes, and his companion will be here in a minute or two."

I looked back down the track in the direction from which they had arrived. A small black woolly object was lolloping happily along in the distance. Shortly afterwards a mongrel of indecipherable parentage arrived and sprawled beside the alsatian in contented exhaustion, receiving several approving licks on his face. They gazed at me together in that crinkly-eyed manner which dogs use when they want to welcome you, tails swishing softly on the ground. There was nothing of the offensive protectionism of guard dogs here. They were happy to share their woods with any other creature discerning enough to appreciate the smells and listen to the wind in the treetops. I chatted to them for a few minutes and we parted on good terms.

By this time the sun was high in the sky and I shed the wind jammer. A rather dull passage through stifling conifer plantations ended abruptly on the brink of a steep hillside. A vista of parched mountain ranges suddenly appeared, row upon row of bare ridges with trees on their lower flanks. The sky was now a harsher metallic blue. This was a Mediterranean landscape. It suddenly dawned on me that from now on the route was downhill to the sea. I was on the final stretch. The end was in sight. It was an odd moment of mixed feelings. Sadness and satisfaction flowed together uneasily. Surely it was not all going to end with a dull tramp downwards through featureless ' garrigue '; that would be too easy. I need not have worried.

As the track descended the temperature rose. The trees were smaller on these sun-soaked south facing slopes and had the look of survivors who had fought for the right to live a rather stunted existence. Empty stretches with just the blackened limbs of bare trees pointing to the sky were reminders of the fires which could devastate the region. The ground was rocky with wild flowers in profusion, recognisable not by the bright colours of their petals but by the beauty of their seed heads. The path took on a dusty whiteness which reflected the heat.

It was one of those irritating days when I needed three maps. Série Verte number 59 showed almost the entire route, but failed by a whisker to explain what happened at a critical junction due south of L'Esperou so Série Verte number 58, or what was left of it after being tucked into my waistband and constantly consulted for nine days, was needed to check the alternative routes at this point. And later in the day I would have to convert to Série Verte number 65 which would take me first to Ganges and then all the way down in a run practically due south to the sea at Sète.

I had parted company with the GR6 that morning, leaving it to continue its journey eastwards almost to the Italian border. The choice had then been between the GR60 and the GR7, both of which led southward to the Herault river. I had chosen the GR60 because it skirted the town of le Vigan by keeping in hills to the north of it. But have you ever found a map which tells the truth, the whole truth, and nothing but the truth? No, nor have I. In any respectable court of law they would be accused of perjury and stuck in jail for a good long stretch. A tight bunching of contour lines will warn you of hills and a splash of green will indicate woods, and a line of blue will indicate a river, but nothing ever tells you what the countryside is really going to look like and feel like. Nothing warns you that the hillside above le Vigan is going to be a narrow ridge with impenetrable bush on its flanks, topped with rock strata which have erupted vertically creating the most excruciating excuse for a footpath which was ever dreamed up by the Comite Nationale de Grande Randonnee. Sharp edges sprouted from the ground like fangs waiting for the unwary walker to overbalance and impale himself. If any smooth stretch of ground appeared it was immediately littered with boulders a foot high which needed wearily stepping over. The rock itself had a viciously rough surface which not only skinned hands and knees but scratched the leather sides of boots and grated away at the soles. I was caught on this exposed spine of nature at midday and battled my way along it in dripping heat until it ended in a nasty chute of loose rocks tumbling down to the village of la Terrisse. The road at the bottom bore the appropriate sign 'D999'. I sat on the verge for some time licking my wounds and considering the next stage of the journey.

Once again the map offered a choice; follow the GR60 into the hills or take a parallel course along the D999 beside the river to Ganges. The road would be boring but predictable; the GR60 was an unknown quantity. After my experience above le Vigan I chickened out and took the low road. My legs had been on the go for seven hours already and had taken a pounding.

The road to Ganges was long and its surface was hard. Occasional traffic passed at speed, and the roadside restaurants were mostly closed as the tourist season had ended. My right thigh had become stiff and painful. The kilometre signs went past more and more slowly and I paused more and more frequently. Fate had ordained that it would be a low day. One cannot expect to travel with the Montpellier hiking club every day.

The Herault river did its best to alleviate the boredom of the afternoon by providing wooded hillsides which fell precipitously to a river cascading over miniature falls and flowing alternately between smooth rock ledges and drifts of shingle. The skyline was scattered with cliff barriers rising out of dense vegetation. A heron-like bird rose from the water and looked at me in disgust, and using its enormous wing span rose at a steep angle to its nest on a crag high above. The sun descended rapidly in the west and for the second time that day I was walking in deep shadow with the sun lighting the tops of the hills above, but this time it was just pleasantly cool after midday heat.

In Ganges the men were out playing boules while the women cooked the evening meal, a sensible division of labour. Boules is such a simple game. All it needs is a reasonably flat area of well drained fine gravelly material, and the only equipment is a set of small metal balls which click merrily when they strike each other. The skill required is akin to that needed for darts except that in this case you are tossing fairly weighty chunks of metal to land with precision either next to the jack or, more entertainingly, on top of one of your opponent's boules knocking it for six. It is an excellent spectator sport with constant action and it is at its best in the cool hour before sunset when dinner with a bottle of wine is known to be the next item on the agenda.

* * * * * *

I grabbed a branch and swung out ape-like into space, dropping with a breath-expelling jolt onto a ledge four feet lower down. This was ridiculous. It was marked as the GR60 as plain as anything on the map and quite well supplied with daubs of paint, in fact there was one right in front of my nose.

I took hold of a convenient tree root, swung 90 degrees to the left and leaned backwards while I walked down a vertical slab of rock. This wasn't a path. It was the sort of stuff Edmund Hilary and Sherpa Tensing had done in 1953 with a nice breeze off the top of Everest to keep them cool. I tried to edge cunningly down a crevice between two rocks and got jammed halfway with my pack so I back-pedalled, losing a good bit of skin off one knee, and went out over the protruding edge instead. When had anyone last checked this route?

The next section was quicker, a slope of loose stones dotted with hardy bushes which you had to grab alternately left and right with a swinging motion, like dancing a speeded up version of Strip the Willow on a sloping dance floor. They ought to have put hazard warning signs at the point where this section of the GR left the road. The gradient eased and, risking a short dash downhill between the trees without any handholds, I swooped past a thorn bush and to my astonishment found myself cantering out onto a well kept tarmac road which vanished to the left round a cliff face several hundred feet high. Panic seized me. There wasn't supposed to be any road until I reached the valley which was now in view some way below me. I brushed an assortment of leaves and insects out of my hair and grabbed the map. Don't say I had taken a wrong turning and gone miles out of my way!

No. It was all right. The map showed a little road which I hadn't noticed. It appeared to zigzag up the hillside to something called Grotte des Demoiselles marked in heavy black print. I looked to my left and realised that there was a car park a hundred metres down the road. Closer examination revealed a restaurant, a ticket office, and all the usual benefits of a tourist trap. A large sign confirmed that I had indeed stumbled on the Grotte des Demoiselles and a selection of coloured postcards advertised caves, stalactites, an electric railway and a guide.

I ordered a café grande and sat down to recuperate. Little did they realise that I had almost entered their caves involuntarily and free of charge through a hole in the roof. I find pot holes quite terrifying, and teetering on the edge of an apparently bottomless hole disappearing into the depths of the earth had got the adrenalin off to a sprint start. It had been an interesting morning so far, beginning with an investigation of the delightful village of Laroque which, although stuck right on the D986, manages to retain its tranquility and character. Its cafes ignore the heavy traffic which must pour down the trunk road beside the Herault River in holiday time and they deliberately scatter the pavements with tables and chairs so that social life may take its course in the evening. From the still waters above the weir a community of old stone houses has spread up the hillside through a little maze of stone-paved streets leading up steps and under archways. Flowering shrubs grow out of the stonework and ancient ten foot walls surround quiet gardens. There are no vulgar lamp posts; instead, elegant lamps are supported by wrought iron brackets discreetly placed under the overhanging roofs. By some miracle the village has preserved itself perfectly without becoming commercialised. I ought not to have told you about it; its a secret between us. Strolling along its upper levels I had come across the GR signs once again and acting on impulse decided to follow them into the hills rather than carry on down the road beside the river.

I had made several discoveries. First, I had found where French dogs come from. They are bred on dog farms carefully hidden in the woods in remote places and run by people wearing ear muffs; at least, I deduced that if they were not issued with ear muffs they would refuse to work there. I was spotted by a family of Spaniels in an exercise cage which commanded a view of the footpath and the exciting news of my arrival was immediately flashed to all points in the camp. A murderous cacophony rent the morning air long after I had vanished from sight, sound and scent. They have special cheer leaders whose job it is to train the younger generation of future guard dogs to produce a really lengthy, anti-social, irritating and unnecessary racket in order to protect all those grim shuttered houses.

My second discovery was a dew pond, a perfect circle lined many years ago with cemented stones, with little ridges forming concentric rings at which animals could stand at the water's edge as the level rose and fell. Flocks of sheep must have roamed the hills in earlier years to justify this beautiful construction, but no domesticated animals were in evidence now. The footpath ran past it on bare limestone through low scrub and occasional patches of taller trees where the path had a thin covering of leaves and it was in one of these stretches that I nearly took a quick trip to the centre of the earth. A side path appeared with no red and white daubs to indicate whether one should change direction or carry straight on so an excursion in both directions was called for. The side path twisted between dense undergrowth for a few paces and ended abruptly at the edge of a black hole which measured ten metres across and was lined with damp dark rocks which plunged to nothingness. There were no restraining strands of wire and no signs of any posts which might ever have carried such safety precautions. I skidded to a halt and waited while my pulse rate fell from about two hundred to something nearer the norm before raising Pentax Zoom 70 with quivering hands. It was no good; you just couldn't get an angle which would convey anything like the horror of the moment. The encircling saplings and rocks provided far too good a camouflage.

And that was why the sudden advertising of the Grotte des Demoiselles came as no surprise to me. The hilltop above had been scattered with similar but smaller apertures, some big enough for a foot to get into, some wide enough for a man to slip down. I sipped my coffee and concluded that the whole place must be riddled with caves. As it was still only nine forty-five I decided that I could just afford an hour for the guided tour if it began shortly. It would be a new experience to travel underground on an electric railway and view the wonders of nature.

"The first guided tour is at ten o'clock, Monsieur," I was assured. "Would you like to leave your pack here?" I purchased a ticket and told the lady that I would keep my pack with me. She shrugged her shoulders but I had no intention of being parted from my passport, credit card, cash, diary and other treasured possessions.

The view out across the wide valley was interesting and I relaxed in the sun for a quarter of an hour calculating where my route would take me through the distant hills to the south. By ten o'clock a group of people were waiting expectantly by the entrance but nothing appeared to be happening.

"The guide is coming, Monsieur," I was promised when I enquired at five past ten with one eye anxiously on my watch.

Boloney! The tour was held up deliberately until ten twenty when a fat voluble Frenchman finally arrived in a fat flashy car and was greeted obsequiously. I snarled inwardly at the wasted time and queued impatiently to board the electric train.

"You are taking your rucksack in, Monsieur? You will have to carry it some way," said the guide. I hesitated. I had thought that we rode round in an electric train all the way but it was too late now to cause another delay. I raised my eyebrows in mock surprise. "I have carried it all the way from the Atlantic, Madame. It is not heavy." Like her colleague she shrugged and waved me through.

We packed ourselves, some sitting and some standing, into the open electric train which was resting on a sharp incline. A lever was pulled and we rumbled slowly up the sharp incline and came to a stop a few moments later at a platform higher up within the hillside. We were now well inside the cliff face but this was the end of the train journey. The remaining fifty five minutes of the tour would be on foot. As we began the three hundred metre climb up damp steps hewn out of the rock and built up in concrete I began to understand the puzzlement of the ticket lady and the guide. A pack becomes heavier and heavier as you walk and clamber very slowly for one and a half kilometres underground. While the other members of the party wrapped themselves in summer waterproofs to keep warm I perspired freely and welcomed the occasional drips of cool water which fell from the dim ceiling above. The guide spoke very little English; I grasped fifty per cent of the content in French and threw in a few questions here and there. A masterful American female with swept back hair and clad in stylish slacks and sweater who had, for an American, an unusual grasp of the French language, offered to translate for me, but I begged her not to bother.

It was worth the time. The centrepiece was an enormous vault of awe inspiring dimensions known as "the Cathedral" in which a mass was sung each Christmas with a choir of thirty standing in a central position while the congregation ranged themselves around the stairway which curved up one side and down the other. It was dark and gloomy enough to serve as the prototype for every French Cathedral. Grotte des Demoiselles was translated as "Cave of the Fairies", so called because the first explorers clambering in by torchlight had been scared by dim figures hovering at the edge of visibility and only later identified as stalagmites with remarkably human shapes.

At the highest point of the circuit we emerged from the dark stairway which twisted round vertical rock faces and came into a pleasant cave with a large roof aperture open to the sky; it was not like the black hole into which I had peered earlier that morning. On our descent we were introduced to the inevitable Virgin and Child as we slipped and tottered cautiously between incredible arches and pillars of limestone in white, yellow, grey and orange. We rode back down the incline in our electric chariot and met the sun again. The masterful American lady rejoined her husband and announced with obvious satisfaction, "I told the guide about everywhere we've been and all the places we are going to." "Well done, honey," he replied, "I'm glad you managed to tell her." A race of people unique upon the earth; the tour would have been a total failure for them unless the guide had been made to understand how fortunate she was to have two such well travelled people in her party.

I sat in the sun once again and checked the map. Below me in the plain lay St Bauzille-de-Putois, beyond it the mountains, and due south beyond them St-Martin-de-Londres which was the day's objective. The valley of the Herault drifted away westwards and once again there was a choice of a speedy but boring journey down the D986 or a gamble with the GR60 into the hills. I decided to gamble.

* * * * * *

Unlike the Monts D'Aubrac or the Causses or the Cevennes, unlike the uninhabited limestone hills of the morning, this mountain bore no trace of man whatsoever apart from the path which I was following. The path, if it deserved such a title, rose and fell relentlessly over rocky screes and scorned the very idea of a smooth surface. For most of its course the best it could offer was a loose rubble of small stones which might have been borrowed from Chesil Bank. The worst it could offer was indescribable but I will attempt to paint a picture for you. It was, of course, hot. The Mediterranean sun beat down out of an azure sky and the heat bounced back effortlessly off brilliant white limestone rock which burst through the greenery in angry outcrops and weathered cliffs. White rocks and stones littered the path in a fierce glare of light. The path searched out each new cliff face and headed straight for any gulley where there was a slope gentle enough to grant a foothold, and then scrambled its way up. Distant mountain ranges formed a backdrop for breathtaking chasms in the foreground. This was unlike anything that had happened before and the grandeur almost became a terrifying remoteness. It wasn't frightening on a hot afternoon with pauses in the shade and plenty of water in my pack but I was conscious that the slightest accident would meet with a grim indifference in this landscape.

The path widened briefly into a respectable track which curved round on a natural terrace below some cliffs and entered a spectacular gorge. Hundreds of feet below was the boulder-strewn bottom of an old river bed with the erosions of centuries now exposed to view. I pulled out the map to check my position and found the phrase 'Ravine des Arcs'. The gorge narrowed and the footpath clawed its way onto a horizontal stratum of rock and then hugged its way across the cliff face with a stomach churning fall on the right hand which I did not pause to investigate. It lost height and came out onto a little promontory where to my amazement there was a signpost offering alternative routes. One could get to St-Martin-de-Londres either by the high road which climbed up the cliffs or by the low road which slithered straight down to the bottom of the ravine. The ravine looked more exciting and was more direct so I scrambled the rest of the way down.

It was like no other path on earth. In the shade at the bottom of the ravine there lay a chaos of smooth moss-covered boulders which had been rolled along the riverbed by the immense pressure of water in another millenium. They measured anything from one foot to six foot in diameter. There was no particular route to follow. You chose your own course and slipped and staggered across the least treacherous stretch which you could see. After twenty metres my boot skidded sideways off a two foot boulder. There was no damage but I sat down to consider what would happen if I dislocated an ankle in this dank chasm. I had not seen another living soul for hours and there was no sign of civilisation ahead. It would be days before anyone came this way and it would need a super-human effort to escape on one leg from this pit to which the sun penetrated for only a brief period each day. The sun was now sinking fast and it was becoming quite chilly. I made up my mind and headed back up the cliff to warmth and relative safety.

* * * * * *

He poked his head out of the caravan door and laughed at me. The word 'snacks' had drawn me like a powerful magnet into the car park by the road and I threw off the pack beside a table while I went to investigate the contents of the caravan. A large basket of blue and white flowers dangled in welcome beside the window hatch.

"You need a drink, Monsieur?" he enquired good humourdly. It was a well stocked caravan and he was dressed in an immaculate white chef's outfit and seemed poised to produce a three course meal at the drop of a hat. I nodded vigourously and mopped my brow. It had been a long haul back up the side of the gorge followed by a stony walk across open country and through the dried up bed of a stream, and the snack bar beside the distant road had looked like the centre of civilisation itself.

"Panaché, s'il vous plaît, " I gasped. It was not much more than a kilometre into St-Martin-de-Londres but a glassful now would taste like nectar.

"You've been busy?" I enquired.

"It's been hectic all day, Monsieur." He waved his hands at the heap of empty cardboard boxes and piles of used paper plates. "But very good for business," he added happily, placing a brimming glass at the window hatch.

I raised it in salute and took a long contented swig before retiring to a plastic chair and stretching at ease. I gazed back at the mountains. Once again it astonished me how whole mountain ranges rose up in front of me in the morning and vanished behind me in the evening. I, an insignificant ant, had crept up and over them and vanished on my way under their steady gaze. It was all right for them to look serene; I was knackered.

The square in the centre of St-Martin-de-Londres has been declared a pedestrian precinct. It is furnished with convenient low stone walls on which to rest as the evening sun slants in from the horizon and silhouettes young couples sitting with arms round each other murmuring endearments while they watch the water in the fountain. Life is taken at a sensible pace. The hotel does not open until seven o'clock in the evening; it has a notice inviting you to call at the bar next door and request the barman to telephone the one part-time member of staff. You have a leisurely drink, book in at the hotel at seven o'clock, have a shower, and go out for dinner at one of the restaurants.

* * * * * *

The bar in Montarnaud emptied in a flash as people crowded out onto the pavement to enjoy a free spectacle. The altercation was developing nicely. The driver of the large blue Citroen turned and reached into the recesses of his car and reappeared brandishing a knobkerrie with which he confidently approached his adversary. There was a gasp from the crowd at this sudden escalation of hostilities and a buzz of speculation as to where he had acquired the weapon. I must confess I had always assumed that knobkerries were the prerogative of hottentots; maybe he was the curator of a museum on his way to do a spot of bartering with a colleague.

The driver of the little Renault, which had slipped bonnet first into the parking space while the Citroen was still manoeuvering backwards, was not to be intimidated by such crude tactics. He too reached into his car and emerged with a metre long loaf of bread. They advanced on each other hurling threats, waving fists, and lunging with their chosen weapons. It looked like being an unequal contest, particularly as the owner of the knobkerrie was at least twice the weight of his opponent. Windows were thrown up in the Mairie, one of whose parking spaces was the subject of the dispute, and the spectators elbowed their way closer to obtain a better view.

I glanced round for the Gendarmerie but they were nowhere to be seen, although maybe an ambulance would soon be of more use.

However, public spirited citizens were now closing in to prevent bloodshed. One brave soul pushed between the two adversaries and begged them not to assault each other over such a trivial matter. They rounded on him angrily, each explaining the affrontery of the other and demanding justice. Other citizens moved in with firm restraining hands and managed to create a buffer zone and institute a cooling off period. The gentleman beside me expelled an alcoholic breath in disappointment and commented " Ce n'est par la guerre! " Loud conversation filled the roadway as each spectator turned to his neighbour to explain who had been in the right and who had been to blame. There did not appear to be a consensus on this point and for a moment it looked as though a whole rash of further disputes might erupt, but then I realised that the incident had simply provided a new topic of conversation to enliven an otherwise routine lunchtime.

Pentax Zoom 70 was furious. "You just stood there and looked! We could have taken some beauties. That chap with the club would have made the sort of picture which magazines go on using for decades!"

"I might have been bashed with a club if I had pushed my way into that lot," I retorted.

"You didn't need to go right in there. You could have stood on the chair and used the zoom," he insisted.

"Well, it all happened too quickly and you were still attached to the haversack," I grumbled.

He snorted. "That's feeble!"

I sat down again in the plastic chair outside the bar and took a long drink of panaché . He was right of course. I should have got in at least one shot, but he was so cocky at times .

The problem today was working out where to spend the night. There were no more mountain ranges to conquer. My route fell in a perpendicular line across the map from St-Martin-de-Londres to somewhere north of Sète, and it was a fast route providing I did not get lost since a series of minor roads and tracks linked neatly with one another all the way. But none of the towns was advertised as having an hotel and the lady who had provided breakfast that morning had been unable to forecast with certainty anything more than a seasonal gîte . It did not worry me unduly as it would be the last night before I reached the coast, and a night in the open would be just another experience provided that I had a decent evening meal to sustain me. Nevertheless I had grown accustomed to the comfort of small hotels and the company which they provided. We would see what turned up.

The country was the Garrigue; not the most attractive part of France but definitely different, a kind of no-man's-land between the Massif Central and the busy coastal strip. The hills were nothing more than undulations compared with the Cevennes behind me and their soil was meagre, supporting nothing more than brushwood. Thorn bushes appeared to thrive and cactus plants were beginning to appear, mainly as adornments in the few cultivated gardens. I examined their vast prickly leaves with interest and respect. It was not a landscape in which to linger. There were no vistas to hold the eye. A brisk four miles per hour covered the ground and permitted me to absorb the atmosphere adequately. It was not hostile country but it was indifferent to the traveller. The only colour came from occasional clusters of yellow flowers by the wayside, the little red blooms at the tips of the cactus leaves, the shining leaves and purple fruit of the thorn bushes, and the blue of the sky.

It had therefore been a bit of a shock to walk into the village of Vailhauques and discover that its south facing hillside had become one vast construction site. Breeze block and stone buildings were mushrooming from the scars left by earth moving equipment. On the steeper slopes of the brief incline the houses projected onto pillars and sheltered shady terraces underneath. Brand new residential roads twisted between retaining walls on one side and a scree of loose rock on the other. In one sense it was an uncouth invasion of nature's wilderness but in another sense it was man making the desert bloom. What on earth had caused people to come and live in this place? If it was speculative building the gamble had come off because the completed houses were already occupied judging from the lines of washing drying fast in the parched atmosphere. But the place was miles from anywhere. The old part of the village was so small that it did not even boast a bar and the Garrigue stretched out in every direction like a desert barrier cutting off the amenities of civilisation.

I stood there in perplexity wrestling with the mystery. Was this the site of the latest nuclear power station? The French have a whole family of these scattered across France and maybe they had chosen this area as one unlikely to arouse local protest. This explanation did not fit; there was no indication of massive engineering works, no advertising of government schemes, no series of warning notices for would-be trespassers. I turned to survey the horizon and found the missing clue. From the slight vantage point of the hillside there was a lengthy view to the southeast and at the edge of visibility little rectangular shapes sprouted from the earth. I checked the map. Yes, as I suspected, they must be the tower blocks of the outer suburbs of Montpellier, and I was standing on the site of a future dormitory town. These householders perched on their newly excavated plots were the vanguard of those who preferred to commute from the country rather than live in the metropolis. I hoped they would enjoy their sun-baked peace and I wondered how many decades it would take to cover the intervening space with urban sprawl.

The outer edge of Montpellier might be in sight but it was not on my route to the Mediterranean and there was still plenty of ground to cover so I had set off again at a fast pace down a long gentle incline to the coast. Maybe it had been too fast. The tendon began to make itself felt again so I stopped and sat in the shade of a tree, crushing a mass of small herbs which gave off a variety of strong scents in protest. I fished out the tube of ointment and did some massage for the first time in ten days. A slight rash appeared as I was putting my sock on again; my longsuffering body had decided at last to inform me that I was allergic to this particular medication; fortunately it decided to wait another week before extending the rash to cover my chest, back, legs, arms and in fact every part of me which was hidden beneath collar and tie and city suit, and by then it was too late for me to be refused entry into the United Kingdom as a cholera suspect.

South of Montarnaud the D roads do a dog leg to the east in order to take in the town of Murviel-les-Montpellier. As I had no burning desire to explore Murviel-les-Montpellier I took the unmetalled track which cut across country avoiding the diversion. It began well by taking me down into a hidden valley filled with vines whose owners were busy harvesting the white grapes and transporting them to the local co-operative. They did not believe in wasted effort. On each journey the tractor-drawn trailer was stacked high with bunches of exquisite grapes, ripened in the sun to a full golden colour. Naturally a few bunches fell onto the road as the trailer jolted along its uneven surface. I indulged myself for several happy kilometres in compensation for the vagaries of the track which ignored the map and took on a life of its own, twisting and turning with every little contour and generally taking three kilometres to cover a stretch of country where two would have been adequate.

Regaining the road above the town of Cournonterral I looked southeast and caught my first glimpse of the Mediterranean. To be precise, it must have been one of the many étangs or salt water lagoons sheltering behind the long ridges of shingle and sand which sweep along that stretch of the coastline. But as far as I was concerned it was blue sea so I sat and contemplated it with satisfaction and had a celebratory Mars Bar. Unfortunately I was not going to be able to walk peacefully down to the sea on sandy tracks between pine trees and splash my way into a quite cove. The way ahead was criss-crossed with a maze of busy roads including a large new motorway named 'la Languedocienne'. Rural France was coming to an end; I would have to pierce the booming coastal belt in order to reach my destination.

I studied the map in conjunction with the view ahead of me. The planning had been sound. There was no point in making for the illusory étang to the east. I should keep heading due south and reach the open sea the following day at Sète. A little sprinkling of small towns lay in front of me at one of which I hoped to stop for the night. Cournonterral looked the biggest but it was already close and I did not want to stop too early. I would visit one of its bars to demonstrate goodwill and then press on to Montbazin which was about six kilometres further on and looked as though it might boast one hotel.

The gypsy encampment sprawled across the shortcut into Cournonterral stared at me suspiciously. Nowadays people did not often follow the old track into the town which took you beside the river and right up to the foot of the old walls, but it was a nice way to approach the ancient town and was almost certainly the original route before the motor car sought out less demanding gradients. I visited a bar and then pushed on in the evening sunlight towards Montbazin. Vineyards crowded the road which was defined by the double line of plane trees stretching out ahead. The low sun brilliantly lit their patchy trunks and brought out a deep green colour in the vines. My pace was slowing markedly, which was not surprising; the map proved that it had been a long day already and might yet turn out to be the longest of all.

Montbazin was another walled town, although more compact and better preserved than its neighbour. It looked just the place to have a nice little Auberge tucked away in a quiet corner. I consulted two ladies who were enjoying an evening gossip. No, Monsieur, there is no hotel in Montbazin but there is one in Gigean which is not far away.

I tramped on mechanically for another two kilometres into Gigean which lay on the N113 and sought directions. Yes, Monsieur, the hotel is just down the hill on the main road.

Down the hill took me right on to the N113 with its steady stream of cars and trucks, and there was the hotel sign a hundred metres to the left, rather tatty and dirty but at least it was a hotel sign and it promised a bed and a shower. The entrance, not unusually, was through a bar; this one was crowded with men who obviously earned their living with their hands rather than their brains. They were a rough looking bunch with one particularly gross individual in their midst, the sort of person whose pock-marked neck runs mysteriously into a close-cropped head without any visible demarcation line. He stood by the bar dominating the whole room without saying a word and beside him, in astonishing contrast, stood the only lady in the room, small, delicately proportioned and dressed neatly and attractively. She appeared totally relaxed and unconcerned by the environment.

I made enquiries of the barman and was escorted outside and into the building by another door, up a flight of stairs to a room overlooking the road. It was spartan; there was no carpet over the linoleum and the fittings were minimal; the windows and shutters fought a non-stop battle to keep out the grime of the N113 below; there was a shower and toilet at the end of the corridor. It looked like being a new experience.

... a rough looking bunch with one particularly gross individual ...

The shower and toilet had been accustomed to rough handling but they worked. I went down half an hour later and enquired where the dining room was. The barman looked mildly surprised but directed me into the dim interior where several tables waited in a canteen atmosphere. I paused at the entrance reviewing my plans judiciously; firstly there was a good chance of getting a better meal elsewhere in town, but more importantly the only other occupant was the neatly dressed lady of exquisite proportions who had been in the bar when I arrived. She was looking at me encouragingly and practically patting the chair beside her. I had a nasty feeling that she was the property of the gentleman with the pock-marked neck, and he had looked the sort of person who might be aggressively protective of his property.

But it had been a long day. Inertia won the battle. I smiled at her politely and took a seat on the far side of the room. Underneath the well manicured surface and undeniably attractive figure there was a hint of steel.

The barman reappeared and I looked up to take the menu. He placed on the table a plateful of heavy looking quiche and a small carafe of red wine and departed. The lady looked across and grimaced at me.

"It's not very appetising. I have left most of mine."

"It does look rather solid," I agreed.

"Are you on holiday?"

I explained how my month's journey was coming to an end and she asked intelligent questions and talked about various parts of France. I struggled with the quiche but finally pushed it aside half eaten. The barman-turned-chef reappeared with steak and chips for both of us, another formidable plateful with emphasis on quantity rather than quality.

"The men need filling up after their day at work," she commented. I concluded that 'the men' had already eaten and were probably now washing their dinner down with several cans of lager. She explained that there was a lot of construction work in the area which had drawn in a large temporary work force.

"What is your name?"

I was tongue-tied for a moment. Attractive ladies do not usually enquire my name in restaurants and I still had an uneasy feeling that the bloke with the pock-marked neck might reappear at any moment and accuse me of chatting up his bird.

"Er, Bill," I said, choosing that version of my first Christian name which blended most naturally with our surroundings.

"And I am Irene," she replied, adding "I am here for a week's holiday."

I forbore to question her selection of a holiday hotel but the mystery was deepening. We continued to chat half in English and half in French as the steak and chips were followed by ice-cream and coffee.

A talkative gentleman answering to the name of Leroy entered the room and joined Irene at her table. She invited me to join them in a drink. Concluding that there was safety in numbers I got up and joined them in a round of liqueurs. Leroy was in the building industry and related at length, and in a strange accent which Irene translated for me at intervals, his problems in organising the assorted gang of Turks, Greeks, and Algerians who were available in the labour market.

"And what do you do, Bill?" he enquired during a lull in the conversation. I had a sudden vision of my large office in a Nash terrace overlooking Regent's Park with its high ceiling and carpeted floor. Surely I must be a parasite living on the backs of people like Leroy who really made things happen, who constructed buildings and roads, who left something permanent for the next generation to use. They wouldn't want to drink with me any longer when they found out.

"Er, I am an expert comptable ," I admitted reluctantly, preparing to empty my glass and withdraw from their scornful gaze.

"Ah, that is good," said Leroy admiringly. "You use your brain. That is very good."

"And you must earn a lot of money," added Irene approvingly. "You are sensible. You got a good training when you were a young man."

I drew a deep breath of relief and ordered another round of liqueurs. "And what do you do?" I enquired of Irene. She made a dismissive gesture with her hands and shook her head while Leroy grinned.

"But you have a job?" I enquired, intrigued by this intelligent and attractive lady who took her annual holiday in a workman's dosshouse in the grubby hinterland to the Mediterranean.

She looked at me and said, picking her words carefully in English, "I am .... dirty." Leroy chortled beside me. I stared at her in puzzlement for a second, then grasped her meaning and joined in the laughter with some embarrassment. We chatted on for an hour or so. Irene had a son of nineteen in the foreign legion. She showed us a photograph of a dark good looking young man whose features bore just a trace of the Indian ancestry whose slight influence added to the physical attractions of his mother.

Yes, the evening had been different. As far as I was aware it was the first time I had spent several hours chatting to a prostitute and buying her liqueurs.

CHAPTER 10

MEDITERRANEAN

It was a mass of roadworks. Diversion signs stood in gangs awaiting the unwary motorist, and half constructed traffic islands littered the ground. Lorries and early morning office workers in their cars emerged unexpectedly from unmade roads while my attention was concentrated elsewhere on navigating stacks of drainage pipes and other hazards scattered in my path.

I was still chuckling over the accommodation of the previous night which I had vacated without waiting for breakfast. It had been a genuine workman's doss house providing the bare essentials for migrant workers drawn into the area by the construction boom, and the joke was that I had mistaken my directions. If I had turned right instead of left in Gigean I would have come to the genuine hotel which my informant had intended. I had passed it that morning, a nice little place standing a little way back from the road on a slight rise. No doubt it would have provided a better meal and a more comfortable room, and I would have had an en suite toilet instead of a one fifteenth share in something on which I had hurriedly shut the door that morning. But it would have lacked the immaculately dressed Irene and the earthy conversation of Leroy. Chez Irene did not rate even one star in the tourist guide but it held a genuine flavour of France which I would otherwise have missed.

The roadworks came to an end and reluctantly gave up their dual carriageway in exchange for an older road which ran dead straight beside the water of an inland bassin , the Bassin de Thau according to the map. It was rather attractive at a distance. Lines of pleasure boats were moored fore and aft beside grassy banks and the actual roadside was fringed with tall reeds. Across the blue expanse of water rose the hump of Mont St Clair, the residential area of Sète, and the whole picture was framed in a forest of little masts. On closer inspection it was not quite as magical. The water was not tidal and litter had collected in corners everywhere, tin cans, plastic bags, and industrial debris of all sorts. It was better to walk along the pavement beside the road and take a detached long distance view.

It was a long stretch of road, but why hurry to the end? The objective today was simply to reach the sea which was not far away after the long hike of the previous day. It was Thursday 28th September and the Atlantic lay six hundred miles and a whole month behind me. The traffic was getting heavier but I did not grudge the noise. I had walked in peace for four weeks and paradise must be surrendered at some point.

There was something nasty ahead where the road appeared to run into an industrial complex to the east of Mont St Clair. What had been at first no more than a hazy smudge was steadily developing into a pall of white smoke which seemed to be drifting right into the town. It grew nastier and more threatening the closer I approached so I sat down for a brief snack before launching the final assault and looked back at the countryside immediately behind me. It was all very well building new towns and new motorways to boost the economy and enable everyone to move faster but there were always casualties. Shortly after leaving Gigean I had walked under the brand spanking new A9 motorway which now ran all the way from the Rhone valley to the Spanish border and had reduced to a matter of hours the journey which would, until recently, have taken a day or two and would once have taken several weeks. That could be counted as progress, but if you wanted to count the cost you had only to walk along those stretches of the N113 whose hotels now stood abandoned, forlorn and empty. There are few more depressing sights than an abandoned hotel with no cars parked outside, no flowers in the window boxes and no voices in the bar. 'La Languedocienne' now swept past imperiously on its separate route with its multiple lanes of traffic, its rest areas, and, no doubt, its ultra modern motels with colour tv and drinks cabinets in every room.

I entered the pall of white smoke generously provided by Sud Fertilisants after passing another factory with the ominous sign ' Guano de Poisson ' painted in giant letters on one of its walls. Emerging on the far side of this environmental dinosaur I stood on a bridge over the railway drawing fresh sea air into my lungs and brushing white dust out of my hair. Presumably the prevailing wind always blew this lot over the railway sidings and warehouses and out to sea. If not, the inhabitants of Mont St Clair and the tourist visitors to Sète must be an unusually long-suffering breed.

Beyond the railway station another world appeared and I realised why my journey was ending at Sète. It was like Venice, but with one indisputable advantage: it was not sinking year by year into the sea. Roads and canals ran together under a Mediterranean sky. Pleasure boats and working fishing boats lay in the water along miles of quays with parked cars nosing comfortably up to the bollards above them. Tiered rock gardens rose above the water where the canals intersected and their colours set off the old stone buildings of a town which had thrived for centuries and was still the second biggest fishing port in France. Restaurants scattered their tables across the pavements where customers drank their coffee and nibbled ice-creams in animated conversation gazing out over the lines of multi-coloured craft and rows of smart apartments basking in the sunshine. Elegant bridges spanned the waterways. I sat down on a corner of some wide stone steps below one of the rock gardens to drink in the scene, and received a drenching when a local council employee arrived to switch on the automatic sprinkler. He apologised profusely as I sprang to my feet with a startled yelp but I still harbour a sneaking suspicion that catching unwary tourists provided the light relief in his daily rounds.

The little streets and squares climbing the lower levels of Mont St Clair were packed with enticing shops and restaurants. I purchased a last selection of postcards, a bunch of grapes and a small packet of luggage labels ready for the return air flight. Sète is the sort of town where you can wander for hours and keep on finding something new, and it was with some reluctance that I headed south towards the open sea expecting to find a sandy beach across which I could finally stride into the water. Instead I found a harbour crowded with fleets of little trawlers, their crews busy sorting out nets and stacking boxes under the watchful eyes of the gull population. Unless I was looking for a coating of diesel oil and fish scales this was definitely not the point at which to end an epic journey by plunging into the water. It was attractive in its own way, in fact totally fascinating, but not quite the spot I was looking for.

Eastwards lay a mass of harbour walls, tall cranes, fuel storage tanks and giant silos before the distant hint of sand dunes. I turned west and had soon exchanged busy docksides for a natural coastline, but it was a rocky coastline with low cliffs and still no easy access to the water. I walked on along the coast road past batteries of hotels and smart apartment blocks with the open sea lapping gently against the rocks below.

At ten thirty a sandy cove appeared at the foot of the rocks, apparently deserted. 'That's it,' said Pentax Zoom 70. 'That's the place.'

'Yes, it looks OK ,' I agreed, 'but who is going to take the picture of me actually at the water's edge?'

'Oh, somebody's bound to turn up,' he assured me confidently. On closer inspection there was indeed someone already down there. A very tanned bald headed gentleman was standing in his swimming trunks with arms folded gazing out to sea. I walked along the road and began clambering down a well worn path through the rocks. 'I hope he's capable of taking a picture,' I muttered. 'This is going to be about the most important picture of the whole trip.'

'He would have to be a bit of a twit to mess it up,' said Pentax Zoom 70. 'Damn it, I set the aperture and the timing and the focus. All he's got to do is a quick zoom to frame you nicely at the right distance.'

I jumped down the last few feet onto the sand. It had been washed overnight by the almost non-existent tide. The water ran gently in and out edging around a few large rocks which formed little private beaches of their own. I walked forward to the line of white bubbles which surged gently back and forth. No, I must not put my foot in the water yet. That important moment must be caught for posterity. I walked casually over to the sun-tanned gentleman.

"Bonjour, Monsieur . Could I please have your help? I have walked across France from the Atlantic coast and have just arrived here at the Mediterranean. Would you please take my picture?" I held out Pentax Zoom 70.

He looked at me for a moment, digesting what I had said and eyeing my equipment. "You are walking across France?"

"I have just finished walking across France, Monsieur. This morning I have arrived at the Mediterranean from Arcachon near

Bordeaux. This is the historic moment," I added for emphasis, gesturing towards the blue sea.

"The historic moment?" he laughed and took Pentax Zoom 70 from me. "Then you have certainly earned a picture of yourself, my friend. Where do you want to stand?"

I showed him where I would like to stand with one foot at the water's edge and demonstrated the zoom mechanism. He experimented once or twice and pronounced himself ready. I poised with one foot in the Mediterranean. I had arrived! Pentax Zoom 70 clicked and wound forward in approval. We took another one for luck.

"That was very kind of you, Monsieur" I said. "Are you on holiday too?"

"I come here from Paris each Autumn after the crowds have gone. In August you cannot see the sand; it is covered in bodies." His hand swept the cove. "I wait until it is quiet. And where are you from?"

"I am English," I explained. "I have taken a month's holiday to do this."

"I was from Italy originally. In 1939 the war started and..." He shrugged and smiled. "I spent the rest of the war in France. And afterwards I liked it so much that I became a naturalised Frenchman."

I nodded. Life as a prisoner of war had obviously suited him, and indeed life in retirement also suited him judging by his deep tan and rounded figure.

"Well, I am going to have a swim now that I have arrived," I announced, depositing my rucksack beside a rock and delving into it for my trunks. I eased off a damp shirt, dusty boots and two pairs of socks, changed into the trunks and waded in. It was bliss. Warm clear water with a sandy bottom changing to rocks and seaweed some way from the water's edge. I swam lazily and floated on my back studying the rocky coastline with its outcrops of modern hotels. Further down the coast each hotel appeared to have its own private beach.

Two more octogenarians clambered down to our cove, each of them well tanned and obviously familiar with his own little strip of sand between the boulders. I swam back in and dried myself unhurriedly. One of the new arrivals preferred to sun bathe stark naked. He was also

'… going to have a swim now that I have arrived.'

sociable by nature and paraded back and forth along the water line talking volubly to the other two. Evidently the trio were the regular daily occupants of this little nook.

It was time for breakfast. Or was it lunch? Anyway, I was ravenous. I tore chunks off a baguette purchased in Sète that morning, spread butter liberally and carved generous slices of cheese. The water bottles were still quite cool. Then I lay spread-eagled on the sand and heaved a big sigh of satisfaction.

It was no good. After ten minutes I was automatically pulling on shorts and shirt, tugging on the two pairs of socks and lacing up the boots. I had disciplined my body for weeks to relax totally in brief catnaps and then to swing into action again. I turned the socks carefully down over the tops of my boots, dusted the sand off my hands, and reached for the arm straps of the rucksack. Then it hit me. It struck me like a physical blow. I had nowhere to go.

I put down the haversack and stared at the sea, then peered down the coast towards Cap d'Agde. It was no good. I couldn't fool myself. It was over.

There was a sudden emptiness. The sun under which I had walked and rejoiced for four whole weeks suddenly began to lose its savage brilliance and became the familiar friendly thing of so many autumns. The excitement was ebbing away with each minute and leaving a strange hurt. What was it that Robert Louis Stevenson had written? 'To travel hopefully is a better thing than to arrive.' He would have known what it felt like. He had walked through the Cévennes with Modestine his donkey in September a hundred years ago and when he arrived at St Jean du Gard and had to take the train home again he had cried on leaving Modestine behind. I wasn't crying, but I was feeling lost and empty.

I sat down on the sand again. This would not do. It had been a wonderful month but it had to come to an end some time. It was just that the mainspring inside me was uncoiling and today there was no point in winding it up again. For a whole month I had pretended I was a young man and had pushed my body eagerly to somewhere near its limits with no other worry in the world than following the map and finding a bed. And now.... and now I was within a few hours of becoming once more the father of four adult children and a commuter on the six fifty five train to Liverpool Street. The trouble was that the last month had been a return to discovery. It had been real living. The rest of life was the sham, the routine played out day-by-day, week-by-week, month-by-month, year-by-year. That was the important idea to hang on to; there could still be new discoveries every year, new experiences every day if I could stick my neck out far enough. Alright, so this was not the end.

I looked down at Pentax Zoom 70 dangling contentedly from his strap beside the rucksack. 'You and I have walked walks which we shall dream of for years, my friend.' He swung gently in the sun and twinkled back at me.

'You and I have looked at dawn skies while the rest of the world dozed in their beds. We have watched the sun rise and smelled the cool morning air together; and we have kept a record of it all.' He nodded.

'We have scrambled up paths where the sheep would have twisted their ankles, and marched where the Romans marched in the days of Julius Caesar; and we have pictures to prove it.' He stopped twisting on his strap and came to rest against the rucksack in a rather pointed manner.

'And we have met some lovely people on the way,' I continued, smiling at recollections of a railway bridge, an auberge in Conques, lunch in a beech wood and dinner in a dosshouse. 'I'm glad I've taken twenty-four reels of film. I'm definitely going to write a book this time.'

'Could I just point out,' said Pentax Zoom 70 with what I thought was an excess of sarcasm, 'that I am the one who took all those pictures and you are the one who missed all the other opportunities like the one of the bloke with the knobkerrie, and that couple on top of the Dune de Pilat, and ...'

'What cheek! I spent hours messing about each day, stopping in awkward places, clambering up banks to get the right angle, walking back along the path...'

'Yes, but I had to do all the brainwork of calculating exposures and apertures and ...'

I looked him straight in the lens. 'If you're so clever, you had better write the book,' I said. That shut him up.

No. We couldn't finish on that abrasive note. I stretched out a hand and picked him up, then lay back and contemplated the cloudless sky above. 'Thanks, Lord. It's been a great month, beyond all my expectations. Thanks for getting us here safely.'